V read 2/2020
"Hunt of the Reaper
ready to buy on amazon

D1409990

BOOKS IN THE RENEGADE STAR UNIVERSE

Renegade Star Series:

Renegade Star

Renegade Atlas

Renegade Moon

Renegade Lost

Renegade Fleet

Renegade Earth

Renegade Dawn

Renegade Children

Renegade Union

Renegade Empire

Renegade Descent

Renegade Rising

Renegade Alliance

Renegade Evolution *(Coming Dec. 2019)*

Standalones:

Nameless

The Constable

The Constable Returns

The Warrior Queen

The Orion Colony Series with Jonathan Yanez:

Orion Colony

Orion Uncharted

Orion Awakened

Orion Protected

The Last Reaper Series with Scott Moon:

The Last Reaper

Fear the Reaper

Blade of the Reaper

Wings of the Reaper

Flight of the Reaper

Wrath of the Reaper

Will of the Reaper

Descent of the Reaper

Hunt of the Reaper *(Coming Soon!)*

The Fifth Column Series with Molly Lerma:

The Fifth Column

The Solaras Initiative

The Forlorn Hope

Resonant Son Series with Christopher Hopper:

Resonant Son

Resonant Abyss

STAY UP TO DATE

Join the conversation and get updates on new and upcoming releases in the Facebook group called "JN Chaney's Renegade Readers." This is a hotspot where readers come together and share their lives and interests, discuss the series, and speak directly to J.N. Chaney and his co-authors.

https://www.facebook.com/groups/jnchaneyreaders/

He also post updates, official art, and other awesome stuff on his website and you can also follow him on Instagram, Facebook, and Twitter.

For email updates about new releases, as well as exclusive promotions, visit his website and sign up for the VIP mailing list. Head there now to receive a free copy of *The Other Side of Nowhere.*

DESCENT OF THE REAPER

BOOK 8 IN THE LAST REAPER SERIES

J.N. CHANEY

SCOTT MOON

CONTENTS

IMPORTANT TERMS AND CHARACTERS

SHIPS

(RWS = Republic of Wallach Ship)

BRIGHT LANCE OF XAD

- Flag ship of the Xad fleet
- Captured from the Union in Flight of the Reaper, TLR 5
- Captain: Cynthia Thomas Younger
- Executive Officer: Commander Bernard Gile

HUNTER OF XAD

- Captain Omon

STRIKER OF XAD

- Captain: Yolanda Dempsy

RWS BATTLE AXE

- With Jellybird scouting new system after Macabre
- Captain Hunger

RWS JUMPING FOX

- Captain: Jaime Peterson

RWS SPIRIT OF WALLACH

- Flag ship of the Republic of Wallach fleet

- Captain: Quincy Drysdale
- Ship the President of Wallach, Amanda Coronas, travels on. (She does not command the ship.)
- Ship that carries General Karn's main army

PEOPLE

A note to the reader from Scott Moon: Jeff and I saw a need for a cast of people and places in this series. I scoured my notes for all seven books so far; my part of the story development is very much stereotypical of most writers and artists—slightly disorganized (chaos!). So please remember this is a living document. Feel free to reach out to us if one of your favorite cast members is missing. A good place to interact is J.N. Chaney's Renegade Readers on Facebook.

Thanks,

Scott

Asis - soldier First Class of Xad

. . .

ANDREWS, Benjamin - Spec ops pilot

BACHMAN - SERGEANT DREADMAX security forces for the Bold Freedom

BUG - A KID from Dreadmax

BEAUFORT - REPAIRMAN on the Bright Lance of Xad and member of EVA work crews

BEN, Amon - Soldier, First Class. Xad citizen. Currently serving on the Bright Lance of Xad.

BRACKEN - WARRIOR of Yansden outlaws

BRIGGS - COMMANDER, Union Spec Ops

CAIN, Olivia Anna - Cain's mother

CAIN, Halek - The Last Reaper

. . .

CAIN, Hannah - Cain's sister

CALLUS, Marley - Union Spec Ops

CORANTH - SANSEIN alien

CRANK - SERGEANT, Union Spec Ops

DAY, Orson - Formerly a Corporal in the Union, now serving on the Bright Lance of Xad.

DEGRON, Tross - Delegate from the Alon Empire

DEMPSY, Yolanda - Captain of the Striker of Xad

DRYSDALE, Quincy - Captain of the RWS Spirit of Wallach

ENVOY - SANSEIN alien

. . .

Esquire, James - James Esquire III, Warden of the Bluesphere Maximum Security Prison

Feist, Theodore - Lieutenant, maintenance and supply officer, fourth watch, section 2 of the Bright Lance of Xad

Gile, Bernard - Commander / XO of the Bright Lance of Xad. Executive Officer for Captain Younger. Citizen of Xad.

Grady, Frederick Eugene (Feg) - Union commando. Friend of Halek Cain in The Last Reaper

Hanson, Kyle - First Lieutenant Kyle Hanson from The Last Reaper. Serves on the Bold Freedom.

Hastings, Elise - runaway, adventurer, was subject to Union experiments

Hastings, Paul - Doctor Paul Hastings, father of Elise. In the service of the Union.

. . .

HUNGER, Dan - Captain of the RWS Battle Axe

HUTTON, Cliff - Admiral of the Wallach Fleet

JORDAN - Sergeant loyal to Marley Callus in The Last Reaper

JUNKBOSS, Michael - Ensign on the Bright Lance of Xad. Controller for Elise during the repair mission of the RWS Jumping Fox.

KALON REGULARS - a military unit of Yansden.

KYLE - COMMANDER KYLE of the Wallach Presidential Guards

LARGO - SOLDIER FIRST Class of Xad

MICHAELS, Britton - Amateur assassin on Greendale

. . .

MOORE, Major Hubert Moore - ship doctor of the Bright Lance of Xad (formerly the UFS Dark Lance.)

NOVASDAUGHTER, Amii - Formerly a Union micro-fighter pilot. One of two girls Cain saved before he lost his arm and became a Reaper.

OBERON, Paul - Lieutenant serving on the Bright Lance of Xad. Special investigator.

OMON, Keeper - Captain of the Hunter of Xad

PETERSON, Jamie - Captain of the RWS Jumping Fox

REJON, Brion - Leader of Xad

SLAB - LEADER of the Red Skull Gangsters on Dreadmax

SLIPDRIVER, Max - fictional character

.   .   .

Sun, Suzan - Warrant Officer on the Bright Lance of Xad. Flight deck control supervisor. Formerly of the Union. Has applied for Xad citizenship and been vetted as trustworthy.

Thane, Byron - former rival of Halek Cain

Thane, Byron II - Byron Thane II, son of Byron Thane

Tross Degron - Alon delegate

Uluru, Sergeant - security chief of the Bright Lance of Xad brig.

Victon - Champion of the Alon

Walker, Kyle - Ensign on the Bridge of the Bright Lance of Xad.

Younger, Cynthia Thomas - Captain of the Bright Lance of Xad. Citizen of Xad.

. . .

Xeres, Samantha - Doctor: Chief Medical Officer on the Bright Lance of Xad. Formerly a Union citizen, now applying for citizenship with Xad.

X-37 - the limited artificial intelligence (LAI) of Halek Cain, the last Reaper.

GLOSSARY

Alon strike group - three corvette class ships, one battle cruiser, and one support ship

Sansein - Aliens first named in The Last Reaper 7, Will of the Reaper

Slayer - Human/Alien hybrid first seen in The Last Reaper

PLACES

GRONIC - PLANET in the Deadlands

NEW SALON - HOMEWORLD of the Alon

WALLACH - HOME WORLD left behind by the people of Wallach after several natural disasters

XAD - HOME WORLD left behind by the people of Xad after hundreds of years of space battles, a comet, and other issues made it unsuitable for human habitation.

YANSDEN – planet deep within Alon space

POLITICS

REPUBLIC OF WALLACH

- President Amanda Coronas

- General Karn
- Admiral Cliff Hutton
- CSL Locke

XAD

- Brion Rejon, leader of Xad
- Captain Cynthia Thomas Younger, highest ranking officer in the Xad Fleet.

PREVIOUSLY IN WILL OF THE REAPER

CAIN and his friends survived a three-way battle between the Alon, Slayers, and a truly alien race called the Sansein. The first betrayed them in the second fall of the twisted nature, except for one hybrid struggling to remain human. As for first contact with the Sansein, it could've gone better. The highly advanced and mysterious creatures now seem to be at war with humanity. Cain holds out hope that there is one called Envoy who may bridge the gap in the future. In the meantime, the fleet is scattered across several systems. The Last Reaper and his friends must find and explore a world neither the Alon nor the Sansein dare trod upon.

1

I HIT my last burpee like a twenty-year-old, then sprinted across the small training deck. Driving hard with my legs and pumping my arms for momentum required all the sprinting technique I'd been refining just for this race.

Elise finished her burpees and began her run for the finish line. It wasn't often I had this kind of lead on the girl, so I needed to win—for her sake. She was getting cocky and needed a lesson. Unfortunately, that was easier said than done these days.

"I'm coming for you, Reaper!" she shouted.

My response sounded like an enraged animal. Elise laughed —actually laughed—as she sprinted ahead of me.

"You should have defeated her, Reaper Cain," X-37 said in my ear when I'd finished and started walking with my hands on my head to open up my lungs. "The distance was short, and your improved sprinting technique combined with raw strength should have given you the advantage."

"Not helpful, X." I tried not to look at Elise, avoiding the trash talking for as long as possible.

"I thought you were going to crush me, Reaper. I guess that lecture on how different distance running is from a life and death sprint—"

"It *is* different," I said, wanting to puke from the exertion of this little farce. "Who cares if you always win on the treadmill?"

"I always win on the track too."

"Don't get cocky, kid."

"You're losing your edge," Elise said, hands on her hips. "Is that the lesson you were going to teach me, because I'm not sure I get it. You don't have to sacrifice your dignity to build my confidence. I'm good. Completely certain of what I can do."

"The Union didn't give me the ability to recover from workouts that they gave you. If I could train three times a day without wrecking myself, I'd be kicking your ass, kid," I said, bending forward to put my hands on my knees.

"Not a kid, Reaper. As for kicking my ass... whatever." She straightened and went to the water cooler we'd put in the corner of our gymnasium. "Is the big scary Reaper sore from our workout yesterday?"

What the Union had done to her and how we met was a touchy topic. I knew she healed quickly. Everything else was either innate or the result of hard work. When she obsessed over a new skill, like flying the micro-fighters, she practiced with fanatic intensity.

Then she talked trash, which I was morally obligated to return with interest—when possible.

"What's the matter, Reaper?"

"Your day will come." I stretched my back.

"Maybe we shouldn't race." She shook her head at my unimpressive level of flexibility. "I don't want to hurt you."

"Doesn't matter how fast you are," I said, laughing with frustration right behind the words. "You have to follow my lead during the mission to Yansden, and that means staying on the ship with Hannah, Bug, and Tom while I go down to have a look. Path will remain here to help you watch the Slayer."

"Briggs doesn't give me a problem," Elise said, already recovered from our little challenge. She had a glow to her skin that was… youthful. "By your own logic, I should go with you, maybe even take the lead, so you can teach me stuff. I'm not going to learn the ropes unless I get my hands dirty."

"Yeah, yeah," I said.

"She has a point," X-37 said to me privately. "Seventeen hours and three minutes ago you told me it was time to start treating her like an adult."

"Don't take my words out of context, X." I found my own water bottle and took a long drink.

"Victon told you there was a secret weapon on Yansden that we need to protect the Wallach-Xad fleet," Elise said, stepping into my personal space.

"Right. But he said weapon, not ship." I was tired of this argument and couldn't understand why no one agreed with me.

Elise shook her head, really frustrated now. "Even if it was a weapon, it would have to be so big it would require a ship—like the fleet paralyzer of planet Xad."

"Slow down, kid. I know more about weapons, and ships for that matter, than you do."

"But you don't know more about ships than Tom," she said, keeping her tone more reasonable than when we first met. She was maturing and I appreciated that.

I adopted my most civil tone, which was probably just north of being a total jerk, but I tried. "Tom agrees with me."

"No, he doesn't, and Path is better at personal combat with any weapon than you are," Elise said, moving to stay in front of me as I turned away in annoyance. "Why aren't we getting his opinion on this Sansein killing super thingy?"

"Path doesn't know how to use them to end wars—as in, he's not an assassin. Thanks for making me say it." I squared up with her. "We're done with this conversation."

"How convenient. You can't stand being wrong," Elise said.

"It's late. I'm hitting the bunk," I said. "In the morning, I'll take a look at Yansden and if I need you, I'll have you come down with Hannah or something."

"Oh, you jerk!" Elise balled her fists and stormed out of the training area.

Several seconds of silence passed.

"Do you really think you will be able to sleep, Reaper Cain?" X-37 asked.

"I guess we'll find out. Elise doesn't understand work life balance. I'm doing my best without cigars—that means rest and relaxation whenever I can get it, because you and I know there won't be any of that once we touch down on Yansden." I headed in the general direction of my room. "Sleep, a good breakfast, and some time on the observation deck, then I'll go to the planet and see what we're dealing with. Have Jelly continue to patrol the system until then."

"Of course, Reaper Cain."

"YANSDEN IS A FASCINATING SYSTEM, REAPER CAIN," X-37 said. "And so far, it doesn't seem anyone in it wants to kill you yet. Recommendation, enjoy it while it lasts."

Things always seemed weird when my LAI made idle conversation. Warning bells chimed right at the edge of my subconscious—a dark and mysterious place where my animal instincts lurked. In my defense, I was still distracted by my argument with Elise. "Why would anyone want to kill me? I'm retired."

"Truly?" X-37 asked, sounding genuinely surprised—a tone he didn't use often.

"I'm pulling your chain, X. I'm going out in a blaze of glory. Everybody knows Reapers don't die," I said. "Or retire. Someone from the Union has to do that for us, in case you forgot the frequent assassination attempts on me and my death row sentence and subsequent incarceration."

"I have retained that information though rarely dwell on it, per one of your earlier requests," X-37 said.

I waved my hand in a tight circle, indicating the conversation was over and we needed to move on. "Call me crazy, but those ore haulers heading to Yansden are really loaded down. Where are their escorts? The Union would have at least a squadron of warships in the area for something like that. And why aren't the Alon raiding them; they have to know this is the situation."

Every ship we'd seen coming from or going to the asteroid belts in the system was pushing four or five times its own mass using a simple but effective technique I thought the people of Xad would appreciate. The situation looked like pirate bait. Something about the arrangement was off. If I'd come for raw materials, I could have made out like a bandit with no resistance.

Or fallen prey to the mother of all traps.

"Yansden is a rich system, developed by the ancestors of the Alon, if the design of their void capable conveyances is a good indicator of who these people are," X-37 said. "My analysis suggests they've been building surplus for centuries. What you're seeing must be the result of a society with an abundance mindset, rather than the scarcity mindset you grew up with."

"What the hell are you talking about, X?" I switched the holo to show a new set of ships chugging along toward the planet.

"The people here are not as paranoid as you are," X-37 said.

"Okay, that makes sense. For a bunch of crazy people."

"It's good that we have these little talks, Reaper Cain."

Something was definitely off with my digital friend. Maybe it was too soon to wonder if X was stalling, but maybe not. There was no reason for the behavior, so it felt random—not a common occurrence with my LAI but it did happen.

"The nine hours of sleep you managed—with my help—have done you good, Reaper Cain. Don't waste it," X-37 said.

"I'm not," I snapped.

"You should relax, Reaper Cain."

"I am."

"You should."

"X, let's stop right here before you start sounding like Elise."

The next thing my limited artificial intelligence said confirmed my suspicions. "I've not consulted Elise on what I should say to you. There is absolutely no reason for me to require such advice."

"You're lying, X."

"How could I lie to you, Reaper Cain?"

"We've covered this. You explained to me in excruciating detail that you could lie to me if you thought it was in my best interest or if the deception served the mission," I said. "Normally, I find this pretty irritating, but I came here to relax and that's what I'm going to do."

"You should." X-37 paused, and when he paused, it was like the silence of an airlock. Not my favorite sensation, even though I understood it was just my perception playing tricks.

I shifted, trying to get comfortable without admitting I was waiting for X to finish the statement.

"You should," X repeated. "Relax, that is." His lack of concern for my mental health was bullshit. "Just take a breath, let it out slowly, and relax—"

"I am relaxing!"

"Your biometrics suggest quite the opposite."

"Because you're being a pain in my ass!"

"Reaper Cain, I was created to monitor your wellbeing and maximize your performance…"

Sometimes, the only way to deal with an advanced computer algorithm woven into your nerve ware was to ignore it. So I did, praying there was no sound deprivation chamber quality silent treatments headed my way. I deserved a vacation even if it was just a couple of hours on the observation deck.

Still annoyed, I selected the panoramic view of the system; computerized images of planets, moons, asteroid fields, and the star in which the focus of my attention grew large enough for me to see—like the *Jellybird* was zooming in with a powerful telescope. It worked best when I was chilled out and going with the flow. Jelly used the same technology during combat situations. In those conditions, the change in perspective could be harsh and jarring—kind of like combat itself.

"Are you listening, Reaper Cain? Shall I discontinue my review of your recovery schedule, caloric needs, and the point by point list of improvements you need to make if you are ever going to win another foot race against Elise?"

I manipulated the holo, touring the system from where the slip tunnel had dumped us to the planet we were approaching in full stealth mode. What I didn't do was patronize my extremely frustrating LAI.

"Would you like to see more of the freight haulers from the habitable planet?" X asked.

"No."

Few things were better than a cigar and whiskey on the observation deck—*if I had a cigar* and if I enjoyed drinking alone. Tom was normally here around this time but was conspicuously absent. Sometimes the rest of the crew was gathered in the lounge to play games of chance or argue and tell jokes at my expense.

"Where is everyone?" I asked. "I thought I'd have company by now."

X-37 answered but I suspected Jelly was also ready with an explanation. The ship AI and my LAI worked well together. "Elise, Bug, and your sister Hannah have descended to the Kalon planet called Yansden," X-37 said. "I'm treating this as a direct question above any of my allowed deception protocols."

"Not funny, X. Work on it."

"That was in no way intended to be humorous," X-37 said.

I stood up, making a fist because I didn't have a cigar to relieve my stress. This had the makings of a serious crisis, but I forced myself to hesitate. Without more information, I wasn't sure where to aim my anger. "X, I'm going to need the rest of the story. Leave nothing out."

"Of course. Right away, Reaper Cain," my LAI said, then continued to stall.

I turned my back on the wall-sized holo screen and headed for the door, still not rushing to failure but definitely thinking about kicking it up a notch. Elise and my friends were loyal and brave—and a huge pain in the ass. I'd made the mistake of guessing their intentions in the past. It was better to know, to choose my reactions based on facts and not to go off half-cocked. Or so everyone kept telling me.

"I'm waiting, X. And this had better be good."

"In my defense, Elise made several convincing arguments in favor of delaying your reaction to her mission. I'll store them for later use if you wish to review those particular discussions and the details therein," X-37 said. "I should also mention that she has learned a great deal from your sister, Hannah, in regard to subtlety and espionage."

"What are you doing, Hannah?" I asked no one.

"From the evidence I was able to gather, or piece back together after defeating several clever encryption algorithms they implemented to block my probes, it seems they've gone down to Yansden with the intent of infiltrating the primary shipyard," X-37 said. "Where they believe the secret weapon Victon mentioned must be hidden."

"Fuck my life."

"Is that a request or an order, Reaper—"

"You know it isn't, X. Just give me a second."

"Perhaps you should punch something," my limited artificial intelligence suggested.

"I'd like to punch you."

"Impossible."

I headed for the armory, picking up the pace now. A calm and reasoned response was good but now I needed to enter the phase I called getting shit done, kicking ass and taking names, or just showing everyone what's what.

"Are you having an episode?" X-37 asked.

I ignored the question.

"HAL, I can do that for you. Just give me a few minutes to get to the equipment room," Tom said. He sounded tired, still recovering from some sort of slip tunnel flu that had been plaguing him for several days.

"I got it, Tom. If you want to come down and send me off, that's fine. But you don't have to. You looked like death warmed over last time I saw you," I said.

"I'm on my way. Feels good to stretch my legs a bit," he said.

X-37 beeped me. "You really should wait for him."

"I think I've wasted enough time, don't you?"

"Perhaps I should not comment, as not to incriminate myself," X-37 said.

I became more and more irritated as I gathered my gear. "I can't believe you betrayed me like this."

"As I have stated repeatedly, Reaper Cain, you were asleep," X-37 said. "This in no way constitutes a betrayal."

"You should've woken me up!" I shouted as I pulled on the under-suit for my gear.

"The Archangel armor will draw too much attention, Reaper Cain," X-37 said. "Please refrain from acting rashly."

"Whatever, X. You're a pushy son-of-a-bitch today," I complained, but I dressed in regular street gear, dumb armor that didn't have all the features of the high-tech union battle load-out. Once I'd checked everything, I packaged the Archangel equipment for drop and saw that Elise had done the same with three sets of gear—two Archangels and one simpler civilian armor I suspected was for Bug.

At least the kid was thinking for the future, which was good unless she expected me to be on the ship ready to send the equipment drop when she got in over her head. "Tom, when you get here can you check the deployment bundles?"

"Sure thing, Hal. I'll be there in a minute," Tom said, not sounding nearly as tuned up about this fiasco as I was.

"It's good we can rely on Tom," X-37 said. "Path has also inquired as to your timeline. He is on his way."

"I don't want everyone on the ship going down to the surface," I said to no one in particular. X-37 would listen, of course. That wasn't the problem. My frustration was with Elise, and to a lesser degree my sister. "I'm just going down there to gather them up. Once we're all back in the same room, we can make a plan everyone agrees on."

"Of course, Reaper Cain," X-37 said. "I've advised the sword saint and he has returned to his meditations."

"I'm still super pissed that you let Elise talk you into this."

"You expressed no need to restrict her movements, or anything that she does. In fact, you said that it was probably time to treat her like an adult," X-37 said. "Had I known this would upset you, I would have awoken you at once."

"Excuses are like assholes, X. Everyone has one," I said, setting my LAI up for a vicious one-up.

"Incorrect, Reaper Cain. I have no physical orifices."

"But you act like one!"

"Is that intended as humor, Reaper Cain? My analysis suggests your verbal attack was a cheap shot."

"Just keep track of Elise and the others." I checked my pockets for anything useful—like the possibility of a lighter and cigars—then headed for the shuttle.

This mission was going to suck. How the hell had I put myself at the ass end of the galaxy with not a single cigar in sight? No one cared about my needs. I couldn't even talk to X about it, because he would just point out that it was a perfect time to quit. "Notify me the moment they have contact with the locals."

"Of course, Reaper Cain. Jelly and I will do our best. There are several environmental and technological factors making real-time intelligence gathering difficult," X-37 said.

"There always are. Do your best." I was halfway across the flight deck when I saw Briggs. "Are you carrying a go-bag?"

"Yeah, Cain. I'm coming with you. You could try to stop me, but I don't recommend it," Briggs said, then showed his fangs. "Awk."

"This is what I get for giving you run of the ship," I muttered, not quite ready for this confrontation. As a ship captain, I apparently had very little authority over anyone. I needed to start laying down the law. It took all my self-control not to just take the entire crew down to this quarantined and probably dangerous planet. Why not? Let's just all get ourselves killed.

"I can hear you, Cain—even when you're muttering like a disgruntled supply sergeant. But you know that." Briggs sauntered toward me, his long legs eating up a surprising amount of distance. The way he was built, he looked like he was taking his time when he was actually moving very quickly.

I studied the Slayer. Over a head taller than me and covered in muscle, he was a freak in other ways as well—his dark blue skin spotted in places and striped in others for very effective natural camouflage. Increasing changes to his vocal cords—and some of the words he used—were also disturbing. "There's no way you can blend down there."

Briggs held up a backpack with extra-long straps to fit his altered physique, a tarp with a hole cut in the center to make a huge poncho, and a wide brimmed hat made from a flat black insulation panel.

"I'm glad you still know how to put an outfit together. Only wish your sense of style had improved." I wanted to smile but wasn't sure how he would react.

"I'm doing my best, Cain." The mutated creature looked forlorn but determined.

"I'm not trying to be an asshole, and I know you'd have my back in a fight, but this has to be a covert mission," I said. "No fighting."

"I could use your stealth cloak. Awk, awk, awk," he said, making the throaty sound that came more and more often when he talked.

Shaking my head, I held up a hand to stop his argument *and* the noise he was making. "You're too tall. Your freaky feet will show. All the kids will run screaming the moment they spot you. And it grosses me out when you shoot tentacles from your forearms at your food."

"I'll stay in the shadows. Awk." The way he said this gave me a shiver no Reaper should ever feel.

I wasn't scared of anything. Except this guy who'd gone from an abomination begging me to kill him to the galaxy's ugliest bodyguard.

"Captain," Jelly interrupted. "My latest sensor check may be reassuring. While searching for Elise and the others, I've learned only one metropolitan area seems crowded and only during certain times of the day. Most of the production facilities are maintained through various automated procedures. What I'm trying to say is that you should be able to avoid crowds of people even in areas with fully functioning power grids."

"So, we'll stick out," I said. "Or get swarmed if we stumble into one of the crowded sections of the city. Kind of a lose-lose scenario."

X-37 clicked several times in my ear. "Jelly was attempting to be helpful, Reaper Cain."

"Fine." I strode toward the shuttle, motioning for Briggs to come with me. "I'm sorry about that, Jelly. This day just seems to be going sideways."

"You're letting me come?" Briggs asked, his question sounding ridiculous because of his size and obvious potential to rip me limb from limb. Looking at my old spec ops commander, I realized he was probably going to do whatever he wanted and there was very little chance I could stop him.

"Yeah, you can come. Maybe you'll like it down there so much I can just leave you and save myself a lot of trouble in the future," I said.

"You don't have to be a dick about it. Awk, awwwwk, huawk." Briggs climbed onto the shuttle ahead of me, grunting and snarling like he did without realizing it.

"He's right, you know," X-37said.

"He knows I don't mean it like that."

"Does he, Reaper Cain? Does he really?"

2

ONCE THE SHUTTLE had cut through the stratosphere, I observed cities full of black buildings that shimmered as though made from glass. Manipulating the controls, I adjusted the resolution until I could see the nearest metropolis on the coast. From space, I had thought it was a vibrant, technologically advanced city full of lights rimming the continents.

Now I realized large swaths of it were vacant and neglected. "Why is the power still on if they're so depopulated?"

"I'm gathering information through Jelly's scans, Reaper Cain," X-37 said. "Most likely, this is the effect of the quarantine that was mentioned earlier. The circumstances around this system's past were shrouded in secrecy by the Alon. The farther you travel from the shipyard, the greater the population density."

I thought about Victon's claim there was a weapon capable of defeating the Sansein on this planet. He'd told me this was where the last hope of the Alon rested. I had a bad feeling that no matter how I interpreted the information, it was going to come back and bite me before this was over. Probably squarely on the ass.

I wanted to believe it was a weapon for a champion and that I could be the champion, doing something good with my life. Everyone else seemed to think it was a ship or a ship's weapon that could be used against our new alien adversaries. I needed to know the answer but was afraid to learn the truth.

"Much of the region's infrastructure is automated, as we've seen throughout the system. It's like most of the people left for distant stars but never turned off all the machines," X-37 said.

"That could be a bad thing or a good thing," I commented, taking another pass along the coast at very high altitudes. "Especially if the machines are running things. No offense, X."

"Taking offense is not part of my programing. There are significant populations of humans, or at least humanoids, on the planet," X-37 said. "I am attempting to gather more data but have found nothing informative as of yet. It is unclear as to why they wouldn't turn off the system wide automations, or at least use the resources being gathered on a scale grand enough to construct another exodus fleet."

"I want to take a closer look," I said. "Let me know if I'm getting picked up by whatever stealth detection technologies they have."

"Of course, Reaper Cain," X-37 said. "I believe you can fly quite close as long as you avoid visual detection. The shuttle has better than average radar avoidance ability, from Jelly's earlier service as a smuggler. I recommend landing the shuttle in an unpopulated, rural area to avoid drone and bot detection."

"Understood," I said. "I'm going to play it safe while you gather as much information as you can. There will be a test on it later."

"There always is," X-37 said.

"Am I picking up sarcasm from you, X?"

"Perhaps a little, Reaper Cain."

The coastal city sprawled for hundreds of kilometers to the north and south. In its prime, it had been densely populated by the look of it. I could see wide highways and heavy railroads leading to and from manufacturing centers.

There were also thousands of skyscrapers constructed from what looked like black glass. The entire scene appeared dusty and neglected. What I assumed had been impoverished neighborhoods were falling apart, more prone to various forms of decay. Herds of animals roamed through one of the cities we passed over.

I spotted the spaceports near automated lifts reaching into the clouds. Most of the population centers seemed to be concentrated there. "Is that where Elise and the others went?"

"It is, Reaper Cain," X-37 said.

"Great. Why can't anything be easy? Don't answer that, X. I was just thinking out loud." Steering away from the city, I found a secluded glen free of technology. Heading straight into the walled metropolis felt like a mistake. The last thing I wanted was electronic interference with my shuttle or an ambush by local security forces.

Briggs stared at our prospective landing zone. "Looks good. Not too far, not too close. Still have to get into the city to find Elise."

"One obstacle at a time," I said, then landed the shuttle.

BRIGGS STARED up at the thirty-meter-tall trees, hands hanging at his side like he'd forgotten he had them.

"You've seen trees before," I said, moving past him to sweep the shadows with my Reaper mask and cybernetic eye. Instinct prompted me to use every tool I had right now, even though I couldn't wear the mask for extended periods. I mean, I could, but I didn't like the inhuman quality of the view. It was better to shove it in my jacket most of the time.

"Not like this," he said, voice straining to sound human. "You were right, Cain. I could live here. Maybe you should just leave me when this mission is over."

The idea didn't sound as good now as I had assumed it would, so I kept my mouth shut.

"Don't you see them, Cain?" Briggs asked.

"I see trees, and animals. Lots of nature stuff." I patted him on the shoulder. "It's very nice, Slayer."

He bared his teeth at me and hissed. "Look again."

I complied, mostly to give X-37 another chance at logging data of our exploration. What I realized after a few moments was that the old spec ops commander was probably onto something.

There was a man-made structure high up in the branches that looked like woven vines or maybe a rope.

"Now you believe me," Briggs said. "What should we do?"

The question reminded me how different this man was than he had been before Doctor Ayers merged his DNA with that of the Sansein. It was hard to say if his intellect was more advanced or more primitive as the changes continued. I wasn't as smart as Henshaw or Tom, but I knew better than to make assumptions. Briggs acted like a brute, sometimes even like a naïve child, but he had his own intellect and saw things from a unique perspective.

The Slayer behaved differently than I expected. Not so long ago, he would've been trying to tell me what to do. Now he was following my lead.

"I'll have X-37 mark the location for future exploration," I said. "We need to find Elise and the others. That's our priority."

He nodded enthusiastically. "Yes, yes. That's right. Good shit. I remember."

I checked my coat, put away my Reaper mask for now, and headed toward the nearest population center. Once we were several hundred meters away from our shuttle, I looked back to make sure it was well hidden. Neither X nor Briggs could see it either, so I felt confident it would be there when we returned.

The city of black glass and dark steel loomed on the horizon, much more impressive from here in the countryside. If I hadn't done the flyover, I might still believe it was a thriving metropolis. Many of the tall buildings had lights to warn away, or perhaps interact with, aircraft and drones. Freight vehicles moved on rails into the city and I even detected a highway that I believed had personal vehicles moving in a coherent traffic pattern.

Briggs kept up easily, but often stopped to watch our back trail. His behavior was a mixture of spec ops commando and animalistic hunter. As companions and bodyguards went, he took some getting used to, but I thought things were going to work out. I was glad I hadn't pushed him out of the airlock during our first argument.

The terrain was best described as rolling hills with sparse forests. We stopped and rested whenever we found a clear stream, drinking from it once I conducted a few field tests to be sure it was safe. The sun was going down and the air was cool.

"X, can you get a read on Elise or the others?" I asked.

"Jelly has been working on detecting their exact location, but it has proven difficult," X-37 said. "If there were an existing civilization that we understood, we could piggyback on their technology. Thus far that has been challenging as we are not certain how to use their fundamental science. To you, it looks like a human civilization. To Jelly and me, it is very strange and unique. Not bad, but worthy of caution."

"I get it," I said, wishing I had a cigar but also knowing I wouldn't have smoked one in any case. Not while on a mission with so many unknowns. Maybe my LAI was right about really quitting this time.

"There are a large number of drones," X-37 said. "Thus far, their flight patterns have been predictable. I think we can avoid them easily."

"I've been on Union and Deadlands worlds that relied on

bots and clones," I said. "Most of the time their economies revolved around manufacturing. So, what you're telling me isn't a surprise."

"It would be outstanding if the shipyard we observed was functional and could be retrofitted to serve the Wallach and Xad fleets," X-37 said. "But this doesn't explain why Victon thought the secret to defeating the Sansein could be found on this planet."

Briggs and I finished our break, drank some water, and moved closer to the metropolis. When we reached the highway, I saw that it was a combination of single vehicles and automated trains. We kept our distance, not wanting to be detected. From time to time, pairs of drones zipped over the traffic, ignoring us completely. It was like they had a job to do and we weren't part of it.

After an hour, we stopped, unable to continue without entering the roadway. The terrain below the elevated highway was artificially rugged, divided by deep trenches, clusters of pipes, and spillways that were dry but that I didn't trust. The last thing I wanted was to be caught unaware.

"What do you think, X?" I remained crouched near a power conduit and signal box at the apex of an on-ramp, ready to move into the trafficway if needed but not yet committed.

"Mathematically, it seems possible for any vehicle to merge with traffic into the city," X-37 said. "Your situation is complicated by your lack of a vehicle. Perhaps you could steal one."

"I need to find one that's not automated," I said. "And I don't see any pedestrians."

Some of the cars looked as though people were driving them,

even though I couldn't see inside their dark windows. Twilight made everything harsh, with running lights casting shadows as the vehicles passed, and the star fields in the sky provided little illumination. Normally, I would consider it the perfect time to move through an urban environment. But there were so many unknowns.

"There is a gatehouse," Briggs said simply. "Or maybe it is a tollbooth. Either way there are guards and they do not appear to be bots."

I zoomed in and saw what he was looking at, a system of buildings on each side of the main roadway where people slowed their vehicles to check in. Humanoid figures wearing rough, grey and black armor with dark red helmets—I really wanted to call them human but I wasn't really sure—approached vehicles and sometimes looked inside of them. I thought one had a dog or similar animal that he used to search for anything suspicious.

"Everything happens with such purpose," Briggs said. "It's good shit. Organized. Probably humans. Not aliens or anything."

"You're right, Briggs," I said. The way my friend talked, it would be easy to tease him. And I guessed we were friends now after all we'd been through. But I thought it was too soon to toy with him. He was still learning how to be human, or whatever he was now.

"Except that vehicle." Briggs pointed at a boxy van-like car probably big enough for several people to be inside. "It's parked on the shoulder of the highway. I haven't seen any like that before. Watch, there are guards going to check it out."

I dialed in my optics and was disappointed that this boxy

vehicle had glass as dark as all the others. It was impossible to see who or what was driving it.

"I bet it will not stay to be inspected," Briggs said with great deliberation.

"I agree with the Slayer," X-37 said.

Moments later, the boxy vehicle accelerated forward, then merged with traffic as though heading into the city. Briggs lost sight of it, but I guessed where it would go and was soon rewarded. It had moved, but not far—just enough to escape inspection by the local law enforcement officials.

More important to our mission, I suspected whoever or whatever was in the van-like vehicle was watching us.

3

BRIGGS and I stalked along the roadway drainage system, looking for a vehicle we could steal or stowaway inside. I circled my finger one time in the air, then pointed into the concrete ditch, indicating it would be our rally point if we had to fall back from an overwhelming attack or other problem. Standard control tactics like this comforted my friend, probably reminding him that we had both been soldiers in the same army long ago.

Darkness fell hard on Yansden and whatever the city was called. The night was without a moon. The distant nebula my friends and I had probably traversed at least in part during recent months was barely visible, almost seeming an illusion.

X-37 identified the glint of satellites orbiting the planet and differentiated them from air capable vehicles traversing the upper atmosphere. Everything seemed very systematic and ordered, but also strangely calm. The longer I spent on the surface of this planet the lonelier I felt.

"I wonder why some stayed behind," Briggs said during one of our breaks. He squatted low, frequently peeking over the top of a safety rail in case one of the slow-moving conveyances could be hijacked.

"I doubt they had a choice." The words felt wrong the moment I said them.

"Quarantine or no quarantine, I don't see anyone stopping the people of Yansden from exploring the stars," Briggs said. "They have technology. They have all the good shit."

"Why do you keep saying that, Briggs?" I asked.

"Talking isn't so easy in my condition," he answered. "Words make themselves. I only steer them. Or that's what it fucking feels like."

"Hey, no worries. Just thought I'd ask."

A pair of security drones raced low over the multi-lane roadway, then veered into the city on a smaller entrance. I didn't think it would work for us, but at least I could see there was more than one entrance into the city. If we didn't find something, the only option would be to land the shuttle inside the metropolis and raise five thousand alarms with the locals. Then the red helmets would be all over us.

"Why do you think people were left behind, X?" I asked. "Why the quarantine?"

"The logical explanation is that workers were expected to maintain the planet for future use or build new ships to follow once the quarantine is lifted," X-37 said. "The main problem with this hypothesis is that I detect no way to enforce the quarantine. The residents of Yansden, with the technological sophistication evident in their cities and manufacturing industries, should also be capable of slip tunnel travel—or whatever they consider an equivalent method of extra stellar movement. Something is keeping the masses away from the shipyard. I advise caution. "

We found a road that entered the massive wall protecting the city. I wasn't sure if it was a wall so much as it was the city itself, merely its outer layer. The structure rose higher and descended lower than I could see. All I knew for sure was that if I stepped off one of the access bridges I'd be falling for a long time.

We watched the less trafficked entrance until we timed how the doors opened.

"It reminds me of a starship, or maybe Dreadmax," Briggs said, staring at the black wall that was either glass or metal with glass pressed against it. "Good... good shit."

"I don't see any real security problems," I said. "Correct me if I'm wrong, X, but I think this is mostly an environmental shield. Maybe even something to do with the quarantine."

Briggs shook his head in disagreement but avoided speaking. I thought he might have something to say but didn't want to risk how his voice would sound. The larger and more inhuman he grew, the more his biology distorted his vocal cords.

"I doubt that it has anything to do with the quarantine," X-37 said. "For such a protocol to be effective, it must be all or nothing. Your first hypothesis is most likely correct, Reaper Cain. Like most planets, wind and weather can have damaging effects on technology. My suggestion is to approach and enter the city when the gate opens to admit one of the automated drones."

"Easy enough," I said.

"Say when, Reaper," Briggs croaked, sounding nervous.

I mentally ran through a list of things that could bother the Slayer, then attempted to reassure him. "Stick to the shadows. We'll go slow. If we see anybody, we can just watch them until we decide how to interact."

"Okay, Cain. That's good shit," Briggs muttered, barely understandable because he was attempting to resist making the monstrous noises that came out when he tried to use human words.

Large vehicles loaded with roughhewn timber approached. The city gate opened automatically, early enough that none of the conveyances needed to slow down. It was a well-timed system. More and more I was assured that this was going to be easy.

"Let's move," I said.

"On you." Briggs hopped to his feet.

We strode quickly toward the opening but didn't run. It wasn't time for that. I'd rather have some gas left in my tank for a sprint if things went sideways. Like they were prone to on nearly every mission.

A pair of vehicles approached on wheels, moving fast. Lights flashed on the front and rear, pulsing white and purple in a way designed to get attention.

"Watch out, Briggs," I said, then started jogging between two self-driving carts full of raw minerals from who knew where. It wasn't a perfect hiding place, but it bought us some time. Briggs stayed close, running in a half crouch to avoid showing his head above the log-carrying trailers that were moving faster than we could sprint.

"Stay in the slow lanes, Briggs," I warned.

"I'm trying," the Slayer responded.

"We're drawing too much attention." What I really wanted was to stowaway on a vehicle headed for a quiet area where we could plan our next move, maybe even make radio contact with Elise, Hannah, and Bug.

"There are additional security elements en route," X-37 said. "I haven't deciphered their language, but the pattern of their communication suggests this is the case."

"I thought you started working on that the moment we entered the system?" I asked.

"Their extra planetary communications are much different than the local frequencies," X-37 said. "Every word is contextual, like idioms or jargon. Even the Sansein with their binary obsession seem easy by comparison."

"Do you have audio of their radio comms?" I asked. "Maybe we can get a feel for their language. Tactical communication has a recognizable rhythm."

"Negative, Reaper Cain. They are using radio waves but also infrared light pulses that are quite effective in terms of security," X-37 said. "I can translate these into language, but there will be a several second delay—and even then, I assume they will speak in codes. It may sound familiar but will certainly be misleading. Apologies, Reaper Cain. I am embarrassed that I have not constructed a functioning codex of their languages. Just when it seems I've hacked their dialects and the foundational principles of their technology, I run into something new. If a machine could be insane, I would say this planet is run by such a thing."

"I bet I can understand their tactical banter, X."

"Doubtful."

"Just keep me updated," I said, realizing I was about to lose my hiding place. The automated timber haulers ahead of us veered off the roadway, then down a track we couldn't navigate. Other vehicles were smaller.

"That is a bus, or something. It's slowing down," Briggs said, barely grunting. "Do you think they will stop for us?"

"I'm not sure that's what we're looking for. Too easy. Can you see people inside it?" I asked.

The Slayer rose onto his toes as he ran, peering into the blackened windows. "Can't see. Really dark."

"Not dark, painted. Why would they do that?" I asked, keeping pace as best I could and looking at places where the covering had been scratched off just enough for the drivers to see where they were going.

"Prison bus?"

The vehicle pulled onto a frontage road where others waited for inspection. I saw the guards and felt exposed. About the time one of the men with a sniffing animal headed our way, moving faster moment by moment, a box-like conveyance on rubber padded wheels careened into the road. Seconds later, the guard diverted toward the disturbance to help fellow guards. Other vehicles joined the bottleneck.

"What's happening?" Briggs asked.

I pointed at a blinking sign above the line of vehicles. "Everyone started pulling in here when that lit up. Mandatory inspection of some sort. Might work in our favor."

We saw our first pedestrians when one of the blacked-out busses disgorged men, women, and children in work gear—heavy overalls, goggles, and grime covering them from head to toe. Some left the roadway, disappearing into a subway system. Others walked along the main thoroughfare, which really pissed off the guards.

"Too many people to bully like that," Briggs said. "Poor planning. Poor training. Fuck, fuck. Bad shit."

"We can merge with the crowd. Keep your head down, don't talk," I said.

"Won't work," Briggs grunted. "Already getting looks."

He wasn't wrong. Even in the poor light, people pointed when they noticed Briggs. The poncho-like cloak he wore couldn't hide his size.

"Go back, hide in the woods. We'll meet at the shuttle after I find Elise and the others," I said.

"No, no. Can't do that. Awk. I'll go crazy. Might wander away and not come back," he said. "Has to be another way for me to get past this place."

The box van that initially distracted the guard started honking its horn again. Soon, all of the guards were pounding on the doors to the vehicle as spectators jeered and made lewd gestures.

"Now's our chance, Briggs. If we're going, it has to be right now. Hunch down, move fast, and get to the subway. I'll try to run interference if anyone gets too curious," I said, already feeling like we were making a mistake.

The Slayer moved with frightening speed, slicing through the crowd, pushing when he had to but never stopping to answer the angry words neither of us could understand anyway. His drab poncho partially concealed his spotted blue skin and misshapen head.

A new set of lights flashed, prohibiting vehicles from entering the inspection area. Then a horn sounded. Pedestrian traffic changed pace, quickly transforming into a mob running for the subway trains at the bottom of the stairs.

Instead of enclosed passenger cars, these were multi-level flat cars, open to anyone who wanted to jump on—or get pushed off.

Briggs hesitated.

"Do it! Jump for the top level. Fewer people up there," I said, instantly realizing my mistake. The top level was for the most agile members of the group—which basically meant kids and their weird pets. The younger the children, the more likely they were to have fuzzy bipedal mammals that looked like they belonged in trees. The creatures hung on the little ones and made me think of the rope bridges we'd seen near our landing zone.

With a Slayer curse, Briggs flung himself toward the slow-moving train, easily jumping higher than any of the normal passengers who were hopping to the lower level. Dozens of people watched his unlikely progress, stunned into inaction.

"Good shit. Fuck, Fuck," Briggs barked after he landed hard. "Awk!"

I leapt to the lower level, raised one hand like they would

understand my words, and spoke with authority that made me want to laugh. "Don't worry, folks. Nothing to see here."

"Gewd ship, fack, fack," one of the people said, wide eyed.

"Strange," X-37 commented as I stared at the speaker who sounded a lot like the Slayer coughing up a hairball.

"You're telling me, X. What the hell is going on here?" I moved through the densely packed workers, found a ladder, and climbed to the top level to look for Briggs. "For a city on a planet under quarantine, this rush hour traffic is the worst."

"That is merely a function of the industry in this area. It is a population center for a reason," X-37 said.

"Not much different than anyplace in the known universe then," I said, walking on the top level of the public transport. Dirty faced children wearing mining, farming, and forestry gear sat in rows—shoulder to shoulder and knee to knee—all of them staring at Briggs. Some of the kids had pet birds and others had four-legged creatures small enough to hold in one of their arms.

"They're scared of me," Briggs muttered.

"I'm scared of you," I said. "Have you looked in the mirror lately?"

"I try not to. Awk," Briggs said, his expression showing me he was more worried about the non-human Slayer word than his recent problem with profanity.

One of the kids leaned forward. "Awk. Hwwwwk. Awk. Awk."

"Delightful," I said. "They speak Slayer."

"Doubt it's a language," Briggs said, staring at the kid who didn't flinch.

"X?" I asked.

"Still analyzing. The Yansden child seems to be participating in some sort of ritual mimicry. Perhaps you should talk to him and see what happens," X-37 said.

"Hey kid, my name is Halek Cain," I said, massaging an ache out of my neck.

"Cain," the kid said. "Cain, Cain, Cain."

"Nice job, X. I think you're onto something. Can we use it to learn their language? Or is it just one more thing to annoy me?"

"I will unravel the dialect before you and offer what assistance I can," X-37 said.

"Thanks. What would I do without you? Don't answer. I already know," I said, looking for a place to sit as dozens of dirty faced street rats stared at me.

THE RIDE LASTED HOURS, sometimes moving at alarming speeds. There were sections of the subway with low ceilings. I resisted the urge to tell the ragamuffin kids to sit down and stop goofing off. They incorporated Briggs and me in their play, darting toward us, touching one of us on the foot or arm, then dashing back.

"One of them is going to fall off and die," Briggs said, not for the first time.

"And die, and die," the kids chorused.

"He speaks the stupid," one exclaimed. Others thought this accusation was both hilarious and horrifying.

Briggs flashed his teeth, driving them back with squeals of terrified delight.

Another child climbed up from where the adults mostly slept and complained in a language I couldn't understand. Silence spread wherever the new kid went. Even the most rambunctious children lowered their eyes and stepped back.

"What's wrong with that one?" Briggs asked, leaning back against the railing.

The child was small, dark skinned, fair haired, and wore a collar that made him appear edged in light—or that was the only way I could describe the phenomena. My normal eye thought he was spectacular, like an angel made real. My cybernetic left eye couldn't track him properly. The image flickered and blurred when he pulled his shirt over the ornament.

"X, what is wrong with this kid?" I asked.

"Which child are you referring to?" X-37 asked.

Two more of the strange ones climbed the ladder—each with their own collar—looked around without a word for the regular children, and followed the first toward the back of the open-topped subway car. It was like watching a funeral march: very somber. Another four followed.

"X, I am focusing on a new group of children," I said. "Tell me what you see."

"Strange, it appears to me that there were individuals where you are focusing," X-37 said.

"They're right in front of me. Right now."

"I am reliant on your sensory input and should thus be seeing exactly what you see. However, it seems my algorithms interpret the information much differently than you do, Reaper Cain. I see a record of seven children that are no longer here," X-37 said.

"What the hell, X? That really creeps me out," I said, focusing on something each child was trying to conceal in hair, or under clothing, or by sleight of hand. I was good, but these kids were masters of deception.

"It is curious." My LAI made several quiet pops and clicks that meant he was processing an unusually large amount of data. "Could this be stealth technology specifically aimed at machines?"

"Tighten your filters, X. You're getting overloaded," I said.

"Correct," X-37 said. "Very clever. The purpose remains unclear, however."

"Let it go, X. Now isn't the time to get sucked into a digital trap." Dread filled me up. Missions without X never went well. I really hoped he could hang in for the duration.

"The train is coming to a stop," Briggs said, sounding like a commando again. "There could be a security check. We should try to get off before then."

"Agreed. As soon as it's slow enough, we jump," I said.

"My analysis suggests that is a risky but necessary course of action," X-37 said. "In poor lighting, you might land on an unfavorable surface or in the path of another conveyance."

"Thanks for the pep talk, X."

"My pleasure, Reaper Cain."

Lights flashed warnings. Dozens of people rose abruptly, gathered their things, and jumped. Before long, it was like escape pods leaving a doomed starship. The kids swarmed off the side like rodents.

"My basic understanding of their language, and of the alert systems of this public conveyance, suggests that there is a point of pay fast approaching," X-37 warned. "Which probably means guards."

"Well shit," I said. "Briggs, are you ready?"

"More ready than you," the Slayer said.

"Then what are we waiting for?" I jumped first, just to prove I wasn't afraid of face planting and breaking my neck. A metal walkway came up too fast. One foot and one knee struck almost simultaneously, causing me to roll about five hundred times.

Briggs helped me up.

"Thanks."

"Someone called security," he said. "The train is stopped now. Armed men are searching it."

A hundred meters ahead of us, I saw what he was talking about—beefy men wearing dark red helmets—some without armor but others in more of the mismatched grey and black pieces. The headgear had seen better days. Each unit was scored down to the metal. Some of the wearers had attempted—with varying levels of success—to paint over the damage. Most didn't seem to care. These were rough men used to getting what they wanted.

I staggered toward a side passage and left the main subway tunnel. Briggs followed. For a while there were workers moving, toward their homes I assumed. Some watched us warily. Others pretended not to see our movements.

"I'm increasingly fascinated by their reaction to us, Reaper Cain," X-37 said.

"Same here," I said. "They look pretty beaten down. I wonder why. Any word on Elise?"

"Not exactly," X-37 said. "But Jelly was able to send coordinates she feels will be useful to our mission."

"Give me details, X."

"I must wait until we have a fresh connection, which is what will be at the coordinates—a zone without radio or infrared interference where we can contact Tom and Jelly." My LAI continued to explain but it wasn't necessary.

Listening with half my attention, I motioned for Briggs to follow as I navigated an abandoned stairwell. Rush hour was over, apparently. Dozens of beady eyed animals with disgustingly hairless tails scurried from corner to corner on four legs.

"What the hell are those things?" I asked.

"Some type of rodent." X-37 paused. "Most animals of this type are natural survivalists. If they swarm in one direction, or otherwise behave erratically, it could be a sign of danger."

"I think I could eat one," Briggs said. Each street corner was marked by boxes I suspected were traffic lights but also power relays and safety stations if my guess was correct. The Slayer circled the first we came to, squinting his eyes and sniffing everywhere.

"That's just like you, Slayer. Always thinking with your stomach," I said, not hungry at all.

"You will not be laughing when you know what I smell,"

Briggs said, clambering on top of the corner box to get a better view of the street ahead.

"Honestly, I'm not sure I want to know." The section of the city we saw now more closely resembled what we had witnessed during our aerial approach over the continent and the coast. Wind blew down the streets, kicking up dust and grit and swirling it into alleys. About a kilometer ahead of us, along one of the wider thoroughfares, I saw high-rise buildings.

Some might've been for business purposes and others for residential use, I couldn't be sure. All I knew was that they were well lit with neon signs I couldn't read.

The section of the city we were now traversing was different. There was less glass and more grayish yellow concrete. The windows on the first two or three floors were boarded or broken out. I didn't see much trash, but there were bins tucked back in the corners where people weren't supposed to see them.

After we'd gone half a block, I finally gave up. "Okay, Briggs, what do you smell?"

"Elise and the others," he said, fighting down some inner impulse for several seconds before he finished the statement. "Awk, Awk. Elise and the others. They're on the move, but slowly, like maybe they don't know which way they should go."

"You're only guessing that last part," I said, unpacking my stealth cloak and spreading it over my shoulders. Not activated, it wasn't that much different from the poncho Briggs had made from storage tarps before we left the *Jellybird*.

The sheen of the material's surface didn't allow dust to stick to it and blended with my other clothing even when inert. I hadn't spent much time considering its appearance without power, because I normally unfurled it and activated it in the same motion.

"Lead the way, Slayer," I said before I thought about the word.

He bared his teeth as he looked at me, not happy with the term. But just when I thought he would say something, he turned and headed into one of the more sinister alleyways.

Another group of the four-legged rodents swarmed out of the trashcan, startling me. I had my finger on the trigger, only stopping myself at the last possible moment.

"Couldn't you smell them?" Briggs asked.

"No, Briggs, I couldn't smell the creepy little alien trash mongers," I said, then moved forward, keeping a better eye on dumpsters, drains, and the slender pipes where I'd seen the little animals run.

"Didn't you hear them?"

"No, I didn't. It's not a competition." I felt like an idiot for arguing with this man who had gone through so much and would never be human again. Handing out apologies wasn't really my style, but I was thinking about it when X-37 chimed in.

"I believe there is movement you should pay attention to near the next intersection," X-37 said.

I zoomed in with my cybernetic eye, not catching whatever my limited artificial intelligence had noticed. We'd gone about two blocks since Briggs mentioned Elise, which probably meant we were getting close. Maybe the pain-in-the-ass teenager couldn't smell as well as my mutant buddy, but I had to admit she was good at these types of missions.

"Listen up, Briggs. We have to be getting close. Let me know the moment you sense Elise or the others," I said. "I don't want her to get the drop on us. We'll never live it down."

"It may be too late," Briggs said. "I think they're getting closer. I think they changed course. Awk, awk. Probably heard us talking or something."

A low whistle arched through the night like a dark winged bird. I stopped moving, stopped breathing, and listened.

Briggs hopped onto another junction box, squatted on his haunches, and peered into the night like the alien hunter he was. "Is that Elise making that horrible sound?"

"I'm not sure. I don't think I've ever heard her whistle. X, can you help me out?"

"Certainly, Reaper Cain," X-37 said. "I do not have the audio file to consult. It was compressed long ago. However, I can say with certainty that she has whistled many times and you have failed to pay attention. I should also point out it is quite melodic and easy to recognize, not horrible as Commander Briggs claims."

"You don't have to make me the bad guy. I pay attention to Elise and my friends. Just didn't know they were a bunch of whistlers." I moved across the street so I could see a slightly different angle of the connecting side streets than the Slayer. For about two seconds I considered climbing up on something like he preferred, but I decided to stay at street level.

The change from evening rush hour to ghost town was

disturbing, even for someone like me. There was a glow from a nearby city over the horizon, but rather than illuminate the impoverished neighborhoods around the darkened space port, the distant illumination caused even deeper shadows. I wondered what anyone else would think if they knew they were alone in the night with the Union's best outlaw assassin and a murderous alien hybrid who could barely control his human and inhuman urges.

"I'm unable to contact her by radio. Something interferes with any signal I send, even if we are close enough. Without Jelly's assistance, we cannot rely on remote communications even if we are very close to Elise and the others. It is safe to assume that Elise is trying to contact us by other means. She'll warn us before she appears so that you don't shoot her in the face," X-37 said.

"Like I would do that. She's not that annoying," I said. "And I have better trigger discipline than anyone on this mission."

"Of course, Reaper Cain. But you should be glad she is following best practices for operations in the field, indicating she did actually listen to your instruction on the subject. I suspect she will repeat the call and wait for a response at least once or twice more."

I waited. The Slayer waited. A breeze blew more of the dark colored grit that was less coarse than sand but not quite dust across our field of vision. When it died down, I heard another low whistle.

I responded with my own two note melody.

"Stay in the shadows, Briggs," I said.

"Ten Roger," he said, pointing to a covered walkway near our position. "This is a good rally point."

For a moment, the man sounded more like himself. The acknowledgment had been a joke in some of the spec ops units. Everybody thought it was nonsensical, but it had been tradition for so long nobody remembered what started the phrase, only what it meant.

I moved forward, showing myself, trusting Elise to take the next step. When she emerged, she was fifty meters from our position, about to cross a four-way intersection that looked like a tactical nightmare—too much open space and too great a chance someone would come down one of the roads and see us.

A vehicle came roaring down a side street, its primitive engine making a harsh electrical noise as the knobby tires made a growling sound on the gritty pavement.

I stepped into another narrow alley, more of an access passage than anything a vehicle could drive into. If I had to run from whoever was driving this mystery vehicle, I'd easily avoid pursuit but would also abandon my friends.

"X, is that the same van we saw outside the city gate?"

"It is, Reaper Cain. I assume you don't need my analysis on this improbable coincidence," X-37 said.

I didn't answer, choosing instead to watch the van as it slowed to a stop and parked in the middle of the intersection. From my vantage point every one of my friends was hidden.

A rush of pride went through me. It occurred to me in a flash how much we had been through and how easily we could handle one vehicle if it was just a straight fight. Unfortunately, we didn't know what we were dealing with on this world that looked so similar but might be the strangest place we'd ever been.

I eased my Reaper mask out of my jacket and slipped it on, increasing the power of my cybernetic eye. I'd mastered use of the device a long time ago but didn't care for it. Something about wearing it put me in a dark mood but now I needed an edge.

X-37 was doing the same thing I was, analyzing the van. There weren't many clues. It seemed like a normal work vehicle, large enough to carry a significant amount of supplies and a crew. Like all the other vehicles in this world, the few windows were blackened. At first glance I thought they were one-way glass, but they'd been painted.

The moment stretched out long enough that I identified an irregularity in the cycling rate of the electric motor.

"X, are you getting that?"

"Yes, Reaper Cain. The vehicle is not in perfect condition. I noticed a similar pattern with other conveyances when we were working our way into the city," X-37 said.

I filed the information for later use. If we had to evade this thing, maybe the limited visibility would be a weakness. If I was going to steal a similar vehicle for our own use, I'd need to deal with the issue before driving fast.

The boxy van rolled slowly forward. "I think it's searching for someone."

"That is a possibility," X-37 said. "I do not believe they're having major mechanical issues that would restrict the speed this much despite its generally poor condition."

It took a while for the vehicle to roll out of my field of view.

The junker was only moving at a walking pace and sometimes stopped. Once it even backed up several feet. Whoever was looking out from inside had a very restricted field of view and was being careful.

"It will be gone soon," I said.

"Correct. However, I am picking up additional radio and IR signals, even if I cannot fully read the encryption. Meta-analysis —volume and frequency of communications—could correlate with a defensive response. There may be additional vehicles moving into the area," X-37 said. "If you listen carefully, you can hear vehicle traffic moving toward us."

"A search party or a quick reaction force?" I wanted to move back across the street and check on Briggs but decided to wait.

X-37 hesitated. "I do not believe it will be either. New data we have acquired suggests this is some sort of shift change. It may or may not be as busy as the rush hour traffic we encountered while entering the city."

"What kind of new data?" I asked.

"The approaching vehicles and pedestrians do not appear concerned about security. Their movements give the impression of boredom with the routine," X-37 answered.

"That might help us," I said, thinking we could blend with the local populace again.

"Doubtful," X-37 said.

Before my limited artificial intelligence could explain further, I saw a light come on each of the corner junction boxes, including the one Briggs had climbed to get a better view of the street.

For a heartbeat, the Slayer was illuminated bright red. I saw him leap back into an alleyway and wondered if any of the approaching drivers had seen him.

"What's with the traffic lights?"

"From what I can detect from the local network, we should be hearing a spoken warning as vehicle traffic increases in this area," X-37 said. "This will happen in a matter of seconds and will effectively cut you off from both Briggs and Elise."

I heard the announcement and thought I knew what it meant. "Some sort of no crosswalk warning."

"Surprisingly, despite my advanced language algorithms, I'm still having trouble with the way these humans talk. I do predict they will be able to unravel our verbal codes easily, which will put us at a disadvantage, unfortunately. I believe the current announcement is a prohibition against pedestrian traffic," X-37 said.

"Great, so now we can't be seen walking about," I said.

"Correct."

"And darting across traffic is out of the question," I said, wanting to punch something.

"Again, correct."

I wanted a cigar. And a glass of whiskey. And a break. "How long is shift change?"

"Unknown."

"Godsdammit, X, you're not very helpful today," I said.

"Apologies, Reaper Cain."

I could barely hear myself think, much less argue with my LAI. More of the vans, freight trucks, and industrial vehicles moved past us almost bumper-to-bumper. None of them looked like they were paying much attention to the road but rather just following a predetermined route. Grime from their travels covered them from top to bottom.

"Are these automated, X?" I asked.

"I don't believe so. They use railways and other guidance mechanisms for vehicles of this size. In one instance, I was able to record a fuel truck being led by a drone that flew a few meters ahead of it when we first approached the city," X-37 said. "Would you like me to play a compressed image of the scene now?"

"No." Unable to cross the street, I backed up until I found an access ladder to a higher level. In a Union city, it might've been a fire escape but this one was almost a chute, not meant to be climbed but only descended. "Why can't anything be easy? I just want to cross the fucking street."

By pressing my feet against the wall and pulling on the fire escape chute, I created enough leverage to shimmy my way upward. Once at the top, I edged along a system of ceramic pipes that I had thought were for plumbing but now seemed more like something to protect bundles of wires.

It took longer than I wanted to reach the streets and look down, but when I did, I was rewarded with a view of Briggs. He was hidden from view at the street level, but I saw him easily—having the high ground on my old associate for once.

"Is he trying to be seen?" I asked.

"Perhaps," X-37 said. "We haven't observed much activity

from the windows, and he might assume that you are looking for him."

"That's a pretty big logical leap," I said. "But I hope you're right."

"He's had most of the same training you have and should know where to look for you if separated," X-37 said.

Staying as close as I could to the wall and checking to be sure no one was looking up from one of the shift change vehicles, I deactivated the stealth cloak and held as motionless as possible. Hopefully, a casual observer would not see me appear if I remained still.

Seconds later, Briggs used a spec ops hand signal to acknowledge he'd spotted me.

I pointed back to where we had come, toward our last rally point. He acknowledged my signal and drew further back into the shadows until I could no longer see him. My retreat across the pipe clusters was more difficult. When I was sufficiently drawn back into the alleyway, I scaled down the wall and started looking for a route through the buildings.

What I found was a new aspect of this society I hadn't suspected. Everywhere was evidence that this place used to be more crowded than it was now. Like many impoverished neighborhoods, the residential apartments appeared to be small and often had laundry lines running between balconies. I also noticed that none of the balconies seemed like they'd been intended to be used in this manner. Hooded light fixtures had been vandalized years ago.

"What do you make of that?" I asked.

X-37 responded a second later. "I believe that the platforms by each apartment window were originally designed for some sort of air conditioning units, before they were converted to living space. The question is, did the residents get rid of the units or were they taken away for some reason?"

"That's a fascinating question, X. Don't let me forget to look into that," I said, picking up the pace now that I knew no one was watching me.

"Sarcasm detected," X-37 said. "But I will put the reminder on your calendar anyway."

This area had once been packed with people and had an open-air market wherever there was space on the ground level. I occasionally saw movement in a window, but no one confronted me.

"I don't think anyone here is going to report us to the red helmets," I said.

"Doubtful, but we have no baseline as to how their society or government works," X-37 reminded me.

"We need a guide," I said.

"That would be ideal." X-37 wasn't able to provide me a list of options, which I hadn't really expected but you never knew with LAIs.

From my hiding place, I spotted the mystery van rolling slowly down a side street free of other shift change traffic. It stopped and backed up once, then sat there for a long time. "Are they waiting for new orders or arguing amongst themselves?"

"Unknown, Reaper Cain."

A warning flashed on each of the corner junction boxes, the

words still as strange and meaningless to me as they had been the first time I saw them. I expected a second wave of workers and was surprised when interior and exterior lights suddenly clicked on. Drab buildings became neon display panels with cinematic advertisements. The alleys were immune to the sudden resurgence of electricity.

"What the hell just happened, X?"

My limited artificial intelligence didn't answer. Music played from a balcony high above us. It sounded like it was coming from a really tame dance club. The entire area was coming to life. Lights appeared in windows, higher and higher until I realized I was seeing people arrive home from work. The behavior wasn't what I thought of as Union or other societies like Wallach or Xad, but it was definitely human.

For about five seconds, I thought of my early childhood—of my mother and father coming home from work, talking about having more kids someday, sharing a glass of beer as they looked off the tiny tenement building balcony. They'd both been wearing basic military uniforms. This memory was strange and precious and hadn't visited me for decades—my parents in love, uncaring of fame or fortune or anything life might throw at them.

On the lower levels I saw kids and their arboreal mammals, laughing as their pets jumped from balcony to balcony. Older kids hooted and whistled at each other. Young women made themselves beautiful while the boys tried to look tough and cool at the same time. The festivities went on for several minutes, then ended when huge screens displayed warnings I couldn't read. Parents gathered their families inside. Balcony doors and windows closed. The noise of life became muted but still shook the walls from the inside.

"X?"

"Apologies, Reaper Cain. The local communication network is being flooded," X-37 said. "I'm seeing a great deal of information. The problem is that none of it seems important or connected to the grid. Very random. Like when you and your friends engage in horseplay and laugh at bad jokes."

I looked around, sensing a break in the traffic. Everything about Yansden changed for me once I'd seen the people being people. What upset me was how short-lived their afterwork socializing had been. "How long do you need to process it?"

"Unknown, Reaper Cain," X-37 said. "Very little of the data flow appears to be critical."

"All work and no play make the people of Yansden dull boys and girls," I said.

"That is an interesting and basically useless hypothesis, Reaper Cain."

"I need to make a move," I said, then edged through the alleyway quickly. There was a shadow in front of a building, an effect of vandalism that had spilled out to a storefront with barred windows. Despite the prohibition against pedestrian traffic, more and more people were jumping from the public transports and flooding into their increasingly noisy dormitory buildings. What no one did was remain on the streets for longer than it took to dash inside.

"I can better serve you if we stop moving," X-37 said. There was now a very rhythmic cadence to my LAI that I didn't like. It sounded like he was being drawn into a bottomless abyss. Probably just my imagination, but I couldn't shake it.

Without waiting or arguing, I darted for the other side of the street as soon as there was a gap in the traffic. An alarm sounded. The vehicles slowed to a stop and began flashing their lights. Drones streaked over the tops of buildings toward my position.

"I need some creative solutions, X," I said, moving quickly into a plaza. Long ago it might've been designed to entertain crowds but now it looked more utilitarian. There were rails set into the concrete to accommodate some of the more useful bots.

I ran quickly for a small amphitheater with weeds and trees growing between the benches. Taking the low ground never seemed like a good idea, so I ran along the top bench until I found a covered section to duck under. Drones zipped past me, some of them racing along dormitory balconies like they were looking for repeat offenders of the curfew.

I hung back and watched the sky for more of the electronic eyes. "I'm having a hard time getting a feel for this place. Who is running those drones?"

"It is an interesting situation," X-37 said. "On the one hand, this society has a very singular purpose of working hard to stockpile resources. On the other hand, they seem to live different lives in private. What connects the two worlds is a fear of the unknown that seems irrational."

"Yeah, I'm going to bet money we find out what that irrational fear is sooner rather than later," I said, moving out of view of drones coming back our way.

I quickly realized I wasn't the only one hiding, and not just from the drones or security vehicles. A group of older kids, practically adults, suddenly ducked into the mini park. I didn't understand what they were saying but thought they were arguing. One of them motioned to get down and soon they were all concealed in some scraggly bushes that had seen better days.

The rush of shift change vehicles was over and anybody who was jumping from public transport to avoid paying had long since disappeared inside the tenement buildings. Music and conversation no longer emanated from windows or balconies. A disturbing hush covered this part of the city.

"I hear something or someone running," X-37 said.

I'd heard it too and was already adjusting my position to see what was on the streets near the mini park. A group of people, or maybe a pack of animals, charged down one of the streets not quite close enough to see from my position. I sensed movement more than I saw it, but there was one thing I recognized from earlier.

Whoever or whatever was running the streets now possessed a ghostly aura I'd first seen around the collars the outcast juveniles on the subway had been wearing. X-37 asked me if I saw anything, then told me to disregard the question a moment later when he caught up. Whatever these creatures were, my organic vision interpreted them differently than X-37's analysis of the same visual input.

"Why do you think we're not seeing the same thing, X?" I asked. "They have some kind of tech you can't lock onto."

"Unlikely, Reaper Cain," X-37 said. "There would be no purpose to only hide from machines and computers."

I disagreed but didn't want to get into this argument with a limited artificial intelligence wired down to the molecule level in my nervous system.

"Why do you hesitate to speak, Reaper Cain?"

"I'm not making this stuff up, X. There has to be a reason I see these Yansden ghosts before you do."

"You are having some sort of emotional reaction," X-37 said. "I suggest you ignore what you see. My analysis will be more reliable."

"Doesn't seem like it," I said.

"When have I ever let you down, Reaper Cain?" X-37 asked.

My LAI had a point, but I needed to get my head in the game. I worked my way across the mini park, easily avoiding the groups of people who were fleeing the moment they saw the runners had gone the other way.

THE VAN we'd seen several times now creeped into the mini park. It stopped near the perimeter but stuck out like a sore thumb and stayed long after the drones came and went. As impatient as I was, I waited and watched. My LAI was having some delusions of grandeur, I thought, but he also had a point. I could count on one hand how many times my digital friend had let me down when it came to sensing danger.

"I have completed my analysis," X-37 said, still sounding a bit overwhelmed. "It seems the locals are fond of doing everything in duplicate which I hadn't accounted for when I began looking at the sudden influx of information. And they are worried about the runners."

"That's great, X," I said. "Very helpful."

"I do my best."

"Are these runners the reason for the quarantine?" I asked.

"I believe the reasons this planet and the system were quarantined by the Alon are quite complicated," X-37 said.

I listened to X and planned my next move. "I'm thinking about taking that van driver out. I'm tired of getting followed."

"It is an option, Reaper Cain," X-37 said.

I hesitated, aware there had to be another way to deal with the troublesome vehicle. "Can you pull up a map of this area with all that new information you were able to acquire during the last shift change?"

"Of course," X-37 said. "Displaying it to your HUD view now. I'm marking the van as an orange icon and the drones as red."

I studied the map of the area and the digital symbols moving across it. "This seems like it was a nice little park before it got turned into a drone junction area."

"It was popular," X-37 said. "Unfortunately, it is also very popular with the creatures they call Runners."

"I'd like to see one up close to see if they're dangerous. The glow-kids we saw on the public transport were weird, but not terrifying," I said.

"Do not make false assumptions about what you have seen so far," X-37 said, then failed to provide any type of detail or explanation.

I crept away from an awning I had used to conceal myself from the aerial drones. The shadows from the inconsistent power grid worked in my favor for once. Far above, there were open dormitory windows, but I didn't see anyone in them.

The van continued to idle, its engine making a quiet, irregular sound that didn't promise it would function for much longer.

"Do you have contact with Jelly or anyone else from the team?" I was worried about Briggs. Not that I thought he would get captured or killed, but that he might go on some kind of killing spree and ruin the mission.

"I am unable to make contact, Reaper Cain."

"All right. I'm bored with that van. Check the local communication networks to see if you can figure out who's driving it and why they're so fascinated with my visit," I said." It's creeping me out."

"Not something that happens often," X-37 said. "But in your defense, Reaper Cain, nothing about Yansden is as it seems."

"Very reassuring, X."

"Truly?"

"No, X. You've been particularly useless on this mission."

A few clicks resonated in my ear. "I'm doing my best, Reaper Cain. Perhaps you should have utilized more teamwork and less complaining. Just a suggestion."

"Let's not go there," I said. "Someone let me sleep while half of my team went rogue, but forget about that. Can you please tell me who's driving that van and what they want?"

"I'm doing what I can. There is more information, but it is far from perfect," X-37 said as I edged away from the van. "I don't believe you will escape cleanly. The shadows are not as deep as you might think and there is no way to be certain the citizens will remain inside after the security drones leave."

I understood that my LAI could measure shadows, and that his predictions of human behavior were often accurate, but sometimes instinct was more important. It was time to go regardless of the consequences.

4

CRAWLING COULD BE undignified but was often the best way to creep toward a target, or in this case, slip out of view. I scraped my right hand, and to a lesser degree, my elbow and both knees.

"I really wish I had my Archangel armor," I said. So far, there hadn't been much need to blend with the local populace. Our only direct contact had been with children on the subway. Adults we had seen hung back, ignoring us or watching us warily.

No one had reacted to the Slayer. They were probably telling stories now, however, that would have long-term repercussions. All I needed was the legend of Briggs the Slayer. How would that help us remain covert?

I kept moving, looking for opportunities, watching for danger.

Once I was clear of the park, I advanced through one of the narrow access ways I was relying on more and more often. My shoulders nearly brushed both sides at once and I often had to duck beneath pipes and other types of conduits. But I wasn't here for comfort or a leisurely stroll.

When I found my way to the street, this part of the city had again become a ghost town. The lights that had come on almost randomly were dimmed in most places. This accentuated other neighborhoods that were having their power cycle fulfilled.

"This city feels half done," I said.

"It would be far more accurate to say it is half empty," X-37 said. "Unless saying it is half-full makes you feel better. My point is that the quarantine has deeply affected the society—probably for hundreds of years."

I paused to study the street, searching for the mystery vehicle that would not stop hunting us. "It doesn't really make much sense, X. If it had been that long, shouldn't they have rebuilt their population base?"

"It is possible they have in other areas while this section of their society remained dormant. It could be that there are laws prohibiting people from living close to the starport that Elise is trying to reach, or there is a societal taboo against trespassing here. Perhaps both."

"I'm sure we'll find out eventually. Right now, I just want Elise and the others back. And Briggs," I said, sweeping my vision across the scene so that X 37 could do his job.

"Thank you, Reaper Cain."

"I hear a vehicle. Are you picking that up?" I asked.

"I've identified it as the same van we first saw," X-37 said. "The driver is very persistent."

"Okay. I've tried being sneaky, now it's time to move fast." Before the headlights could come around the corner, I sprinted toward a new street. The mystery van gunned its electric motors and came around the corner, intent on running me down this time. The cat and mouse game seemed to be over.

Unfortunately for my adversary, I had a good enough lead to do what I needed. I cut through one of the narrow passages that were so useful, climbed to another level, then dropped onto the roof of the van as it slowed to figure out where I had gone. The really great part was that none of my friends were around to hear how hard I was breathing or to listen to me swear.

Gripping the handle on the top hatch, I yanked upward as hard as I could, intent on opening the thing. This van wasn't a military vehicle, but something just for work. I guessed the top hatch was merely for the sake of convenience and not someplace they had intended to mount weapons or surveillance equipment.

All I wanted from the portal was to get inside and figure out who was following me and why. I could hear the metal creak but couldn't get it open cleanly. "I'm gonna rip this thing apart!"

After snapping out my arm blade, I jammed it into the seam around the hatch.

A speaker box hissed and popped with static as whoever was inside shouted at me. None of the words made sense. "Can you help me out, X?"

"I believe he said: don't do that! It's hard to fix that kind of damage. What are you, crazy?"

I hesitated, taking advantage of the moment to look around

and ensure no one was sneaking up on me as I dealt with this problem. "That sound like a kid to you, X?"

"It did resemble a young voice," X-37 said. "At this proximity, I'm able to access the vehicle's radio. Making sense of what it transmits may be a problem, however."

"That's what I thought," I said quietly, then raised my voice to address the child or children inside. "Tell them they can talk to me, or I can rip this entire vehicle into its component parts."

"They seem alarmed at my voice coming through their radio speakers, but I captured their attention. If I've interpreted the spokesperson's extensive use of profanity, he's saying you can't do that," X-37 translated.

"I bet he can," another voice seemed to say in the background. Or maybe he was just cursing me.

I was reminded of Bug in the surveillance tower on Dreadmax, which made me worry about him, Elise, and Hannah.

"Hey, Mister, who are you talking to? And why are you speaking stupid," the first voice asked.

Understanding the words wasn't as comforting as I thought it would be. And who was this brat to call me stupid? "Don't worry about who I'm talking to. You probably don't want to know."

"You sound funny," the voice said. "But a couple of things. First of all, don't mess up our truck. Unless you can buy us a new one. And second of all, you can't speak stupid."

"What are you talking about?" I asked.

"He doesn't get it," another voice said.

The first voice came back. "We call it speaking stupid when

you use the language the Kalon don't like. It'll get you thrown in a jail cell. You've seen the Kalon Regulars. The ones with the big red helmets. You can't stay here long without them throwing you in a lockdown box."

"Wouldn't want that," I said looking around to make sure no one was sneaking up on us as we had this delightful conversation. "This is your last chance. Then I'm taking this door off the hinges. You can complain to the Kalon Regulars or whatever."

The kid yelled, "Don't do that!"

"Then get your asses out here where I can see you. I need transportation," I said.

"Just step back a bit," the first voice said.

I complied and watched the hatch creak open. The hinges hadn't been oiled for a long time.

Inside were four children ranging in ages from twelve to sixteen. "Why are you following me?"

Surprisingly, it was one of the middle children who spoke up as their leader. "The other one was scary. Watched him eat a couple of rats. Which was disgusting and made us all think he might eat us."

"Yeah, I saw some of those. Didn't know that's what you call them," I said. "Where's the scary one now?"

"Not far," the leader said. "We could probably take you to him if you have something worth trading for."

"How about I don't snap your little necks," I said, too tired for this.

They retreated inside and shut the door.

"That was poorly handled, Reaper Cain," X-37 said. "The good news is, however, your conversation went a long way in helping me decipher their various languages."

Using my enhanced optics, I peered easily into the shadows below me and saw them crouching down in the vehicle. "You followed us for a reason. That means we can help each other. Let's work together."

The leader of the children babbled something at me I didn't understand.

"We were doing so good," I said. "Go back to speaking stupid or whatever you call it so I can understand you."

They laughed nervously, then nudged the leader forward to be their spokesperson. He looked back once or twice, but eventually climbed out and sat on the edge of the hatch where I could examine him.

Like most of the people on Yansden, the kid was dressed in work clothing that had seen better days. It was too big—cinched at the waist, rolled up at the wrists, and bunching at the ankles over heavy work boots. He had goggles pushed back on his head and spots around his eyes that were slightly cleaner than the rest of him, but it was probably an illusion. His bulky gloves were tucked through a loop on his waist area.

"What are you looking at?" he asked, clearly doing the same thing to me.

"I'm looking at you, kid," I said. "What's the point of working so hard? I never see you people do anything with the resources you're gathering."

"What do you mean?" He glanced at his friends, as though unsure about the entire encounter.

"Never mind," I said. "I'm assuming all of the raw materials are going to shipbuilding at some point."

The kid shrugged.

"What's your name?"

"Manager, like my dad and his dad," the kid said.

"Why are you following me and my friends?" I kept my gaze on him so that X-37 could record and analyze his nonverbal behavior. But I could already see a rebel doing things he wasn't supposed to just to be difficult.

"I can't tell you, stupid," he said, crossing his arms. "Got to take you to my sister. She's old. She knows everything."

"Just a tip, kid. Calling someone stupid isn't a compliment," I said.

"I know that," he said.

"Great. This is going to be loads of fun. I can't wait for you to meet Elise and my sister," I said.

"I've also been wondering how this will go," X-37 said to me privately.

"Do you know where my friends are?" I asked.

"We've seen them, but the big scary one's the only one around here," Manager said. "He's not invited. Can't believe he's your friend. Saw him eat a rat in one bite."

"Deception detected," X-37 said.

"It's okay," I said. "He almost never eats troublesome kids like you."

That made the whole group laugh, but they remained as

81

cautious as ever. Maybe they thought I was going to catch them and feed them to the Slayer. Before long, we were driving slowly with me riding inside their crappy little vehicle.

"My sister will know what to do with you," Manager said. "She knows everything."

5

I KEPT my fingers on my leg as I rode near the back of the van, watching each of the kids carefully. X-37 was on higher alert as usual. So far, it didn't seem these little street rats suspected I was communicating with my limited artificial intelligence.

Which led me to wonder if they knew what such a thing was.

The oldest kid in the vehicle was the driver. He was also the biggest and very sullen. I got the feeling he hated everything about the entire incident. Whenever the vehicle had to stop, which was frequently, he stared at me.

"That one does not seem to appreciate your unique personality or your many talents," X-37 said. "Perhaps you should explain to them about Reapers."

I responded to my limited artificial intelligence with hand gestures. "Bad idea, X. Just pay attention. I want to have a good read on this planet and the people here sooner rather than later."

"Of course, Reaper Cain," X-37 said. "But it is unlikely that these children know where a super weapon is hidden."

Manager squatted on the seat across from me, our knees close together, and when he leaned forward, he was close enough I thought he might try to pick my pocket.

"We're only interested in you because you're strange," he said.

"Thanks, I think." I thought about slipping on my Reaper mask to see how these kids reacted but decided against it.

"We watched your sister and her friends too," Manager said. "Kind of funny that we both have sisters. I mean, it's probably not that funny, but you know what I mean. No offense, but you're scary. Hard to talk to."

"You don't seem to be having a problem with it," I said, stretching one arm across the back of the bench I was sitting on. This allowed me to lean away from the kid a bit and I hoped it made me less intimidating. In reality, all it did was emphasize how I could fill up most of the interior of the vehicle all by myself if I stretched out.

"My analysis suggests you should not trust these children," X-37 said.

I tapped out a quick response. "They're sketchy. I don't trust them."

After about two more stops and three random turns through the neighborhood, the driver cursed. He looked back and stared at me resentfully.

"What's the problem?" Manager asked.

The driver spat to one side, which I thought was disgusting

given that we were inside the vehicle and not out in some field. "The monster is still following us."

Manager pointed at me. "You tell him to go away."

I shrugged and looked toward the hatch of the roof, then to the back door to the van. "Might be easier for me to just lean out and shout at him. I can barely fit through the hatch."

"No tricks," Manager said. "I don't trust you. Just because we're using your stupid talk doesn't mean we are stupid."

"Stupid is as stupid does," I said.

"What kind of sense does that make?" Manager demanded. "Just don't try to hold the door open. He can't fit in here anyway and I don't want him to eat us."

"I don't need his help now that you guys are giving me a ride," I said. "As long as I can trust you. I can trust you, right?"

They all nodded frantically. Manager waved one hand at his friends as though to demonstrate their collective sincerity. "You can totally trust us. Absolutely."

"Oh, good. That's a big relief. Let me just send the Slayer back to the shuttle," I said, noting how the word Slayer alarmed them. After an inappropriate amount of theatrics, I opened the back door and leaned out, whistling softly to signal my inhuman partner.

"I hate that sound," Briggs said from the shadows. "Part of me knows it's just a whistle, but it hurts my ears."

"Yeah, sorry about that. Just so you know, the locals can understand our language. They call it stupid, like that's an actual name for the dialect," I said.

"Stop talking so much," Manager said. "Just send it away."

I waved at the kid to be patient and continued to look into the shadows where I could sometimes see Briggs and sometimes couldn't. "Just head back to the shuttle. I don't need your help anymore."

"Very convincing," X-37 said. "But if you want him to recognize the hand signal you gave him to disregard what you said, I suggest you make it more obvious. The shadows are very inconsistent now that the residential dormitories are being shut down once again."

I gave the hand signal again. Briggs responded with the croaking sound I thought was acknowledgment. Either way, the mission had to continue. I had intended to come down here by myself so if Briggs went off and did whatever Slayers do, I'd just improvise.

To my surprise, Manager and one of the other kids climbed out and scouted around the vehicle to make sure Briggs had left.

"The children are either very brave or not as afraid of Briggs as they claim," X-37 said. "I wonder how they would feel if they realized he was still following us."

"He could still be out there," Manager whispered to his friends.

I pretended not to hear.

The neighborhood appeared more and more dilapidated as the van worked its way closer to the spaceport. It was pretty clear that several factors were working against the area. X-37 was able to decipher some of the signs that warned against trespassing this close to the restricted zone. There were still hovels tucked into buildings that were all but falling down, but they were fewer and farther between now.

The driver stopped for a column of pedestrians who were marching the way we had come from with their heads down. None of them talked. Like the rest of the residents of the city, they wore heavy work gear but also carried backpacks.

Manager saw what I was looking at. "Those are the poorest people. Have to go to work for several days at the time. Got to carry changes of clothing and rations. None of them can afford the cafeteria at the mines or the timber fields."

I nodded. My conclusions hadn't been much different. "Why are we going this way? Seems like this is the worst neighborhood in Yansden."

"That's because it's close to the spaceport. Lots of rules against going there, and if you listen to some of the oldsters talk, it's dangerous when the ships take off. Engines cook you when they blast off."

"Makes sense. What doesn't make sense is that they have launch pads of that size in the middle of a residential district," I said.

"Don't know about that," Manager said. "This is the way it's always been. Where else would they put it?"

I didn't answer. X-37 was recording the conversation, not that I thought it was groundbreaking. Long ago, during other missions, I'd learned to talk to the regular people anytime I went to a new city or ship. They often had details that weren't included in a mission briefing. Sometimes the minutiae of daily life could be helpful.

In this case, I was pretty sure I was being hustled. These kids weren't trying to help me. They were taking me to someone who would try to rob me or cheat me. That's the way it was in these types of neighborhoods. They did what they had to survive. I knew the life.

"We're almost to the fence," Manager told me. "May not look like much, but you have to follow the rules. There are other reasons this neighborhood isn't safe. Sometimes they come at night, sometimes they come in the daytime, but you never know which."

I leaned forward to peer through a small slit in the painted window and saw a tall chain-link fence with crude razor wire at the top.

"Two questions," I said. "Why does everyone paint their windows? And what do you mean when you say they come?"

"We don't paint the windows." Manager laughed. "Rival gangs do that. Every time you stop in a new area, they spray the window so you can't see their territory. Always been that way. Just what they do."

"Why don't you scrape them off so you can see out?"

"Wouldn't do any good. Just get covered up again." He looked out one of the small slits and then sat back to finish talking to me. "You don't know who they are?"

"Not a clue," I said.

He studied me a moment longer. "I believe you. I guess you are really new here. We call them the Neverseen."

"I think I have seen them," I said. "They're kids with light in their hair and clothing, almost like they're backlit."

My new friends laughed nervously. Manager eventually leaned closer to me and spoke in a low voice. "They ain't Neverseen, but they will be. They're more stupider than stupid. Went too close to the starport."

"Interesting," X-37 said. "This may link several disparate facts together. The quarantine is starting to make sense now."

"For you, maybe," I said to my limited artificial intelligence, inadvertently confusing Manager and his friends.

"Not just for us, for anyone. Can't go too close. You get the sickness. And there's no getting better," he said.

We drove along the perimeter of the compound. I was surprised to see the chain-link fence was well maintained. Crafted from stainless steel, it had also been sunk into a solid foundation. I kept looking for gaps in places where someone had dug underneath it and found nothing. Someone obviously patrolled the perimeter and made sure no one had cut their way inside.

I also saw guard towers every fifty meters. Most of these fortifications looked empty, but I did see movement from time to time. With few exceptions, the guards were young—normally teenagers about the age of Manager.

"Listen, I'm not trying to rush you, but we need to find your big sister sooner rather than later," I said. "I'm on a schedule and I need to talk to her about child labor laws."

"Is that supposed to be a joke?" Manager asked.

"Sure, maybe a little. But let's stop screwing around and get to it. If all we're going to do is drive around and look at fences, I can do that on my own," I said.

Manager signaled the driver, who picked up the pace. I

wondered if Briggs would be able to keep up but trusted him to find a way to get it done. He was a well-trained professional with some high-powered alien DNA to help him out in the strength and speed department after all.

The main gate was more heavily fortified than the towers along the perimeter. Nothing about it was original or clever, but it was solid and manned by armed guards. The men and women I saw here looked a bit older, maybe in their twenties, and stood like soldiers.

The van stopped.

"We see you, Manager. You know the drill. Open up and let us have a look," the lead guard said.

Manager and his friends complied. I kept my hands visible and tried not to look threatening. The security force kept their distance, a pair of them walking completely around the vehicle and looking in through open doors and hatches. A third man watched from the tower, his rifle pointed at me.

Eventually, the two men on the ground climbed into the vehicle and searched everything. No compartment of the van was left unchecked.

"I'm putting together the Yansden dialect with what they call stupid—basically your language, Reaper Cain," X-37 said. "Would you like hints and prompts until it clicks for you?"

I signaled yes even though I thought I could grab the meaning of most local conversations, even if expressing myself in the Yansden tongue would remain difficult for a while longer.

"Inspect the undercarriage," the leader said.

I was relatively certain he hadn't said, "Kill everyone. We don't want Reapers up in here!"

His subordinate grumbled but complied quickly and with a professional level of thoroughness I respected. When they were done, they waived Manager and the rest of us through the gate without further conversation.

"Why do you look so nervous, Manager?" I asked.

"Bringing someone inside the fence is a big deal. Not everyone has the privilege. I mess this up, and I'll get a demotion," he said.

I crossed one leg and leaned back as far as I could in the small space, completely relaxed. "No worries, Manager. You'll get no problems from me."

His body language wasn't exactly confident, and I suspected he knew how badly it would go for him if he cheated me.

6

THE VAN CONTINUED to drive slowly down a narrow road with a tall chain-link fence on each side. The setup reminded me of a prison camp. At the end of the long passage, there was a second gate with more guards. None of them wore uniforms, but they were all armed and serious.

"These fences wouldn't stop a vehicle or a serious attempt to breach them, but would easily contain most casual trespassers," X-37 said. "I haven't found the same level of decay here as in other parts of Yansden. Whoever is in charge here takes security seriously and uses what resources they have available."

I gave X a thumbs-up, which caused Manager and the others to look at me strangely.

"Why do you fiddle with your hand so much?" Manager asked. "You got a nervous tick or something?"

"It's better than talking to myself," I said.

"You're weird, man. Maybe we should've brought the monster instead." He then stood and went to lean over the driver. They spoke quietly and I couldn't quite make out what they talked about. Not that it mattered at this point.

Before long, we were passed through the second gate and into a courtyard. Apparently, somebody had called the watch, because a lot of armed men and women arrived to greet us. I counted eleven adults broken into three fire teams or small squads.

"Why the big welcoming party, Manager?" I asked.

"You've got weapons," he said. "And there's something not right with your eye. And some of us think you're a Kalon robot because of your arm."

"Fair enough," I said.

"You're dangerous, man."

"If you only knew." His reaction to my words was very satisfying. The color drained from his face, just like it did from the rest of his friends' faces. None of them seemed overly confident now.

A woman about twice the age of Manager approached. She was short and tough, but not unattractive. I estimated she was probably between thirty and thirty-five, and she had hair that would be considerably lighter if she washed it. Her brown eyes were clear and alert.

"Focus, Reaper Cain," X-37 said. "I haven't had to babysit you for some time."

"I don't know what you're talking about, X," I said under my breath, knowing exactly what my limited artificial intelligence was implying.

"The sudden variation in your biometrics profile indicates you are forming a romantic interest in this woman," X-37 said.

"Just stop," I said. "And for your information, overalls and dirt don't normally indicate it's date night."

"I'm not sure I understand your logic," X-37 said.

"X, I said stop." My conversation was drawing looks and I didn't want to explain right now.

"Stopping," X-37 said. "I have a list of pickup lines available should you need help in getting a date. Not that I'm condoning such an action at this particular moment in our mission."

"I'm gonna kill you, X," I said.

"That is unlikely, Reaper Cain," X-37 said.

Putting aside my frustration with myself and with my limited artificial intelligence, I reassessed the situation. During the brief distraction, little had changed. The guards worked as a team, but I didn't think they had formal training. They were well armed, but not with anything I couldn't handle.

If I brought my Archangel armor, I could've walked through this little outlaw hideout at will. Not that I was second-guessing X. He was probably right about leaving it behind. So far, I hadn't seen an opportunity to mingle with the local populace beyond this group, but that didn't mean I wouldn't need to at some point.

A large number of my missions for the union had been in cities, often strange semi-rebellious places where I had to learn who was important and who wasn't, who had power, and who only made promises.

"I thought you said your sister was really old," I said.

Manager looked at me indignantly. "She is old!"

"You wouldn't be trying to ambush me, would you, Manager?" I asked. "You tell me your sister's old, when she's not. You take me to a safe place, then have armed guards surround me. I'm not liking the vibe you're putting off, kid."

"That's not my fault," he said. "That's because of the Neverseen. We have to be protected."

"If not for the impending confrontation, this would be a good time to pin him down on the details of these mysterious creatures," X-37 said. "I will file the details for future reference. You may, of course, ask his sister directly unless you're wanting to talk to her about other things."

"X, shut it," I said. This was the first time I'd clearly spoken to my LAI out loud since joining the van kids. Manager and the others looked at me like they thought I was probably crazy and definitely someone they shouldn't have brought into the stronghold.

His sister stopped, lifted one hand, and motioned for me to step out of the vehicle. The inward wave resembled someone summoning a dog or a lonely subordinate.

And yet, I wasn't really that annoyed. Maybe X-37 was correct. Maybe I needed some time off to go on a date or something. At the very least find someone with a good cigar. I wasn't quite sure how I had sunk so low that I literally had nothing to do but work.

"They shouldn't have brought you here," she said but I didn't think she meant it. It was part of the act.

"I could leave." I turned back toward the double gate and

looked at all the security measures that prevented me from leaving this compound.

"Don't be difficult," she said. "What's your name, stranger?"

"Halek Cain," I said, making no move to approach. "What's yours?"

"You don't get to ask that."

"Her name is Tatiana," Manager said, probably just to be an annoying little brother. She gave him a deadly look.

"Nice to meet you, Tatiana," I said. "I'm not here to cause problems. Some friends of mine went missing in this area, and I'd like to make sure they're okay."

"That's very noble," she said. "Come with me."

"Well okay," I said and followed. We left Manager and the others behind. One of the squads of guards followed us but the other two stayed to defend the gate area, like they thought there was some sort of alien Slayer freak following me who might try to force his way in or something. Why was everybody so paranoid?

"Your little brother implied you had all the answers," I said. "Are you not the person in charge?"

"I am not in charge. Melina is in charge. I'm taking you to her," Tatiana said.

I pretended to be chastised but was scanning everything about this place so that X-37 could make a decent analysis. They were fond of chain-link fences. Tatiana led me through a maze for several minutes. When we emerged on the other side, I found everything about this group was conducted inside a giant warehouse that had probably been intended to manufacture starship parts at one time.

Equipment that could be removed had been removed, but there were still rails on the floor and reinforced pillars supporting the ceiling high above. There was glass in the skylights that was broken or discolored by age. I saw birds fly in and out and wondered if there were more of the rat creatures in the shadows.

"How many weapons do you have?" Tatiana asked as we walked across a large open space toward a dais near the middle.

"More than one."

"So, you're a smart ass and you speak the stupid," she said. "We don't normally make guests put their weapons in a locker, but I think you might be an exception to the courtesy."

"I'll keep my weapons."

She stopped and faced me. The squad of guards behind us spread out, making a pincer formation between whatever she was going to do in them. Stepping closer, she spoke almost privately.

"I'm not taking them from you because I don't want any of my friends to get hurt if you resist," she said. "You might think that makes me look weak but it's my decision and you would be wrong."

"You made the right call, if it makes you feel better. I'm not here to hurt any of your people or to take anything from them," I said. "Trust me."

She looked me in the eyes for a long moment, her expression nearly unreadable. I thought she was tough, but not as hard as she was pretending to be. "I know."

"That's it?" I asked. "You're just going to take my word for it?"

"Correct. Let me ask you this. Why would I do that, why

would I trust you even this much?" she asked. "And in case you're wondering, that was a test question. I want to see if you're as smart as you are big."

I thought about it for about two seconds before I had the answer. "You've already run into Elise and my sister."

Tatiana crossed her arms. "That's her name? We haven't exactly had a long conversation, but the boy was easy to catch."

"Bug? Better not mess with that kid. He's tougher than he looks, and I owe him my life."

"So that is his name? I thought he might be having a joke on us," she said. "No one here likes to speak your dialect. The kids call it stupid, because almost everyone who uses it gets in trouble with the authorities. We're not supposed to talk about old times or the quarantine or anything you represent."

"Very mysterious," I said. "I've got nothing to do with whoever put this place under quarantine. I'm just like you, I'm here to help my people."

"And how would you do that, Cain?" she asked.

"My people have enemies. I was told there might be technology here that can help us." I decided it might not be best to talk about interstellar space travel or super weapons just yet.

"We live in dangerous times." She turned to lead me the rest of the way across the room.

I followed. "Agreed. I'm serious, Tatiana. We don't have to be enemies."

She didn't answer, but merely stepped aside at the foot of the steps. What awaited above her was a dais fit for a queen, if an old one dressed in overalls. Once upon a time, it had been the foundation for a large piece of machinery, but now it was the seat of power for this collection of outlaws.

The woman was tiny, probably even smaller due to her age. She wore the same drab overalls that had been patched too many times over the knees and elbows. Her hair was probably gray but had the color of dirt ground into it.

She had her own guards, but they gave her space, standing one step down from the top level. Since the dais was a large oval, they surrounded anyone who came up to talk to her. None of them spoke to me but they all looked like they were ready to fight.

"What is your name, stranger?" She asked. "You probably have me at a disadvantage because I imagine that Tatiana has already told you who I am."

"My name is Halek Cain," I said. "I'm here looking for some of my friends."

She nodded, then had some sort of silent conversation with Tatiana. I wondered if they were related but couldn't be sure. "I am Melina. They put me in charge because I'm so old."

"There are worse criteria," I said.

"If you're trying to flatter me, it needs work. We rarely take weapons from our guests. What would be the point? With you, I think I'm going to regret that decision. Not many people scare me like you do," Melina said.

"Doesn't have to be that way. Just tell me where my friends are and how I can get to the spaceport," I said.

"You can't get to the spaceport. My children have probably told you about the Neverseen and made them sound like ghost stories. You may have even observed some of the touched ones in the city. But I promise you, go to the spaceport and you will regret it."

"Sounds like a bad situation." I looked around, hoping to see Bug or Elise or Hannah somewhere in the large room.

Melina hobbled toward me, then around me, taking a good look at me from all sides. I could tell that Tatiana was growing impatient. The guards around the dais, however, only watched. They might not be trained like Union soldiers, or like Path, but I wasn't going to underestimate them.

"You've been in many bad situations." She pointed at my left arm. "How is it possible that you are part machine? It does not look easy to control."

"I've had it for a long time. My people have different technology than you do," I said.

"There's no doubt we are very different. Just the way you talk makes it hard for us to communicate even though there is at least one dialect we share, old as it is," she said. "You know what the kids call it?"

"Yeah, I know."

She snapped her fingers without looking away from me. "Bring the one called Bug."

Two of her people immediately complied with the order.

"Thanks." I turned slowly as though killing time during the wait, but what I was actually doing was giving X-37 another chance to scan the room despite the dark corners. There wasn't really a good way to light the entire place given the amount of damage it had sustained over the centuries.

"I'm the elder of our tribe. Which means I'm educated and

remember as much as there is to remember about the past. Nothing mentions you or anyone like you," Melina said.

"Who's in charge of the city?" I wondered if I was doing the right thing by talking to this person. My question caused Tatiana to flinch where she stood just at the edge of my peripheral vision.

"There are several councils," Melina said. "I used to be able to promise meetings with them, but they have revoked the privilege regardless of the price petitioners are willing to pay."

"Isn't there one person more in charge than the others?" I asked. "I may be able to help, but I don't want to go around talking to dozens of leaders and wasting my time."

"Let's leave that discussion for a time when we are certain we are not enemies," Melina said.

A new guard entered the room, clearly one of Melina's more trusted soldiers, and approached, walking straight past me without acknowledging my existence. He bent close to the old woman and spoke softly enough that it was difficult for me to hear.

Unfortunately for him, my own hearing combined with the analysis X-37 could perform, allowed me a pretty good idea of what they were saying.

"He is not to be trusted. His monster seems to be hungry," the new guard said. "We have not been able to control the two young women. The boy who calls himself Bug is being escorted here but he is annoying his guards severely and might wind up locked in a cell before long."

"That is disappointing. We need to keep track of the girls.

They've been outside the fence for too long." Melina then waved him away as Bug was escorted into the room.

"Hey, Reaper! Good to see you here," Bug ran toward me and gave me a hug. The moment we made contact, I realized he had slipped a handful of cigars into my jacket.

At that moment, I loved the kid like he was my own son. Always thinking of other people.

"Why does he call you a Reaper? That is what they call the angel of death among our people," Melina said.

"You're probably not going to believe me if I tell you my old bosses just thought it sounded cool," I said.

She almost smiled, which made her seem less ancient and severe. I actually respected her for not succumbing to my wit, strange as that sounded. "No, Reaper. I wouldn't believe that at all."

I nodded, then skillfully withdrew one of the cigars Bug had passed me. As a stalling tactic, it was one of my favorites. Most people thought it looked pretty cool, or if they didn't, they never said anything to my face. The problem was, my benefactor hadn't provided a lighter.

I patted one pocket after another, then glanced back toward Bug.

"Problem?" Melina asked.

"You got a light?"

She moved slowly toward me, drawing out the moment and setting me off balance. When she looked up at me from her new position, I realized how tiny she was.

"It seems only appropriate that I provide a light for my own cigars," she said.

I shifted uncomfortably. I hadn't been too many places where theft was tolerated. In this type of situation, I wouldn't have been surprised to learn the punishment was death or getting thrown into some sort of monster pit. Xad came to mind.

Melina patted me on my arm, smiling reassuringly. She spoke in a low voice. "Do not concern yourself, Reaper. He didn't steal them, but I can see from your reaction you expected as much. We bartered for information and I learned more than enough."

"I think I'd rather he stole them," I said.

"Ha, you say that now. But no one likes a thief. Better an assassin than a thief," she said.

"What the hell did he tell you?"

"Calm yourself, stranger. He said mostly good things," Melina said. "Now if you will excuse me, I'm old and very tired. Please keep track of your friend so that he does not get himself into much trouble. I fear that he has been acting like a big shot since the moment he arrived."

"My recommendation is to rest, Reaper Cain," X-37 said.

"I'm also looking for two young women." Getting something to eat and closing my eyes for a bit was appealing, but that was why I was here.

"They were here, but they slipped away as soon as we turned our backs on them," Melina said. "I wasn't able to talk to them as much as I would've liked."

"I really don't have time to take a break," I said.

She extended her hand and one of her guards brought her a

cane, which she leaned on as she walked away from me. "Do not be in so much of a rush. I'm old. I know what I'm talking about. You may move about the compound so long as you listen to the guards when you encounter them."

I watched her leave and looked to Tatiana, almost expecting but definitely hoping she would give us a tour of the place. When she turned away without a word, I was a bit annoyed but kept my cool.

"Looks like it's just you and me, Bug," I said.

His smile was as big as I'd seen for a long time. "Hey, no problem, Reaper. I know my way around. The people here are all right."

7

AT FIRST, we walked through the oversized building, exiting the main room and traversing several hallways that seemed to lead around the perimeter. The layout reminded me of the large hangers on Dreadmax where I had first seen Elise.

"I'm glad you made it," Bug said. "I was getting bored. Nothing is really happening here. Not like back in the fleet. Do you think the Sansein are going to come here and kill everyone?"

I shook my head. "I doubt it. This place has been here for a long time. No one wants anything to do with it, which is probably a bad sign for us. They had to have quarantined the place for a reason."

"Yeah, it's really dangerous here. If your enemy is boredom," Bug said.

"First lesson, kid. Don't get complacent. These people are scared of something, and even if there isn't some sort of super monster out there, whoever's in charge runs this planet like a prison camp. That means someone has enough power to enforce the rules. It also means people are afraid to step out of line and will toss us to the wolves for a very small reward."

"Yeah, I know. I'm not a kid. I grew up on Dreadmax, remember?"

There wasn't much to say and if I argued with him, I was just going to reinforce his belief that I didn't trust his judgment—which I did and didn't, depending on the circumstance. "Where are Elise and my sister?"

Bug's face reddened. I could tell he was trying to think of something clever to say but gave up. "They ditched me, all right? Which is dumb, because they could've just left me on the ship if that's what they were going to do."

"Maybe you annoyed them." There wasn't a good way to explain that I didn't need him to look after the girls, but the girls to look after him. He was just old enough for this type of statement to be a crushing blow to his teenage pride.

"What if we split up? Maybe Elise set me on a mission," he said.

"Did she send you on a mission?" I asked.

Bug shook his head no.

"What about Hannah? Did she have something she wanted you to do?" I asked.

Again, the answer was negative.

"So, like you said, they ditched you, probably because you annoyed them or were slowing them down," I said.

He stopped, backed away from me, and shouted, "I wasn't

slowing them down! I don't slow anybody down. Maybe you're slowing me down!"

I backed him up against the wall, suddenly aware of my mistake but lacking sufficient time to correct it. This was one of the many reasons I wasn't suited for parenting. "Settle down, Bug. I know what you can do. I was on Dreadmax and you saved my life more than once. Don't get your shorts in a bunch."

I wasn't sure if this mollified him, but at least he stopped causing a scene.

"I'll show you around. This place can be confusing. There aren't any signs or painted lines like on a starship to show the way to the head," he said.

We walked in silence for a bit, steering clear of the locals when we saw them. For their part, they gathered in small groups and watched us wordlessly. Melina and Tatiana might not be afraid of us, but I thought everyone else was.

And why wouldn't they be? We didn't dress the same, talk the same, or have anything to do with their lives of work and toil. With my cybernetic arm and my eye, it didn't seem like they knew what to think of me. Apparently, that type of technology was unheard of in this place. I hadn't forgotten Manager's concern I might be a Kalon robot. If they thought I was a machine sent to harm them, it would definitely cause trust issues.

And there were already whispers of the Slayer following me. Depending on which overheard conversation I was listening to at the time, the alien hybrid was either my dark servant or was hunting me to get revenge for some crime against his people.

Bug's mood slowly improved. "I can get us whatever we want, even extra food. Or cigars."

"Great, how about you find me a lighter," I said.

"That'll be easy." He walked briskly and encouraged me to match his pace. "I charmed the old woman and I'm working on some other people who have stuff."

"I'll believe it when I see it," I said. "All I know is that I don't have a lighter and you lost Elise and Hannah."

"I didn't lose them," Bug said indignantly, then lowered his voice. "I just can't talk about it here."

"Why not?" I asked the question without breaking stride.

"Elise told me not to let these people follow her," Bug said. "She said if I messed up, it would ruin the mission."

"They ditched you. Probably only gave you those instructions to make you feel important," I said. "Unless they're planning on stealing from these people, I don't think anyone's going to care where they go. They certainly aren't going to follow her to the shipyard. They're afraid of the place."

"Why do you have to talk so loud?" Bug asked. "You might be right, but why tell everyone?"

"You have a point," I said. "I guess I should be glad you're practicing good operational security. Even if it's totally unnecessary. What would've made the entire mission better would've been including me in the planning stage. Oh, wait, I told none of you to go down to the planet."

This time when I stopped, Bug made sure to stay out of arm's reach. "You can't do everything, you know. We're trying to help defeat the Sansein too."

"And the Alon," I said.

"What?" The expression on Bug's face was priceless.

"Don't forget about the obvious threats. Just because Victon was Alon and sent us here, doesn't mean he was our friend or that his people aren't going to continue their war against Wallach and Xad."

"I know that," Bug said. "What exactly do you want me to do?"

I made a final assessment of the outlaw hideout. I wasn't buying the altruism of Melina, but that didn't matter right now. I came here for one thing, and that was to find Elise, Hannah, and Bug.

"Listen carefully, Bug, because I'm gonna ask you one time: Can you take me to Elise and Hannah?"

He looked around first then moved toward one of the large doors that opened into another of the hangar-like maintenance buildings. From our current location, we could take more of the chain-link corridors to the maze and either leave or go deeper into the compound. The lighting was gloomy and inconsistent.

"I can take you to Elise and Hannah," he said quietly. His youthful cockiness was gone now. I wondered what type of adult he would be if he lived that long. The kid had come a long way since squatting in a security tower on Dreadmax. "Just act like you're giving me a lecture or something, and we will work our way toward the South gate. The guards might not like it. No one goes that way unless they are trying to get to the shipyard."

"Just lead the way." I didn't want to keep up the act all day. "If they try to stop us, let me handle it."

No one paid us any mind until we were about to leave. A pair of tough looking fighters stepped forward. One was considerably older, his gray hair thinning on his head. He wore one shoulder pauldron and the lower half of a cuirass. I wasn't familiar with the materials, but I imagined it was something like carbon fiber or a metal alloy with a non-reflective surface.

"I got word you might move this way, stranger," he said. "You don't have no business in the starport. Not that anyone does. Save yourself some trouble and head back."

"My business is my business." I held his gaze. His partner backed him up, but in the end, they stepped aside, and we left the compound.

Bug led me into one dark alley after another. I marked the main spire of the spaceport and used it like a guiding star, always keeping track of our progress. X-37 frequently updated our maps. It wasn't long before my guide became cautious, slowing down to search for any type of possible ambush.

"We should be getting close," he said. "Elise said I should whistle to let them know I'm coming."

"Or so she can avoid you."

Bugs eyes went wide, then he cursed. "I was wondering where the hell they went."

"I'll move ahead fifty meters. Then you whistle and let's see what happens," I said.

"Okay. I can't believe they would do something like that to me."

Once I was away from the kid, I slipped on my stealth cloak and started searching for Elise and Hannah in earnest. Bug started whistling without any results about the time I activated the Reaper mask.

The edges of my vision took on the distinctive blue tint I associated with the device. The effect was minimal but reassuring. A quick scan of the area revealed nothing.

I moved even farther away from Bug.

"Are you certain you wish to leave the boy behind?" X-37 asked. "You've only just reacquired him."

"I didn't acquire anyone, X. We talked about this. Just try to keep tabs on him." I searched the darkness. When I still found nothing, I focused on each doorway I came to with increased infrared sensitivity.

The combined power of my cybernetic eye and the mask would make this an almost unfair contest, but it had limits. I couldn't see through walls, for example, unless there was a fire or explosions—and even then, it was inconsistent.

What I was able to put together were images of anyone hiding in shadowy recesses or behind other insubstantial barriers.

"We are approaching the coordinates Jelly earlier advised would be best for communication with her," X-37 said.

"It's about time." I'd almost forgotten this was one of our short-term mission objectives. This planet and its deceptively neglected industry were really throwing me off my game. Compared to Union cities or even the dives in the Deadlands, this place looked like it should be a walk in the park. At least at first glance, that is.

So far even the simplest problems had been frustratingly difficult to handle, and I still wasn't sure why the place had been quarantined or what made everyone so terrified of the spaceport.

"I'm not seeing Elise or Hannah, so go ahead and contact Jelly." I put my back to the wall to avoid surprises.

"I'm searching for a connection," X-37 said. "One moment."

I waited until I started feeling exposed, and then moved to a new position. There were pros and cons to staying on the move, but I didn't like to be static while in unknown territory. This wasn't time to camp like a sniper. I was still in search mode.

"Good evening, Captain," Jelly said.

"It's much better now, Jelly. Good to hear you. Have you figured out the communications network of this planet?"

"To some extent, Captain. When we entered the system, X-37 and I went to work diligently. We encountered several layers of encryption, but also something else," Jelly said.

"We identified a doubling that seemed unintentional, much like how our sensors perceive the Sansein. But even with that knowledge, neither of us could understand how the system's communication networks work. It's a simple problem that should not be this difficult," X-37 said.

"What I've discovered while you and X-37 were out of communication with the ship is that we overlooked the obvious. One of the layers of encryption is actually not encryption at all. It's a function of decay on a level we hadn't accounted for," Jelly said.

"I apologize, Reaper Cain. The ability to piggyback on local communications networks and their computers is still slightly beyond our reach despite their relatively low version of Alon technology." X-37 updated my tactical map, and I saw two dots moving into the area.

"It looks like Elise and Hannah are on the move." My HUD also showed Bug was nearby, heading toward Elise and my sister on a parallel course to my own. "Let's scoop up Bug then have a reunion with the runaways."

"I suggest continued surveillance," X-37 said. "Re-contacting the boy is an unnecessary complication at this late stage."

"Agreed." I started to move. Sneaking up behind Bug was more difficult than anticipated, but I was back in the zone now. All of my friends were good, but they'd pissed me off and I wasn't about to get ditched again.

X-37 and Jelly provided overwatch and guidance. Working together, we were soon witnessing a reunion between Bug, Elise, and my sister.

They argued over a large piece of equipment, apparently thinking that Bug should help. When he finally agreed, the three of them hobbled around the corner.

"What the hell are they up to, X?" I asked.

"Jelly will be able to answer that question, but she is going to lose contact with us soon," X-37 said.

"They are taking parts to a ship they intend to steal," Jelly said. "My orbit is taking me out of the ideal communications encryption gap. I'm sending X-37 other possible locations where we can link up."

"Thanks, Jelly." I crept into visual range of the three conspirators.

"What are you doing here, Bug?" Elise asked, apparently not for the first time.

"You know."

Elise cursed under her breath. "Then where is he?"

"Are you waiting to make a dramatic entrance, Reaper Cain?" X-37 said.

"No, X. I was just trying to decide if I'm ready for more grief from the kid," I said, then moved into the open.

Elise saw me a fraction of a second after my sister Hannah did. True to her nature, my sister kept silent, probably knowing that Elise would carry half the conversation we were about to have.

"Well look at you," Elise said to Bug, planting both fists on her hips as she stared me down. "Led him right to us."

"I'm sorry, Elise," Bug said.

"Too late for that now, Bug. We counted on you."

"You shouldn't have ditched me!"

I held up a hand, silencing my young protégés. "What are we doing here, Elise?"

"Are you going to try and take over the mission?" Her resolve was easy to see in her expression.

I thought about my answer, carefully considering the effect my words might have. She waited. Off to one side, Hannah and Bug looked back and forth between us.

"I was mad as hell, Elise. And I'm still not excited about this kerfuffle. But it is what it is, and I don't want to argue," I said.

"Are you going to start bossing everyone around?" she asked.

"I might, but I'll try not to," I said. "Good enough?"

She shrugged. "Sure, I guess. Whatever."

I glanced at the ship parts they'd been lugging through the abandoned city. We were just on the edge of the spaceport now, and there were several small launch and landing pads. Probably for maintenance vehicles and support craft rather than warships or exploration vessels.

Elise pointed at our destination. "I'll be honest, Reaper, I don't know if the ships are the weapons Victon told you about, but they'll help the Wallach and Xad fleet a lot. The technology is straightforward but in very good condition despite the way this place is falling apart. These are pretty new components and resources."

I crossed my arms, trying not to offend her, and nodded thoughtfully. "That's a first. Don't get mad, but I'm sure this isn't what Victon was talking about. He said it was something a champion, meaning one person, had to use. But all of this is good, and we might as well keep doing what you were doing until we figure out the rest."

"I can live with that, Reaper," she said.

8

"ALL RIGHT, fine. What the hell are you trying to move? If we're going to do this, I'd rather not be out in the open for too long," I said.

"We're pretty sure it's a battery," Elise said. "We tried two other batteries with the shuttle, but Hannah thinks they might be vehicle specific. Some type of security protocol."

"Makes sense." I squatted next to the device they had been dragging down the street. It was about two meters long and a quarter meter thick at the widest point. At each end there were connector couplings. "I can help you carry it, but I have a better idea."

"I'd love to hear it," Elise said.

"Give me your best whistle and see if you can get Briggs here. But go easy. It hurts his ears."

Elise put her fingers in the corners of her mouth and let out a whistle that made me flinch. "The Slayer is right. That's a horrible sound."

"Is it?" X-37 asked. "I'm curious to what makes it so bad. Is it the frequency or the volume?"

"It's just unpleasant, X." I watched for the Slayer, anticipating his approach and wondering how many local rodents he'd eaten since we started. I was about ready to eat one myself if I didn't find some food.

"I like it," Bug said. "It's beautiful. Music to my ears, Elise. Really."

Elise rolled her eyes and ignored the kid from Dreadmax.

A short time later, I heard Briggs issue his response—a tortured howl that sent shivers down my spine. "Like that's more comforting than a whistle. I'm glad he's on our side."

"I'm not certain you're doing the commando a mercy by letting him live." Hannah seemed sad, her tone much gentler than what she was suggesting.

"Did you know the test subjects before they went through the DNA splicing?" I asked.

My sister nodded. "Some of them were very protective of Mom and me."

"Well maybe it's good I didn't kill him," I said. Hannah didn't comment.

Briggs came into view, moving cautiously through the night. "I heard the sound and came right away, Reaper."

"Sorry about that. I know you hate it," I said. "But I wanted to make sure we got your attention."

"I'll live," Briggs said.

"Can you help me carry this shuttle battery?" I asked.

Briggs sauntered over toward it and looked down. A moment later he gathered it up in his arms, then hefted it onto his shoulder. "I can carry it."

"Outstanding," I said. "We'll cover you. If you have to, drop it. Our first priority is staying alive, and the second is figuring out what the secret of Yansden is."

"He's still stuck on the idea of a super weapon," Elise said.

The Slayer snorted noncommittally.

We moved out, watching for Manager's people, the Neverseen, and the Kalon Regulars of Yansden. The sun started to come up, casting long shadows across the abandoned spaceport ahead of us.

"The shuttle is a good idea," I said, hoping to avoid an argument with Elise.

"Well, thanks. But you still think I'm wrong. Admit it," she said.

"I was the one who fought Victon. He said he was the champion who could use the secret weapon on Yansden to defeat the Sansein," I said. "I don't know how else to interpret that."

To my surprise, Hannah jumped into the argument. I'd expected Elise to give me trouble, but I forgot how persistently logical my sister could be.

"And how exactly could he have known anything about this planet?" Hannah asked. "They've been under quarantine for centuries. Anything he suspected had to be basically rumor, or worse yet, a myth."

"You should listen to your sister," Elise said.

"Great, now I'm outnumbered," I said. "I already agreed to do things your way, mostly. We'll get these resources to the Wallach and Xad fleets. What more do you want from me?"

"Don't make us the bad guys," Elise said. "Our plan is basically a sure thing. I don't even know what your plan is. What is your plan, exactly? Tell me more about this super-secret weapon only a very special champion can use."

"Now she's just being ugly," X-37 said. "My analysis suggests that she is trying to provoke you."

"Thanks, X. I'm not used to getting that kind of support from you." Wanting out of the argument, I went to help Briggs carry the battery, but he scowled at me.

"My brother always has a hard time admitting he didn't know what he was talking about," Hannah said.

"I should've left you in the cryo-tube," I said.

Hannah laughed. "I was wondering how long it would take you to come to that conclusion. But admit it, you're glad Elise stands up to you. I remember when you first joined the Union military. You were always frustrated with people who lacked strong convictions and the will to carry them out."

My sister's words hit home. She saw me as I was and not as I had become. There wasn't time to fully appreciate what having her and my mother back could mean, even though I had practically already lost them. The fleet was scattered, and Elise and Hannah were right. We needed these resources. The exodus fleet, wherever it went, would always be in jeopardy until we had a base of operations and a place to manufacture new ships and parts, and to produce food for long voyages.

Maybe Yansden could be that place. If my hunch was correct, the quarantine was old and no longer needed. Or that was what I hoped.

For the first time, I really saw myself as something more than just a Reaper.

"Let's just stop arguing," I said. "We can do both. If there are things our fleet can use, great. But I know there is a secret weapon someplace on this planet. The only reason Victon or others like him haven't used it is because they aren't allowed to come here."

"Because there is a quarantine for a reason," Elise said. "Which means we could already be poisoned or something."

"You're not wrong," I said.

I stopped talking and considered what Elise and my sister were saying. Maybe I was wrong. Maybe I was an arrogant hothead too stubborn to listen to reason. I'd always been a loner, even before I was singled out for Reaper training. Depending on who you listened to, I hated to admit failure and tried to do everything myself.

These thoughts and others filled my mind as I watched Hannah, Elise, and Bug work on the shuttle. When their efforts ended in frustration, I felt guilty. Not so long ago, I might've made a sarcastic comment. Now I realized they were working hard, totally committed to doing the impossible. I had no right to diminish their efforts with my poor attitude.

"Perhaps you should scout the area while they finish their work," X-37 said.

"That's a good idea, X," I said, then told Elise that's what I was going to do. She nodded without a word and continued working to fix their fuck up. Sweat dripped in her eyes, forcing her to wipe it away in frustration.

"Slayer, come with me," I said. Neither of us flinched at the name. Soon we were stalking into the shadows, creating an ever-expanding circle around the shuttle. We focused most of our efforts on the spaceport where the alleged danger should come from if the prohibitions against traveling here remained valid. I still wasn't exactly sure why there had been a systemwide quarantine.

"Not even the Sansein come to this place," Briggs observed when we took a rest break.

"I've been wondering about that too," I said. "I half expected everyone on this planet to be covered in radiation sores or some-thing. But since they aren't, maybe it's not so bad here."

"Reaper optimism is a strange thing," Briggs said. "Awk."

We found the first set of bones a short time later. Patrolling each side of a wide boulevard that seemed designed to move heavy machinery, I saw the corpse about the same time the Slayer smelled it.

"Old bones," he said. "Probably someone or something dragged them here a long time ago."

I zoomed in on the scene with my cybernetic eye and my Reaper mask, asking X-37 to record and analyze everything we found here. Images popped up on my HUD. X-37 marked several more bodies that I wouldn't have seen on my own. Some were little more than bone fragments or scraps of hair. The only thing I knew for certain was that we'd definitely arrived in the

place no one wanted to go. Human remains, in all their varia-
tions, disturbed me but there were other remains as well. I saw a
femur too large to be from a man. Something with sharp teeth
had been gnawing on it.

"You should head back and warn the others," Briggs said.

I studied his posture, and the way he faced the most likely
direction of the threat. Whatever had caused this seemed to
radiate from the starport.

"What do you think, X?" I asked.

My limited artificial intelligence took a full minute before
answering. Once his scans were documented, I saw several new
markers in my heads-up display. There was a pattern to where
the bodies had fallen, even accounting for the ones that had been
dragged afterward.

The victims of whatever happened had been running, and
from my experience of post battle scenes, they'd been in *panicked
flight*. We scouted several more streets and discovered the closer
we move toward the center of the starport, the more bodies there
were.

"Let's head back to Elise and the others. I'm strongly considering having Jelly pick us up."

"That's good shit," Briggs croaked. "Can she send the
shuttle?"

"We'll have to pick it up later," I said. "I'm afraid it would
run into trouble if we tried to pilot it by remote. The other option
is to have Tom send down the Archangel gear in a pod."

I STAYED out of my friend's way, choosing to watch the shadows and listen to X-37's frequent updates on their progress. Briggs, in one of his moods, hid on a rooftop somewhere—or maybe he was just gone this time.

Elise stood from her work abruptly, shooting me a glance. I readied my HDK Dominator and glided forward, looking for whatever she'd sensed in the night. Somewhere distant, Briggs howled like a Slayer talking to the moon.

Elise backed away from the frustratingly nonfunctional shuttle, creating distance between Hannah, Bug, and me. My sister didn't seem to have much tactical training, but she picked up on what we were doing and angled toward the cover of a building. Bug was left standing alone for half a second, but his own survival instincts quickly kicked in, inspiring him to hide under the shuttle.

"Help me out, X," I said. "Can you get anything off the local security grid yet?"

"Only meta-analysis, but I think I can assure you we are not dealing with the Kalon Regulars. I believe these will be soldiers of Melina."

I scanned the area with the combined power of my cybernetic eye and my Reaper mask, quickly confirming my LAI was correct. Armed men and women advanced through the shadows toward our position. Most carried firearms I suspected they had crafted themselves. They worked together, covering each other as they crossed open areas. With some real training, they might become a high functioning military unit.

Until then, I wasn't impressed. That didn't mean I wasn't

wary. The will to fight could make any group of armed men and women dangerous.

"X, please tell me that you can communicate with Elise's earbud," I said.

"It would be a lie," X-37 said. "You're going to have to rely on more basic techniques."

"We really should've brought the Archangel gear," I muttered. "Next time we have a link with Jelly, tell Tom to get everything prepped for a supply drop."

"Of course, Reaper Cain," X-37 said. "In the meantime, it seems that Melina's goons are surrounding this area. They see at least one of you."

"Which one of us?"

"Analyzing data," X-37 said. Two seconds passed. "I believe they are converging around Hannah's position. I'm unable to see her, so I can't describe what she is doing wrong. Perhaps you should offer her some training in the future."

"I'm sure she'll love that," I whispered, then slipped to a new position, hoping I could protect my sister and the rest of my friends if this went bad.

Melina's soldiers stopped and solidified their perimeter. An additional squad arrived, followed by a vehicle that was in surprisingly good repair. Its electric motor barely made noise and its tires didn't look patched.

I waited and was glad that none of my companions had broken cover during the tense silence. Once this group had the area under their control, Melina climbed out of the vehicle.

She walked to the center of the intersection, adjusting her

coat against the chill, and then looked up. "We know you're here, Reaper. Please come out and talk to me."

Hoping that my companions remained hidden, I emerged from the darkness to face the woman and her soldiers. The men and women were loyal to the old woman and surprisingly well-disciplined despite their lack of formal training. No one said a word. All remained alert and stayed at their posts, each watching a different zone.

X-37 commented on their tactics. "They do better when they're stationary, it seems."

Melina didn't hear my LAI. "You found a rather valuable shuttle battery, I see. It won't work the way you're trying to use it, so we'll take it back to our compound and salvage it."

I didn't argue, which caused her to raise an eyebrow.

"You have a problem with that, Reaper?" she asked.

"Nope. Not even a little bit," I said. "It's junk. Unless you're going to provide a shuttle we can use. Maybe an escort to the center of the spaceport."

She laughed. "You've seen the bones by now. It's foolish to go that way."

"Why are you here, Melina?" I asked. "We don't owe you anything and you're taking a risk coming this far, if what you're saying is true."

"You are a stranger, but you're human. I don't think you're tainted by the spaceport. So, it's my duty to help you. And I do hope that you would be grateful and perhaps repay our kindness."

I glanced over my shoulder, checked my weapons, and stalled

to see how patient she really was. "I'm on a mission. I don't really have time for this. If you can't help me get to the spaceport, I think we're done talking."

"You *do* want to talk to me, Reaper. Trust me," she said. "The Neverseen don't come every night, but I believe they will be hungry now. And not just for meat. The more you tamper with the technology, like that shuttle and its battery, the more they are aroused. Their connection to the spaceport and the city is complicated. There is still a reason for the quarantine."

"Now we're getting somewhere," I said. "I could use some answers. If you're not going to help me, at least tell me what's happening on this planet."

"I'm willing to enter into a parlay of sorts. But we must return to the compound. You may have a death wish, but none of my people want to die at the hands of the Neverseen or their touched ones," she said.

"What do you think, X?" I asked.

"I believe it would be wise to gather more information. I would also feel better if we had already arranged the Archangel supply drop, but no plan is ever perfect," my limited artificial intelligence said.

"Agreed." I held Melina's gaze when I spoke to my LAI, which only slightly confused her. Some of what I said probably made her think I was crazy, but in the end, she got what she wanted.

Elise, Hannah, and Bug emerged from their hiding places and we allowed Melina's soldiers to surround us and escort us back into the compound.

9

THE TRIP back to the compound was uneventful and we were soon within the tall fences. We watched our guards carefully, fully aware we were badly outnumbered. I also noticed that there were no kids around when we arrived, almost like Melina expected there might be trouble.

"I'll talk to you alone, Reaper," she said.

"Not a chance, old woman," Elise said. "We're not splitting up anymore."

"That's an interesting stance considering how hard you worked to stay away from your benefactor," Melina said. "But as you wish."

She motioned us into the main building, then toward the platform where I had first met her. She took her seat, arms resting on the oversized chair like a queen on a throne. Tatiana and several other high-ranking members of her tribe, or whatever this was, joined us.

"If we are going to have a council meeting, then I need my best people here," Melina said. "You're a dangerous man, Reaper, but your counsel is made up of children."

Neither Elise nor Hannah fell for the bait. Bug, I was less worried about. He was sarcastic and witty over a radio mic, but less outgoing in person. He sulked like a moody teenager and it was almost embarrassing, except I didn't have time for that. All I needed was for him to shut up and listen, and given the awkward nature of this confrontation, that was exactly what I would get from the Dreadmax kid.

Tatiana crossed her arms, standing next to Melina but slightly back. Two other men and one woman who didn't reveal their identities arrayed themselves similarly behind the old woman.

"How did you come to be here, stranger?" Melina asked. "And before you assume this won't be a fair trade of information, I know that you have questions about the Neverseen and the spaceport and probably a great many other things."

I milked the moment for all it was worth. Lifting my cybernetic arm, I was tempted to extend the blade but decided better of it. Instead, I worked my fingers to show how complex and dynamic the augmentation was.

"Long ago, I was a soldier. The story of how I lost my arm is irrelevant, but the organization I fought for was able to give me this." I looked around, sweeping the darkness without letting them know what I was doing. To my surprise, they didn't have any hidden soldiers waiting to ambush us if things went bad. "They also fixed my eye."

"Interesting." Melina seemed less than satisfied. "I can tell that you're going to withhold many secrets. That is unacceptable."

Elise stepped forward, motioning me to silence. "We lived under the control of an intergalactic government called the Union. Not everything they did was bad, but most was. What Cain isn't telling you is the cost of his augmentations."

I hoped she would skip what had been done to her during the early stages of the Lex project, back when scientists like her father really didn't know what the hell they were doing. What the Union had wanted was complicated—I still wasn't certain how far her healing abilities went. Explaining any of this to Melina and her quasi superstitious band of ne'er-do-wells was a recipe for disaster. Just the idea of ancient Earth Tech was probably more than any of us could handle, especially this far into uncharted space.

"We are on the run from the Union," Elise said. "It doesn't matter why, only that they're far from here and unlikely to catch up to us now. During our travels, we met others who had their own enemies and we helped them. Now, we're part of an exodus fleet seeking to escape the Alon. Once, long ago, I think it might've been your people."

Melina nodded sagely. "That is possible. Our people are the Kalon, a word that sounds very similar. But why would they bring you here?"

"They told us this planet was off-limits along with the rest of the system," I said. "We came hoping to find something to fight them."

Melina and the others consider this without talking. They exchanged looks but didn't discuss what we had revealed.

"Tell them the rest," Hannah said.

Melina and her counsel faced me expectantly, fear clearly written in their expressions. "Yes, Reaper. Tell us the rest."

"You're not going to like it," I said.

"I imagine you are correct. Nevertheless, we must know what type of evil you brought to our world," Melina said.

"Do you have any suggestions, X?"

Melina narrowed her gaze when I said this but didn't say anything. I could feel her suspicion.

"I suggest just getting it over with, Reaper Cain," X-37 said. "Don't reveal any more information than is necessary but also be aware that if you hold back, they will know."

"What the Union did to me"—I lifted my Reaper arm again —"was an experiment. They are obsessed with developing weapons and warriors to use them."

"Or perhaps they combined them," Melina said. "I can't promise you that my people will accept what you are, Reaper."

"I guess that's my problem," I said.

"I almost want to tell you to stop," Melina said. "I fear that what you're about to reveal is worse than anything I will tell you about Yansden."

Tatiana watched me with an intensity that made me uncomfortable.

"There was a scientist who was fascinated with the possible existence of nonhuman aliens," I said.

"Nonhuman aliens? Not so long ago, I would've thought that a ridiculous proposition because you and your friends are the only type of aliens we've ever had visit our planet," Melina said. "At least, not for many generations. That's another story, I fear."

"You better have a good story when it's your turn," I said. "This scientist found genetic samples from what he believed was an alien race and combined them with test subjects."

A murmur went through the group of Yansden people. Melina slashed her hand downward to silence them.

"How is that even possible?" she asked.

"I'm not a scientist. Genetic manipulation is not impossible where I'm from," I said. "But the point is, we found the aliens and they were pissed off about the entire incident. They're also trying to kill us. For some reason, they've avoided your system. Which makes me want to know what is wrong with this place."

Melina took her cue and began with practiced efficiency that almost made me embarrassed for our poor presentation. "The records of our people are extensive, if not available to all citizens. As you might've guessed, we in the compound are outlaws, people who live far too close to the starport. Once, ages ago, that was not such a bad thing."

"She has made this presentation many times before," X-37 said. "I believe they have a tradition of oral knowledge. Which is interesting, given their level of technological achievement. Digital storage would be much more efficient. Their choice suggests a caste system of knowledge stewards. Admittedly, their infrastructure is in poor repair, but it would be possible for them to retain some technology for important tasks."

Melina continued, unaware my limited artificial intelligence was talking to me. "The oldest of our records suggest we were once travelers as you are, and that this world belonged to others before us. There are ancient ruins in the wilderness with evidence of this truth, but no one goes there. The question that many have is, if we are not from this planet, how did we get here?"

I waited for more.

"As it turns out, this longing to know where we are from was our undoing. Two factions arose: those who wanted to explore the galaxy the slow way, and those who wanted to cheat against physics and the laws of nature."

"I don't think this is going to go well," X-37 said. "I wish that Tom and Henshaw were here to hear the story."

I signaled X-37 that I agreed but tried not to be obvious about it. Earlier, the kids had noticed me fidgeting and I didn't want to distract Melina from telling the full tale.

"Two fleets left our system. They called themselves the Alon and Manna. We do not know what happened to them," Melina said. "Our scientists experimented with different methods of traveling great distances. The ships they launched were supposed to travel farther and faster than anyone thought possible."

"Like a slip tunnel?" I asked.

"I don't know what that is, but perhaps those who left did," Melina said. "What I know, what we all know as part of our history, is that the spaceport you want so badly to explore warped reality somehow. There was radiation sickness, but that's long past."

"But something in the spaceport has everyone afraid to go there," I observed.

Melina nodded. "Politicians have been promising for generations that the creatures haunting the spaceport would die out, but they seem to be breeding rather effectively."

"What about the touched ones, or the Runners? I've heard your people mention both," I asked.

"The touched might be redeemed; their situation requires a longer explanation. The Runners hunt anything with blood and drag them back to their master," Melina said.

"Avoid the Runners. Check," I said.

"Was that a joke?" Melina asked, not amused. "Never mind. I will continue. One of the many ways our leaders, and when I say that I'm talking about the official leaders of this planet, have promised to end the threat was by sending killer drones to seek the monsters and destroy them. They are on the third iteration of the death machines."

"I don't like the sound of that, Reaper Cain," X-37 said.

I wished that Elise could communicate with me via her earbud as we had on other missions. I was starting to understand why there is so much interference with radio and infrared links.

"I've seen a lot of drones," I said. "None of them seemed particularly dangerous. Mostly for traffic control or maintenance."

"They are strictly regulated, and currently down for renovation. The Neverseen learned to trick the drones. You have witnessed the touched ones, people from outside who thought their lives would be better in alliance with the Neverseen. The abominations in control of the spaceport gave these misguided souls just enough technology to hide from the drones and send them to run errands, scout for Kalon Regulars, and gather other resources," Melina said. "Make no mistake, Reaper, they are all dangerous in their own way. Do not think you can help the touched ones. They've made their choice."

I pulled out a cigar, considered it, and tucked it in one side of my mouth. I didn't light it, because Bug still hadn't come through with a burner, but it made me feel better. "Have you ever seen one of them?"

"They are called the Neverseen for a reason," Melina said.

"But you have to know something," I said. "Are they humans, animals, robots? Big? Small? What kind of stories do people tell about these mysterious ghosts?"

"The most dangerous are those that have retained human form. But they also have their pets," Melina said.

"Sounds scary." I wanted answers and this woman was telling me ghost stories.

Melina crossed her arms. "Someone give him a lighter. He looks ridiculous with that thing hanging out the side of his face."

One of the men handed me a small metal box. I stared at it, not exactly sure how it worked. After a few seconds, I opened the top half—then stared at a wheel of flint.

Tatiana explained, sounding frustrated, "You have to flip it open or it won't have enough friction. Stop being so nice to it. Get rough."

I closed it, then snapped it opened until I had a flame. "Nice."

Tatiana shook her head, reminding me of both my sister and Elise. It was good to know that I frustrated all women equally.

"Keep it," said the man.

"Thanks. I owe you." I noticed that my words made him uncomfortable.

Whatever, I thought.

A speaker box near the ceiling sounded an alert tone. Melina and the others faced it but didn't seem alarmed. She smiled, then faced me. "Brecken's patrol has been successful, or so it seems. Let us reconvene near the front gate. Tatiana, please escort our guests."

"Yes, grandmother," Tatiana said.

She waved a hand for us to follow her and we did.

APPARENTLY, whoever Brecken was and whatever type of super-secret patrol he had been on was a big deal in the compound. People flowed out of their barracks to see what was happening at the front gate. I had a pretty good idea I wasn't going to like it.

"Do you think they could have killed Briggs?" Elise asked.

"Maybe." I took a puff of my cigar as we walked. "That's more likely than him getting captured, I think."

"What are we going to do?" Elise asked. "We can't just let them do something like that."

"What do you propose?" Hannah said. "Punish them for

killing a monster that they probably think is going to eat them when they sleep? There's a good chance we are the villains in this scenario. They didn't ask us to come to their planet."

"She's got a point, kid," I said.

"I know, but that doesn't mean they get to hunt our friend. And before you say it, I know he's never really been super cuddly and nice, but he's on our side," Elise said. "We have to help him if we can. And I'm not a kid, jerkface."

"If he's not dead, we'll help them." I joined the rest of Melina's people in the courtyard closest to the front gate.

More and more people gathered. I gave Elise and the rest of my friends a hand signal, indicating we should spread out but not too much. If Melina and her people wanted to lock us up, they were going to have to work for it. At the same time, we needed to work as a team. To do that, especially with our comms situation, we needed to be close enough to see each other and exchange nonverbal signals.

The mood changed. Throughout the compound, the lights were dimmed and replaced with red illumination—something often seen in the cockpits of airships or armored cars during combat. Seconds later, powerful floodlights were pointed out from the guard towers. Street after street was searched until we saw a group of the Runners dash into an alley and disappear.

"Am I crazy, or do those things remind you of Briggs?" I asked.

"Didn't get a good look," Elise said. "They were almost running on four legs but were about the same size. What color do you think they were? I didn't like the way the lights reflected off of them."

Melina and her bodyguards approached me. She pointed beyond the perimeter of the compound. "That is why we brought you here. It's not safe beyond our fences. Those are Runners."

"Looks like a swarm," I said. "Are they attacking the compound, or just harassing your guards?"

"They have not dared to attack us directly in years," Melina said.

Tatiana caught my attention. Her look was concerned but I also thought she was ready to fight if she had to. "They know Brecken and his team are coming in."

I moved ahead of the others, closer to the fence. It was tempting to follow the searchlights, but I tried to focus on other movement instead. "The search beams are doing more harm than good."

"Yes, but they make the people feel better." Tatiana took me by one arm and pointed. "There, do you see it?"

Right where she pointed, one of the Runners stopped and stared at us. It stood on two legs and had two arms, but it was much taller than I had anticipated. Lean to the point of ridiculousness, it nevertheless had a huge rib cage and broad shoulders. The color was deceptive. I suspected it's skin, or hide, or whatever was somewhat reflective—not unlike my stealth cloak when it was turned off. It was like the creature couldn't decide if it wanted to reflect light or absorb it.

10

MEN, women, and their children crowded into the area but kept their distance from us. Some pointed, all of them talked. Brecken and his squad drove through the final gate in a procession of vehicles: a fast car with roll bars, a flatbed truck with the cage, and another of the smaller off-road vehicles bringing up the rear. The first and last vehicles had crew-served guns with belts of ammunition running into large metal boxes. None of the vehicles had much armor, but I suspected they were for raiding, not for fighting pitched battles.

Inside the cage, Briggs held the bars with his oversized hands, scowling whenever he flexed his claws. Once, when a guard came too close, he shot a tentacle toward the man. Apparently, this wasn't the first time they'd been through this dance because the man barely flinched—only moving back far enough to be safe.

The civilians watching, however, squealed in terror or delight depending on their age and desire to see a spectacle.

"Melina," I said. "That's my companion. I want him out of that cage."

"He looks more dangerous than anything we've seen from the spaceport quarantine zone," she said. "I'm not sure you're thinking clearly if you count such a creature as an ally."

"Looks can be deceiving," I said.

"He's one of the experiments, isn't he?" Melina stepped closer to me and lowered her voice. "He's half human and half alien."

I shrugged like it didn't matter. "I'm not sure it is exactly half, but either way, he saved my life way more times than you have. My loyalty lies with my friends."

"As it should," she said, but didn't seem happy.

Elise, Hannah, and Bug looked grim. The crowd around us grew moment by moment. X-37 had a hard time keeping track of their numbers but was able to warn me of their mood—like I needed help with that.

Kids laughed and squealed, playing games much as those on the subway had. The difference was, they never quite touched the cage this time. Guards stood with their weapons held at port arms, discouraging approach for any reason. What they couldn't stop, however, was the occasional thrown bit of rotten food.

I leaned close to Melina, causing her guards to flinch and grip their weapons more tightly. "This is a dangerous game. You're lucky he didn't kill ten of your soldiers when your lieutenant captured him."

She didn't respond, which made me believe that there had in fact been casualties.

"I'm not quite sure you understand what I am." I used a hand signal to ask X-37 what the status of the Archangel drop was.

"Ninety-three seconds, Reaper Cain," X-37 said. "Path insisted on accompanying the equipment, which necessarily slowed the descent vector. We didn't want to incinerate the sword saint."

"I know your type," Melina said. "You come in here and try to steal my best people, lead them away on some quest that will get them killed. They have to know I'm in charge. Everyone must understand which of us will keep them safe."

Hannah stepped in when I expected Elise to challenge the old woman. "So, this is a show of strength?" She raised an eyebrow in appreciation. "Not bad."

Melina became suspicious, signaling her people. Brecken immediately ordered his people to pull tarps over the cage, hiding Briggs from view. It was a pretty good tactic but wouldn't be enough to save them. Melina and her lieutenant had effectively taken Briggs out of our communications loop since this mission seemed destined to be low-tech—for about half a minute.

I wanted to light a cigar so bad I could barely stand it, but that would interfere with my Archangel mount up when the time came.

A whistling sound ascended toward our location. More and more people looked toward the sky. "I hope we can do this peacefully."

Melina's eyes widened as Path and the supply bundle streaked toward the courtyard.

"Get out! You have to get out! Brecken, put the beast and the Reaper outside the fence!" Melina screamed, waving her arms as she raced around the courtyard giving orders. Her uncharacteristic panic set the crowd and her soldiers off balance.

Children started to cry and some of the parents were smart enough to leave with their entire broods in tow. Others watched in fascination as Path and the Archangel bundle slammed into the ground. The shockwave scared the crap out of me because it seemed impossible my sword wielding friend wouldn't be damaged even though he absorbed the impact by crouching very low with one hand out to catch his balance.

A circle of dust expanded across the surface of the courtyard around him and our gear. The concrete cracked underneath his armored boots.

"Gear up!" I shouted, running for my unit.

A guard blocked my progress, but I shoved him hard with both hands, sending him flying. One man aimed the rifle at me but hesitated and missed his chance. Elise, Hannah, and Bug all ran to their gear as each unit open like a clamshell.

"You are point thirty-eight seconds ahead of Elise," X-37 said, his tone almost encouraging.

The second I was inside, I activated the armor, causing it to close and run field expedient systems checks. Lights blinked in my new HUD display as haptic feedback pads vibrated in my gloves, but also several other places throughout the armor that I normally didn't notice.

Path stood with his sword held ready, turning to face the men with guns and a horrified crowd that couldn't decide whether it should flee or stay to watch this disaster.

"I'm going to help Hannah and Bug," Elise said the moment she was ready.

I moved beside Path and we stood back to back, ready for anything. "Get it done, Elise. I want this to end without any actual fighting."

It felt like forever, but it was only seconds before we had completed our transformation. Melina's top lieutenants, including Brecken, had started ordering civilians out of the chain-link plaza. Groups of different sizes disappeared into the maze of fences, most watching from a safer distance. If bullets started flying, they'd be injured but I was hoping it wouldn't come to that.

Melina gathered herself and approached, shaking off Tatiana's restraining grip. "So, I suppose that is *your* show of force. Impressive, Reaper."

I didn't respond, aware of how intimidating the Archangel armor looked when I didn't talk. Each of our units was slightly different now that we'd learned to customize them. I decided to stay with flat black, while Elise utilized a mixture of dark colors to create a camouflage not unlike the Slayer's skin. Hannah's Archangel armor was almost identical to mine, with a dark red stripe down one side. Bug, who seemed amazed he wasn't in some sort of modified EVA kit, didn't know how to change his Archangel armor's appearance and thus remained a shivering statue of gold technology.

Three more full squads of soldiers arrived at a run. Some even had armor. I heard a vehicle approaching that sounded as though it was on tracks, which I suspected was their biggest hitter probably rarely used.

"Don't be stupid, Melina," Elise said. "We're not here to fight."

The woman's lips curled back over her teeth. She cursed us with words not in the stupid dialect. Her guards shifted their positions, alarmed at what she had said.

"I've kept these people safe for a long time." Melina moved in front of her bodyguards who were trying to stay between us. "You can't just drop down out of the sky and doom us all."

"We don't have time for that," I said.

"Very convincing," X-37 said, causing a giggle from Elise now that we could all hear my limited artificial intelligence because of the Archangel armor. It had been designed for extreme conditions and had its own comms network. As long as we could see each other, we could talk, and probably then some but I wasn't sure.

"I don't need your help, X."

"Very good, Reaper Cain. I have a diplomatic negotiation script ready if you need it," X-37 said.

"You should have told me about your ability to call armor down from orbit," Melina said. "If I'd known your full capabilities, things might have gone differently."

"That's kind of bullshit," Elise said on our squad comms. "I'm not sure I like this old woman. She should step down and let Tatiana take over."

"Correct me if I'm wrong, but we are not here to ferment rebellion," X-37 said. "My analysis suggests we should contract a guide and continue with our mission. There is a thirty-seven percent chance Melina or one of her people will still be willing to accommodate us so long as we conclude this incident without bloodshed."

11

Two ARMORED VEHICLES crowded into the fenced area, one on wheels and another on treads that made a lot of noise. Each vehicle had one of the crew served machine guns like the light recon vehicles Brecken had used to escort the vehicle carrying Briggs's cage. The last few groups of Melina's fighters that showed up carried axes, machetes, and wrenches.

"She has assembled every man and woman of fighting age she can command," X-37 said. "A more seasoned military commander would not have shown her hand in this way. I suggest caution. She may give orders that make no sense to someone with proper training."

"It's like dealing with a street gang," Hannah commented.

"It's stupid is what it is." Elise pointed at the Runners outside the fences, who were barely visible now. "Don't they want our help with those things?"

"We're not here for that." I wanted to say more but Melina continued the conversation unaware that we were having our own private dialogue.

"This was poorly done," Melina said. "I've lost face because of your duplicity. You should have told me you had robot armor at your disposal. Now I look like I don't know what's going on."

"We should've done a lot of things," Elise said. "Starting with not wasting our time with you."

"Easy, Elise." I hoped I wasn't about to set her off. She hadn't been this worked up for a while. "We're going to the shipyard no matter what you say, Melina."

This angered her more than I expected. "I know you will! And you leave us to deal with the consequences. You must not awaken what sleeps there just like you must not draw the wrath of the Kalon Regulars."

"Now that's ominous," I muttered.

I imagined that beneath the Archangel helmet, Elise narrowed her eyes like she was ready for a fight. "Yeah."

"The Runners sleep during the day?" I asked.

Tatiana answered. "Sleep is not the right word, but they are less active. In the morning, I will lead you to your destination. Bracken will also come."

"You're overstepping yourself, Tatiana," Melina said.

"Just let me do it, Grandmother. It'll get them out of our stronghold and maybe we will learn something," she said.

Brecken stepped forward, standing beside Tatiana, who I strongly suspected was his sister, and looked us over. I wasn't sure, but I thought he was less than pleased to be outdone.

I clapped my hands together, which was much more impressive in my Archangel gear. "Great. It's settled then. We'll kick back, get some rest—smoke a cigar or five—and head out in the morning. One big happy squad of adventurers. Maybe we can all be friends when this is over."

"I do not like you much, Reaper," Melina said.

"He takes getting used to," Elise said. "But while we're on the topic, I'm not your biggest fan, old woman."

"Be careful with that talk, kid," Melina said.

"Not a kid." Elise leaned forward with a clenched Archangel fist, causing the guards to draw back.

Melina, on the other hand, stood steadfast. "Since you're so keen to help them, Tatiana, show them where they can spend the night. Their Runner will be released outside the walls in the morning. If we put it out now, it won't stand any better chance of surviving than the rest of us."

"Yes, Melina." Tatiana motioned for us to follow her.

Brecken watched, then gave orders to the other lieutenants, squad leaders, and soldiers of the compound. "Return to your units. The danger is over for now."

One of the men whose name I didn't know stepped forward. "My squad has the fence watch tonight."

Bracken nodded. "Very good, Christopher."

We followed Tatiana through several wings of the chain-link maze, eventually arriving in a vacant building that had seen better days. It's only qualification as a dormitory was that it was within their secure perimeter. I wasn't sure it even had power, but that might've been a side effect of the citywide rationing schedule.

I removed my helmet. "Where did you get all of these fences?"

Tatiana answered, though I had half expected her not to. "I'm not sure. We've been here for generations. At least one section of it was some sort of security installation or prison. No one really agrees on which."

"Why the maze?" I asked, suspecting I knew the answer.

"Sometimes they get in. We know the maze. It gives us an advantage and we can close off sections to minimize the death toll. Also works for Kalon Regular raids. Sometimes they get this idea they will take out our leadership and bring us back under their influence," Tatiana said.

We walked in silence for a while, during which time I saw enough of the compound people to realize they were cleaner and more civilized than the hordes of slave-like workers we'd first encountered in the city. These people were really living, not just breaking their bodies to accumulate resources.

"Thanks for volunteering to guide us," I said.

"Don't thank me yet." She sounded almost sad. "You won't be welcome among us when this is over. I'd hoped you would be."

"Yeah, me too, Tatiana," I said. There really wasn't a way to explain this was how things almost always went with me and my crew.

Path volunteered to stand guard, as I knew he would while the rest of us slept.

SUNLIGHT CUT DOWNWARD through a high window, revealing the building interior to be every bit as sad as it had looked in the dark. Dust drifted lazily. Hannah stood guard in her Archangel armor while Path finally slept.

I crossed the room, forming words in my head, wanting to rebuild a relationship from another lifetime. She towered over me in her new gear, standing stiffer than necessary because she'd never been properly trained in its operation. "How do you like that armor?"

"I feel like a giant. Using it is a bit intimidating. Don't expect much from me—if we have to fight that is," she said.

"You never were a fighter." I regretted the words instantly. So much for rebuilding our relationship. Her reaction was impossible to judge, but I thought she shifted slightly inside the armor, barely noticeable from my point of view.

"There are different ways to fight," she said. "What you mean is that I wasn't in the habit of punching people who pissed me off —like someone else I know."

"Guilty as charged," I said, feeling like maybe it would be okay—like she was better at this family relationship stuff than I was. "We need to get ready. The sooner we're done with this place the better. I hadn't expected a huge welcome, but if we haven't convinced Melina and her people we're the good guys by now, we could be in real trouble."

"At least we have the right equipment now," Hannah said.

Elise, wide awake and alert within seconds, stepped into her uniquely styled Archangel gear. "We could have more problems than we're anticipating. I thought about what Melina told us last night. The Neverseen have stealth technology specifically to avoid drones and sensor tech. How is that going to affect our equipment? This stuff won't do us much good if we're going to be blind."

"She has a point." Bug got out of his bed roll and stared around like somebody had driven over him with the truck. "Sorry, I don't wake up well. Oh, why is the sun so bright?"

Path, in stark contrast to the kid from Dreadmax, awoke and geared up in almost the same motion. It was disturbing.

"Aren't you going to take a piss first?" Bug asked.

"That is possible while wearing the armor," Path said. "Have you not learned the way of it?"

"Well yeah. Sure, I mean yeah." Bug was obviously lying.

"Elise, can you help him out?" I asked over the Archangel comms.

"Sure thing," Elise said. "Why not? It's only like the third time I've explained the basics of powered armor to him."

I quickly examined each part of my equipment, paying special attention to the weapons and sensors. I hoped we wouldn't have to fight, but I knew we would need to see and hear. So far, Yansden had been problematic for our *superior* technology.

We started working together as a team, and by the time Tatiana and Brecken arrived, I felt we were as ready as we would ever be.

"Good morning, Cain."

I glanced her way. There was something in Tatiana's tone that made me wonder if she wasn't expecting more of a response from me.

I wasn't good at this sort of thing, wasn't good at anything that didn't fit neatly into a mission. We weren't meant to be friends. Melina had already decided we would be rivals, and maybe even outright enemies.

Which really sucked. There was something about Tatiana that made me forget some of my problems by her mere presence. It was like I could be a normal person if I just knew what to say.

"Good morning, Tatiana. I think we're ready," I said.

She studied me for a second, then nodded, waiting for us to follow. She wore a tactical kit that was nevertheless a joke compared to how we were outfitted. Brecken was the same, and just as serious as he had been when we first met.

Squads of guards escorted us to the southern perimeter of the compound where we headed out toward the spaceport.

I walked beside Tatiana, towering above her in my Archangel armor. I felt like a mechanized warrior escorting a child, but she didn't seem to be the least bit intimidated. Sometimes I wondered how strange we must appear to her and her people. In many ways, our technology seemed to have similar roots, but as X-37 had explained to me many times, the differences were more than they appeared. It was like we were all using a different operating system. Every society of humans I'd met since Dreadmax had evolved differently, though their wants, needs, and behaviors changed little.

Ahead of us, Brecken and Elise scouted the way. Hannah, Path, and Bug brought up the rear of our column.

"There isn't much danger yet," Tatiana said. "But I like the way your squad stays alert."

"Do you go on patrols with Brecken and the others?" I asked.

"I was our lead patroller before I relinquished the job," she said. "Melina asked me to be her apprentice. That was two years ago. I still try to go out—to keep my skills sharp—but not as much as I would like."

The skyline of the mountains beyond the spaceport rose up like a picture.

"It's a beautiful view," Tatiana said. "Someday I'd like to visit there."

"You never been?"

She shook her head. "Even in the daytime, it's dangerous to travel this close to the spaceport. Going around would take days, and that would mean sleeping outside the compound perimeter. If I went into the city, the Kalon Regulars would have me working in a mine before I could shout for help. City life is safe, but you have to follow a lot of rules. In any case, I'd never make it to the mountains."

"What can you tell me about Kalon Regulars?" I asked.

Ahead of us, Elise and Brecken stopped but didn't tell us not to approach so I assumed they wanted to show us something. Tatiana saw this as well, and for a second, I was worried she wouldn't answer my question.

"The Kalon Regulars are the elite soldiers of Yansden." She held up one hand when I started to interrupt. "They aren't what they used to be. During the days of legend, their caste was raised to fight from birth. I'm sure they have something like this among your people. Now they are just men and women who inherited red helmets. The rest of their armor was lost long ago and is a mystery. Some think there are armories in the ruins beyond the wildlands.

We reached Elise and Brecken too soon. I had more questions but no time to ask them. A flock of small birds burst into the air from a distant building. I thought I heard a surge of energy, a system that had a circuit breaker about to give out.

There wasn't a single thing that alarmed me, but lots of small details that made me uneasy.

"Do you hear a vehicle coming from the general direction of the compound?" X-37 asked.

We both heard the same things, but my human brain focused on different things than my LAI. For a microsecond, I thought I understood how the Neverseen and touched were able to evade the drones but couldn't articulate it.

"I don't believe it is part of the disturbance," X-37 continued.

I waited to see if Tatiana or Brecken had detected the vehicle and learned our reaction was slightly faster than what our guides could perceive without technology. Motioning to Path, then Elise, I set up a defensive perimeter. Bug and Hannah remained in the center, probably not even knowing what we were doing.

Tatiana and Brecken looked tense, but not alarmed. She motioned for us to remain calm. "This isn't unusual. Not good, but we should be okay for now."

"How about we don't take any chances?" I said.

Brecken spoke to me for the first time. "We expected this. With your foray toward the spaceport, and other recent activity, the Neverseen would be more active. Even during the daytime."

"Why is that?" I asked.

"They need technology, or at least they are compelled to scavenge for it whenever it's detected. This exertion makes them hungry and they have to hunt as well," Tatiana said. "My brother and I have wondered if your technology, especially the equipment drop, wouldn't bring them out of their holes."

"My little sister was right, as usual." Brecken adjusted his grip on his shotgun. "We should be ready for anything."

"Elise, can you see the vehicle?" I asked, analyzing what Brecken and Tatiana had said but also aware of the larger situation.

"It's the van," she said.

I knew immediately which van she meant. Manager and his crew didn't have enough sense to stay inside where it was safe. Scavenging on the city side of the compound was one thing, but creeping toward the spaceport was another. I wondered if the kid and his crew were going to get in trouble for this with Melina.

Tatiana strode toward the van where it parked. She shouted something in a dialect I couldn't understand, pointing with one hand in a manner that seemed more than a bit insulting. Manager and his friends eventually leaned out of the vehicle, looking rebellious but worried.

"It's okay, Tatiana," Manager said. "We're family, right?"

"You're supposed to do what I say," Tatiana said. "And I told you not to leave the compound until I got back. So did Melina."

She looked sharply at Brecken, who spread his hands like he didn't want anything to do with the conversation.

"I've got a vehicle," Manager said. "If they attack, me and

my friends are probably the only people who will escape. Unless you're nice and ask for a ride."

"Your sister might have a point, Manager," I interjected.

"That's really cool armor, Reaper," Manager said. "I can't believe how bad ass that stuff is. We want to see you use it."

"No, you don't," Tatiana said before I could say the same thing. "This isn't a joke, little brother. No one comes back from beyond this point."

"I know," Manager said. "That's why we wanted to see what happened. I mean, we wanted to see someone break the curse. You know what I mean."

Closer this time, another flock of birds burst from an abandoned building. An animal shrieked, then another, and finally a third.

Tatiana's expression became even more grim. "Just stay with us, Manager. Let us protect you. None of your shenanigans this time. The Neverseen Runners are coming."

12

A HOT BREEZE pushed down the street, buffeting my armor. X-37 highlighted the sensor readings in my HUD display so that I would appreciate the phenomena. A quick glance told me that Tatiana and Brecken had also felt it. Their reaction suggested they expected it.

"That doesn't seem natural," I said.

Tatiana motioned for me to walk with her, and also gave her brother a tactical hand signal I thought I understood. Elise and Path ensured that the rest of my team was moving well, watching for threats, and not getting too spread out. Several times I heard Elise remind Hannah and Bug to always be searching for cover in case we needed to bunker down in a firefight.

"It's not natural," Tatiana said. "Some people argue otherwise, but our oral history says it is caused when vents from the spaceport are opened. The real question is why this happens. If the elders are to be believed, the heat vents were originally designed to accommodate large ships blasting off."

"That's pretty standard in this type of setup." I scanned the terrain and gathered more and more information for X-37 to store and analyze. "Most Union ships of the size you're probably talking about are built in orbital space stocks. This is a much older way of doing things."

"You talk as though we have a common history," she said. "I admit it is one of the things most intriguing about you and your friends."

"X would tell me I'm making a lot of assumptions," I said.

"X?"

I motioned for everyone to stop, then edged towards one of the streets where I thought I had seen movement. Tatiana followed. Elise asked if I needed help and I told her no. Two minutes later, X-37 and I were both convinced if there had been anything lurking on the side roadway, it was now gone. The occasional gusts from the starport heat vents were blowing random bits of debris away from its center, causing minor confusion with my motion detectors.

We took advantage of the moment to reassess. It was something we needed to do often in this uncertain environment. Slow and steady would get us to the spaceport. Even I didn't want to rush if I didn't know exactly what I was getting into.

And I wanted to talk to Tatiana more.

"I'm not the person you think I am," I said.

She laughed. "You have no idea what I think."

"Fair enough. What do you think about my mechanical arm?

Does that make me a freak? Are your people going to think I'm some sort of monster the longer they look at me?"

She took her time answering, and I had the advantage of being able to read her body language since she wasn't encased in a protective shell. "Everyone has their own opinion. And their own fears."

"What about you?" I asked, signaling everyone to start moving again.

"I think you're a dangerous man, but I don't believe you intend to harm my people," she said. "Don't press. You'll only embarrass me."

"My mechanical arm and eye, cybernetics technically, aren't the only things the Union did to me in order to make me what they wanted," I said. "I have a computer-assistant."

"Like something you carry around?" she asked.

I shook my head, a motion that was less obvious with my helmet on though it still worked. "They put it inside me. The details are hard to explain. But it can never be removed. I call it X, or X-37."

"Does it hurt?" The way she asked the question made her seem young.

"Only when he tries to make a joke. That's pretty miserable," I said.

"Reaper Cain, are you going to disparage me when I cannot present a defense of my character?" X-37 asked.

"Did he, it, just make a joke?" she asked with a smile.

"Yeah, sort of. How did you know?"

She returned her attention to the next street we needed to

follow. "I can tell a lot by the way you walk or stand. You're transparent."

"I can honestly say no one has ever accused me of being transparent," I said. "What do you see ahead?"

"Nothing, which is a problem. With the heat vents blowing in our faces and the animals moving toward safety, there should have been an attack by now—even if it was just a probe," she said.

"Makes sense," I agreed. "Everyone look sharp. Tatiana says there is something unusual about the Neverseen's reluctance to engage us."

"Maybe it's because they see five strangers that look like robots," Hannah said. "And let's not forget the Neverseen developed ways to evade drones and other machines."

"Yeah, Reaper," Elise said. "Way to miss the obvious."

"Speaking of the obvious. X, can you pull up a window completely free of enhancement? Something as close to me not wearing a helmet as possible?" I asked.

"The Archangel armor is capable of doing this; however, you may be slightly disoriented," X-37 said. "The visual mini screen will be the easiest. Auditory input will be much more difficult to differentiate as long as you are inside a closed unit."

"Just do it, X. I'll figure out the rest," I said. "Elise, let's switch out for a bit."

I expected her to argue with me, to complain that she was perfectly capable of running point, but she didn't. It was like we trusted each other or something. Instead of fighting, she started experimenting with using some low-tech options in case the Neverseen targeted our tech like they did the Kalon bots.

"I'll go with you," Tatiana said. "My big brother needs rest as much as your protégé."

"Agreed," I said. At face value, taking the lead was no more strenuous than any other part of the formation, but psychologically a person could get dull and make mistakes.

Once Tatiana and I were a hundred meters ahead of the others, we entered a new section of roadways that required us to climb a short set of stairs. X-37 examined them closely and advised me there were vents worked into the design.

I squatted down and peered inside, expecting to see monsters clawing to get free. Tatiana joined me, shining a handheld flashlight into the darkness below the surface.

"This is farther than I've ever been," she said. "I've seen this rise from a distance and always wondered what it looked like underneath this level."

"I don't see anything on infrared or with motion sensors." I directed my helmet to flood the area with light.

Shadows evaporated. Tatiana drew back slightly and raised one hand to protect her eyes.

"That's somewhat more powerful than my flashlight," she said dryly.

"I don't use it much. Normally we rely on other technology—infrared, nightvision, and motion detection algorithms."

"I'm not sure what any of that is, but it sounds useful," she said. "If it wasn't so reliant on technology. The Neverseen are masters of stealth. What people like my brother forget is that they are also good at evading human eyes. That's why all of the children have pets to alert them of danger."

That reminded me of the little creatures we'd seen when we first encountered the people of the city. Something else occurred to me. "Have you ever been outside the city?"

She shook her head. "Few people have reason to go anywhere else. You'd have to talk to one of the farming crews or the wood-cutters. There are miners who pass through the area on rail transport, but they wouldn't know much more than they could see from a train."

"There's a lot more to this planet than your fenced in compound," I said.

"I know. If things were perfect, we could go places and see new things. As it stands, survival is always our main concern."

"Let's get moving." I led the way up onto the next runway. I felt exposed. There weren't any buildings or junction boxes for a hundred meters. I could imagine all manner of ships landing in this area. It seemed like a support zone, or an area for small and medium ships to launch into orbit. There were several support structures that had been damaged or looted over the centuries.

"There," Tatiana exclaimed, one hand flying to the pistol on her hip. After a brief reconsideration of the situation, she let go of the weapon and pulled her rifle around to the front of her harness, gripping it like her life depended on it.

"I'm not sure what she's looking at," X-37 said, sounding slightly concerned.

"I see it, Tatiana. Stay behind me. My armor can protect both of us." I wasn't sure if she would listen. My experience with my sister and Elise told me this type of chivalry wasn't always appreciated.

Advancing, my **HDK Dominator** merged with my armor. I searched for targets but only saw another blur of movement. Something was happening near the next set of buildings, some sort of maintenance or fuel depot from what I could tell. There was also a haze of dust covering the area now, the effect of the heat fence blowing out grit and grime as we made our approach.

"Elise, Path, do you see anything?" I asked.

"I'm picking up movements, but I can't tell what it is," Elise said. Her vantage point wasn't as good as mine because she was back a way, but I trusted her judgment and her instincts.

"Nothing behind us," Path reported.

"We should move quickly." Brecken barely opened his mouth when he spoke, tension coloring his words and his actions.

"Agreed," I said. We rushed toward the next point of cover, a dangerous proposition considering that was where the movement had originated.

"We might have to fight whatever's waiting there, but we can't stay out here in the open," I said.

"We're not arguing with you." Tatiana was breathing hard as she and her brother matched our pace. The moment I started to slow down, she gave me a dirty look.

"It's not that far," she said.

"Elise, get up there with me so we can clear these buildings," I said.

"On my way, Reaper."

Moments later she was beside me.

Tatiana fell back nearer her brother and the rest of our unit that had tightened up the moment Elise and I sprinted between the buildings, weapons out, ready for action.

"There!" Elise shouted, a heartbeat before she fired her HDK rifle at a blur twice the size of a man and running fast. The image flinched but kept moving laterally across our field of vision. Before I could shoot, it was behind one of the short buildings.

Path arrived a second later. "I'm needed here."

The three of us spread out. More of the Neverseen flashed across side streets, through windows, and along fire escapes.

"We need to get to the high ground," I said.

"On it!" Elise scurried up a metal ladder then jumped the final distance. Path climbed another building with equal ease. I cruised between buildings, hunting for the enemy through my weapon sights.

"Talk to me, kid. What do you see?"

"I think there is one just ahead of you, trying to outrun you," Elise said. "You can catch it if you put on a burst of speed."

I slowed down, checking to my right and left. "Feels like a trap."

"You can get this one!" Elise shouted.

"Elise, stop and look around. What else do you see from up there?" I asked.

I slipped sideways, finding a good shadow to observe from. The Neverseen were masters of stealth, but two could play at that game. I was about to turn the tables on them if I could.

"Shit, you're right," Elise said. About a street over, the way you were heading, there's a mass of them. Godsdammit they're ugly," Elise said. She seemed to be moving to a better position.

"I also see them," Path advised. "I am ready to attack when you are, perhaps catch them in a triangulation of fire."

"That's the plan," I said. "Bug, are you with Hannah and the others?"

"We're here," Bug said. "Can we give your girlfriend and her brother hand radios?"

Wanting to argue with his labeling but knowing we didn't have time, I told him sure. Shapes crept around the corner, moving along the short buildings, keeping to the shadows just as I was but on the opposite side of the street.

"I've got eyes on the Neverseen," I said. "Tatiana, can you hear me?"

"I hear you, Cain," she answered.

"How many different kinds are there?"

"No one really knows."

Moving slowly, careful not to draw attention with excessive movement, I added my stealth cloak over top of the Archangel armor. It didn't cover me entirely, but I could use it to improve my hiding place.

Across the street, a half-dozen monsters moved forward. There was one in the front that looked like some sort of four-legged animal with a foreign head and a mandible like a bug. The other five seemed to be trying to control it or prod it forward. But they were nearly as strange as it was.

The skin of these creatures, and their clothing for the

humanoids, shifted and blurred. I could see the light in their eyes at times but other times they were just too hard to look at.

"X, are you getting all of this?" I asked.

"My readings are confused, Reaper Cain," X-37 said. "I am proceeding cautiously, because during my previous attempts I was overloaded with data. Information overload seems to be one of the primary mechanisms they are using to confuse the drones and other machines hunting them."

"Good to know." I sighted the monster through my HDK. "Elise, Path, I will initiate the ambush. Make sure you're in position to help. I'll be in a lot of trouble if I have to do this by myself."

I briefly described what I was seeing and waited for them to tell me if there were any others.

"I'm pretty sure there's at least one more group, but they're not close. If we're going to do this, now's the time," Elise said.

What I was about to attempt was known as a sniper-initiated assault in Union military parlance. But contrary to how this was normally done, I was close enough to go full auto from the first round. With the four-legged monster in my sights, I pulled the trigger and dumped half a magazine into its body.

The monster reared back onto his hind legs, thrashing right and left and looking for who had caused it so much pain.

Elise and Path attacked from above, their targets less well selected than mine were. I couldn't say for sure, but I was fairly certain they were aiming off of my rounds, saturating the area with bullets and hoping to hit something.

"What you need is the chain gun," X-37 said.

"Yeah, that would be fantastic." I darted toward the corner of the building to take cover. "That thing didn't go down!"

"You are correct. My analysis shows that you hit the largest of the Neverseen 37 times. It seems to be wounded, but it is still fighting and extremely angry."

"I see them now," Elise shouted. She leaned over the edge of the building, no longer worried about being seen, and unleashed hell on the group of Neverseen that were now pursuing me. Path did the same, but moments later jumped off the building and landed amongst them, slashing right and left with his sword. Elise followed, and I stopped, turned around, and went back to a fight that seemed more and more like a really bad idea.

Path closed the distance on his nearest adversary and slashed upward with his sword, a strike that should have beheaded the humanoid. As close as we were, and with all the confused movement, it was difficult to describe them as human. Recent experiences prevented me from jumping to conclusions.

What I saw were large, humanoid shapes, wearing clothing that distorted what I could see of them. They didn't seem to have guns, which was nice.

Path continued to drive his enemy back, striking again and again despite the lack of effect. Elise attacked her enemies with a sword in one hand and fired her pistol with the other. I thought one fell to the ground and crawled away but couldn't be sure. I had my own problems.

The enraged four-legged beast lunged at me, snapping its viselike mandibles toward my face. I dodged backwards, causing it to miss. It slashed with its horns.

Aiming my HDK Dominator, I fired the moment it opened its mouth toward me. The bullet struck it in the throat, causing it to spin away from me and run into the darkness spewing blood.

Two men that had been driving it forward attacked me. One had an electrified pitchfork, and the other a single edged blade that had been cut from sheet metal. The crude blade deflected off my armor. I kicked the first man, launching him backwards.

When the second came after me, I saw he was wearing a powered mask. Cords ran down his back and each of his limbs. Low intensity light pulsed in a rhythm that threatened to give me a seizure. I fired my HDK Dominator. Only a few of the rounds made it through the layers of clothing, body armor, and color shifting material he wore.

Stepping closer to the man, I held my weapon down to one side and scooped under his armpit with the other. With some quick footwork, I tossed the much larger man over my hip, body slamming him on the concrete.

He screamed threats or insults and came to his feet, immediately charging despite the gunshot wounds and body slam that should have knocked the wind out of him. Bracing my feet, I struck his chest with the palm of my Archangel gauntlet, stopping him in his tracks.

One of his companions rushed me.

I spun in a tight circle, heel kicking my new opponent right below his sternum, launching him backward.

"These guys don't have shit for weapons, but they won't quit," Elise said, running to my side.

"There are more of the Neverseen approaching," X-37 said. "The integrity of your armor won't last forever."

"Thanks, X."

"Of course, Reaper Cain. I am here for you. Would you like me to go through all of the reminders I have set for items that need your attention?"

"No time for that, X, but maybe you could do something useful like tell me what kind of tech these assholes are running."

"I'm not sure why you are having so much trouble with fewer than a dozen of the Neverseen," X-37 said.

I pointed to where I wanted Path to hold a position, then did the same for Elise. Tatiana, Brecken, Hannah, and Bug stayed behind us. The van was gone to who knew where. I hoped Manager was smart enough to head back to the compound.

"Look again, X," I said. "There have to be fifty of them coming around the corner."

"Are you certain?" X-37 asked.

I lunged forward to meet the first of the Neverseen, ripping his hood down. What I saw was a pale, hairless head with beads and rings stitched into his skin from chin to crown. They pulsed with light just like the cords woven through their clothing.

"Oh, there is another one," X-37 said. "Good work, Reaper Cain. Their cloaks must work when in contact with the tech imbedded in their bodies."

I shoved the wide-eyed freak backward, then retreated to maintain the scrimmage line I'd set with Elise and Path.

"Now if you will just disrobe the rest of your enemies, I will be able to help you track them," X-37 said.

"Yeah, whatever, X. We seriously need to talk," I said. "Why aren't they rushing us? They have the numbers now."

"Is disrobe not a word?" X-37 asked.

"Later, X. Why are they hesitating?"

The crowd split to create a wide lane down the middle.

"I don't like this," Elise said.

"Look at the bright side," I said. "So far, our armor has held, and they don't have machine guns."

"Look out, Cain," Tatiana said in a voice that spiked my attention. "They have one of the big ones."

The ground shook as the beast approached. Smoke swirled ahead of it. All I could see for several moments was a wall of shimmering distortion.

"What the hell?" I demanded.

"Remember when you told me the Union conducted experiments that went badly?" Tatiana asked.

"Yeah. Are you going to tell me what exactly we're dealing with?" I asked.

"I'm trying to," she said. "It's hard because we don't really know. A long time ago, they experimented with dangerous types of space travel and extra dimensional shields for their ships."

"How is that possible?"

"I don't think it is," Tatiana said, backing up as the stomping came closer and closer and the parting crowd of Neverseen humans got more and more worked up. "But they tried, and it did all of this. Their ship plant exploded. Nothing has been good on Yansden since then."

"I believe I can detect unstable energy signatures," X-37 said.

"Not unlike radiation. It is a complete unknown. There is nothing in my database on these power frequencies. Please treat this situation as extremely dangerous."

"Godsdammit, X! What do you think we're doing?" I shouted. "Tatiana, go with Hannah and Bug. Everyone run for the compound. We'll hold them off."

A horrible voice shrieked at me from a building top. "You go, Cain. I'll fight it."

"You're not that scary anymore, Briggs," I shouted as the Slayer joined us. "Where the hell have you been?"

"I hate this place," was his only answer.

13

THE NEVERSEEN CHANTED and rhythmically shuffled their feet, sounding like an ocean wave breaking on the shore. It also had the effect of gradually moving the entire mob toward us. My focus had to be on the big baddie coming down the middle of the street, so large and hideous that it was sucking air into it with enough force for me to feel the draft. But I was also worried about becoming enveloped by strange and determined enemies.

"So far we haven't been able to do much damage," I said. "I'd like to call it a stalemate, but I think this thing might just be big enough to swallow one of us whole."

"I volunteer not to be eaten," Elise said.

Agitated, Brecken moved closer and closer to our line like he was going to get in front of us. "I don't think this is the time for jokes."

I could see his nervousness, and as much as he didn't like it, I thought he was the type of person who felt obligated to be in the thick of the fight even if he clearly had less effective armor and weapons. The man had a large rifle, but it required a lever on one side to chamber each round. If our fully automatic HDK rifles weren't having an effect, I couldn't see what his weapon would do.

"Hannah, Bug—the two of you are going to have to step up. You don't have weapon skills, but you have armor. Watch out for our hosts and shield them if you can. Especially from the mob that is surrounding us," I said.

"Of course, brother," Hannah said.

Bug made some kind of joke, but I ignored it.

When the Neverseen monster roared, I could feel it even inside of my armor. There was a smear of light that I suspected was it opening its jaws and ruining part of its concealment effect. The huge beast pushed off the ground and charged.

"X, what's the chance my armor can withstand its bite?" I asked in a rush.

"It's coming!" Elise shouted, firing her weapon into its flank.

"Reaper Cain, I strongly advise against this course of action," X-37 said. "I estimate its bite strength to be sufficient, if it catches you at an advantageous leverage point, to bisect you with or without your armor."

"So, there is a chance it will hold." I sprinted forward.

"What are you doing, Reaper Cain?" X-37 asked.

"I've got an idea."

"Famous last words."

I picked up speed, closing the remaining distance. Despite

what I'd just said, my timing was off slightly. I did a stutter step, waited until it roared again, and then lunged into its jaws. Maybe I would've felt more confident if I could see it clearly enough to accurately gauge its size, but it was time to get busy with this thing.

I sprung into the air and crashed into its teeth, grabbing its upper row and driving one knee into its lower mandible. Something horrible happened then, something I hadn't expected. Its tongue battered me like an enraged python on a suicide mission. As horrifying as the experience was, I'd hit my adversary exactly where I wanted.

"Yes!" Ignoring the ropelike tongue, I got both feet under me and shoved downward as I also pushed up off my hands. Bones popped, teeth broke free, and the monster made a shrieking sound that hurt my ears even inside of my sound canceling helmet.

The rest of the battle was hard to track. I was just a tad busy. The giant Neverseen monster thrashed side to side, trying to throw me out. When that didn't work, it slammed its own face on the ground, which shoved me deeper into its gullet. One foot slipped on the blood and slime, losing all traction. This left me with two hands and one leg to resist its strength.

"Something is happening, Reaper Cain. I strongly advise you to get out of the beast's mouth," X-37 said.

"Working on it!" Desperately, I tried to hold its mouth fully open with one hand and one leg while drawing my sidearm with my right hand.

"It's running toward the spaceport," X-37 said. "But more

important to your rapidly diminishing chances of survival is that there are fewer and fewer of the human Neverseen and more and more of the large monster versions joining its rampage."

I fired my pistol until it was out of ammunition and I had no way to reload it.

"You owe me, Reaper!" Briggs shouted.

"What's he doing, X?" I asked as I holstered my pistol and put both hands and both feet back to work trying to keep the Neverseen behemoth from crushing me.

"That is a very good question, Reaper Cain," X-37 said. "Unfortunately, I am also a bit busy. I just received a confusing distress call from the center of the spaceport."

"Later, X."

"It's very compelling," X-37 said.

I wasn't trying to be difficult. Under other circumstances, my limited artificial intelligence would've had my complete attention.

The best I could tell, Briggs was on top of the monster, writhing and slashing at its neck and throat area. It was probably my imagination, but I thought I could hear his tentacles whipping out and back. Unlike a real Sansein, the hybrid aliens had tentacles with hooks and serrated edges rather than razor-sharp arrowhead blades.

The monster screamed and I recognized its fear.

When the monster I was mouth-riding finally plowed into the ground and started its death throes, I had no idea where we were. X-37 populated my HUD with red dots of enemies all around us. And they looked like large dots.

"You have a very short window of opportunity. The other

non-humanoid Neverseen are wary of you because of the noise this one made as it died," X-37 said. "Or that is what I believe to be happening. Also, the distress beacon has disappeared. I'm afraid whoever was crying out for help is gone."

"Now I have guilt." I was joking, but I was also disturbed by the sudden development in what had seemed like a difficult but basically straightforward mission. Five minutes ago, I had all my friends in one place and one group of enemies to defend from. There were choices to be made.

"Briggs, we're getting the hell out of here!"

"Awk! Good shit!" He sprinted the way we had come, I thought. My sense of direction was a little bit skewed right now.

Staggering after him, I looked right and left, witnessing shadows that circled me like hunters. Some of them were taller than the two-story buildings of this section. Others were small and fast. I hoped some of the tiniest ones were just rats fleeing danger but suspected that nothing in this area was benign.

Important distractions filled my mind as I ran. Where were my friends? Had they made it back to the compound? What about Manager and his van?

The ground vibrated as more and more of the large Neverseen stomped down streets looking for us. The further we got from the spaceport and the distress signal, the more of the human sized Neverseen we encountered. One group flooded into the street ahead of us.

"I'll lead, stay right behind me," I shouted at Briggs.

"Awk! Awk!"

"Fingers crossed, X." I put all the speed I might have otherwise dedicated to defeating Elise in the sprint into my charge. Slamming into the first row, I knocked a half dozen of them sideways with the weight and strength of my Archangel gear. My progress quickly slowed near the back of their pack, however.

"I'm not certain what that expression means," X-37 said.

"What?" I asked, not even sure what I had just said to my LAI. All my attention was focused on breaking through, and once I'd made it, Briggs and I rushed away from the growing horde of freaks chasing us.

"I've identified the distress call and why it was so strange," X-37 said.

I lengthened my stride, finally in a position to use raw speed. We were crossing one of the wide-open landing platforms with no cover. Small support ships to the main spaceport lay on their sides, ruined long ago. Briggs matched my pace, then pulled ahead slightly. He was grunting and making all kinds of strange Slayer sounds that might or might not have been him taunting me.

This really wasn't a good place for trash talking, so I ignored it.

"It's Envoy," X-37 said.

"Of course it is," I said, not believing I had heard X correctly.

"He's not sounding like himself," X-37 said. "I'm running options for assisting him, since he is the only Sansein that has ever shown as any kind of benevolence and could be the key to the future of humanity."

"I love how you take a perfectly impossible situation and make it even more screwed up," I said.

"Please be advised that I am ignoring your banter at the present moment," X-37 said. "The stealth technology overload tactics of the local beasties is, to put it in your vernacular, giving me a headache."

I jumped over a rail track and caught up with Briggs, who was almost to a row of maintenance buildings near the edge of this particular landing zone.

"Zero solutions found," X-37 said.

The words stunned me, nearly causing me to lose my stride. I knew this was something X-37 could say to me, but I'd never heard it. It had been kind of a joke during the early days of Reaper training.

"I am analyzing his final message and recording relevant data points," X-37 said. "The rest will be compressed for long-term storage given my current processing demands."

Breathing hard, I was getting frustrated with my LAI. "What did Envoy say?"

I already felt like crap for not helping the alien. He had fixed our starship, after all.

"First and foremost, he wishes to warn us that his brother Coranth is coming and he is angry," X-37 said.

Up ahead, I saw Elise shooting at a smaller group of Neverseen and almost laughed. Unable to drop them, she began hitting them in the feet, which seem to discourage them more than anything we had done with body and head shots. The others were there as well, including the white van. It was like they were waiting for us or something.

Not the best thing they could have done for their own safety, but it made me feel warm and fuzzy inside.

"Envoy continues to send warnings. He wishes to reiterate that his brother is obsessed with exterminating the abomination," X-37 said. "He also implied that if we could take control of the central spaceport, it would be worth our time."

"Coranth may have a harder time carrying out that threat," I said. "This is a pretty rough neighborhood."

14

CORANTH'S SHIP dropped down from the atmosphere, far in the distance. The only reason I noticed it was X-37 alerting me to its presence. To me, it was just a setback far off in the corner of my viewscreen.

But once I noticed it, I could feel an impending sense of doom. There was more at stake than my safety or the welfare of my friends. The Yansden system should've been a boon to the exodus fleet, but I was quickly coming to understand the quarantine was here for a reason. It almost felt like the place was just cursed with bad luck. What had Envoy found that he thought was so important?

"X, keep me apprised of the Neverseen," I said, even though I could hear the larger ones in the distance and sense the smaller ones creeping around us, looking for a way to take advantage of our isolated position.

More and more of my attention was drawn toward the Sansein ship sweeping across the city, never hesitating, and never having the slightest problem with the Yansden defenses, drones, or other electronic countermeasures that had been wreaking havoc on our communication systems.

The ship in all its strangeness shot across the landing fields, so low that it kicked up dust behind it. Banking slightly, it raised just enough to dart over our heads and disappear behind a row of short maintenance buildings.

X-37 and I both saw the tops of the lumbering Neverseen move toward the landing site then disappear. Roars of outrage quickly turned into screams of pain and then silence.

"What the hell is that?" Tatiana asked.

"One of the aliens we pissed off," I said.

The Yansden woman I was coming to respect more and more looked grim and at a loss for words.

"You're going to wish we never came," I said.

She looked at me, an ember of heat in her gaze. "Don't assume you know what I think."

"Look on the bright side, Reaper Cain," X-37 said. "Perhaps Coranth will draw some of the Neverseen that seem to be extremely interested in killing you."

"Yeah, that'd be great. But we both know that's not how luck works for us," I said. "If the tide shifts toward where that ship landed, we head for the compound and warn Melina and the others to prepare for an assault."

"Good plan, Cain," Tatiana said. "With one minor modification. Manager, get in that van and get your little posse back to the compound immediately. I'm not fucking around this time. If you don't go, I'm gonna punch you where it counts."

"Hey, sister. No need to get rough. I get it. You don't think we can fight, and that's fine," Manager said.

"Too much talking, not enough getting out of here." Tatiana pointed and said several rude sounding words in one of the dialects I still hadn't quite mastered.

Before long, Manager and his friends were speeding away in the van. I wish I could've sent Bug and Hannah back with them, but their Archangel armor was too big for the vehicle.

I was glad they had the protection but dreaded the moment when they thought they could fight—because they couldn't. Armor and weapons didn't make a warrior.

I looked at Elise and Path, wishing that it was just the three of us on this mission. My protégé seemed to be thinking the same thing but wasn't about to admit it. I caught her looking at me without talking trash, which meant, in my experience, she was feeling guilty. She might not admit I was right, but sometimes we arrived at an understanding.

"Why didn't you go back with your brother?" I asked Tatiana.

"I've got work to do here," she said. "You still need to get to the spaceport. Brecken and I are the only people crazy enough to guide you."

"They're coming, Reaper Cain," X-37 said, reinforcing his words with several flashing alerts on my HUD.

"Stay behind us." I half expected her to argue but she didn't.

"Elise, Path, Briggs—we're going to have to do the fighting

and we have to make sure they don't want to fight us anymore," I said.

"I think we can do that," Briggs growled.

No sooner had he spoken than the first swarm of Neverseen came around the corner and bolted across the open space between our corner of the landing zone and the other buildings. Intermixed with their ranks were larger, four-legged creatures with mandibles and horns. Slightly farther back were three huge creatures so big that their stealth fields wouldn't hold.

Tatiana and her older brother muttered something in their native language that sounded like a prayer for deliverance.

"Elise, how is that foot shooting working for you?"

"It doesn't kill them, but it slows them down. Disabling them may be the best we can do," she said.

I adjusted my position, aimed, and began to fire. After a few tries, I was able to start skipping rounds across the pavement and into their feet and lower legs. The advancing mob of Neverseen slowed dramatically. Some even left the field, darting away in between the buildings around the perimeter of this landing zone.

The three of us did as much damage as we could, slowing them down significantly. Some of the injuries we caused took the weakest of our enemies out of the fight. When they came close, they drove the four-legged monsters ahead of them, ripping off the tarps they had used to improve their concealment so that we could see how monstrous they really were.

"What causes that type of transformation?" Elise asked in horror. "Radiation?"

"I'm not detecting significant or dangerous levels of radiation at this moment," X-37 said. "The genetics could've been damaged generations ago, however."

I called Tatiana on the handheld radio we had given her. "What are the chances we can summon reinforcements?"

"It's a possibility, but I believe they would be better served staying behind our defensive perimeter at the compound, don't you?"

"Yeah, I'm just thinking out loud. The entire reason we're standing here is to give your brother a chance to get back and warn them," I said.

"I just hope he doesn't get creative," Tatiana said. "The stupid kid thinks everything's a grand adventure."

"Here come the ugly ones." Elise opened fire on the first of the four-legged monsters. Its skin was stretched in places and bulging in others. It looked like it might've been striped at one time, but the color was hard to identify. Some kind of mixture of black and dark green. But there were also random streaks of pink or orange on some of them.

"X, can you get a hold of Jelly? See if she can help. Maybe Tom can send down some bigger guns or something," I said.

"I am working on it, Reaper Cain," X-37 said. "It seems that the arrival of Coranth made our communications problems even worse."

"Tatiana, what about the Kalon Regulars? If this is a major crisis, would they respond in force?" I asked, then fired a three-round burst at my nearest enemy, striking it in its four legs but barely slowing it down.

"No, and if they did, they'd have to come through the

compound to get here, and that wouldn't go well. My brother and I are going to climb on top of a building and provide fire support. Our weapons are slow, but we will do our part if we can."

"Sounds good," I said. "And don't take this next part the wrong way, but stay out of trouble. If you get swarmed, that will only make everything more difficult. I'd rather you run away than need rescue."

"Don't worry about me, Cain. I see the reason in your words. But watch yourself. Don't ever think we need your help," she said.

"She has broken the communications link," X-37 said.

"Fine," I said. There were plenty of targets, so I started shooting, counting my ammunition and hoping I wasn't going to run out.

One, two, and three shots rang from the rooftops. The advancing Neverseen were getting closer. The only thing that was keeping us alive this long was their reluctance to suffer what we had done to the big one.

"Reaper Cain," X-37 said. "You need to focus on your job. "Please stop looking toward Tatiana and Brecken's position."

My LAI had a point. I reloaded, then checked in with Elise and Path. "How is your ammunition holding out?"

"I have enough, but only if we go soon," Elise said.

"My situation is much the same." Path said. "I prefer to engage them with the blade, but there are too many."

Off to one side, Briggs bounced on his toes, opening and closing his clawed hands.

"Settle down, Slayer," I said. "You're probably going to get a lot more chances to fight than you want."

"All I want to do is fight and kill," he said. His chest rose and fell from his heavy breathing, and I could see the veins pulsing in his neck and on his arms. Adrenaline had to be driving him toward a killing frenzy. Which was probably exactly what Doctor Ayers and Vice Admiral Nebs had hoped for when they created Briggs and the other hybrids.

"I think it's time to fall back," I said. "If the Yansden kids haven't gotten their van back to the compound by now, I don't know what else we can do for them."

"It may be too late," X-37 said, right as two of the four-legged Neverseen bolted across the final distance. Something had inspired them to a desperate last charge.

"Path, Briggs, you're up!" I dumped rounds into the charging pair of monsters, trying to keep them occupied while my friends moved in with their blades and claws.

Briggs was there first, leaping into the air and landing on the back of the first beast. Path arrived a heartbeat later, choosing to attack the same opponent so that they were concentrating all their killing power on one enemy. He slashed across the hamstrings of the first monster, sending fountains of blood into the air.

Briggs wrestled the animal by its head, twisting it until it fell sideways. The scene was horribly violent. I lost track of Path in the chaos. There were still other targets to shoot. Elise, Tatiana, and Breckon kept up a steady stream of fire. I pivoted and launched several rounds at one of the extra-large behemoths that were getting too close for comfort.

It slapped aside its own kind to rush forward.

The second four-legged beast in our perimeter slammed into Path, launching him through the air.

Briggs rolled off his victim and leapt at the second four-legged monstrosity. It caught him with his horns and flung him sideways. By this time Path was up with his sword and racing forward.

My HDK Dominator ran out of ammunition. Instead of reloading, I drew my pistol and sent several rounds at the eye of Path's opponent. I couldn't tell if I hit what I was aiming at, but the creature flinched and Path jammed his sword into its throat, then he ripped it sideways to cause horrific damage.

"You need to break contact with this mob of Neverseen," X-37 said.

"Really, X? I hadn't thought of that," I said, panting to catch my breath, something that didn't happen often even during a hard fight.

"Sarcasm detected. I am really trying to help. It seems you slipped very deep into the fog of war. It is harder and harder to devise a coherent strategy to deal with this problem," X-37 said.

"Tell me about it," I grunted, holstering my pistol and reloading my HDK Dominator. "Time to go, everyone!"

"Tatiana," Elise shouted. "You and your brother have to go first!"

Without answering, Tatiana and Brecken climbed down from

their building and ran the direction the van had disappeared toward.

"Elise, you're next with Briggs," I said, shooting, watching my ammunition counter drop, hoping nothing else went wrong.

"Okay," Elise said. "Come on, Slayer."

"Awk. Awwwwwwk!"

Path and I retreated slowly as the growing mass of Neverseen swirled out of the way of one of the big ones.

"This planet is a terrible place." Path looked toward where Coranth's ship had landed and killed two of the Neverseen behemoths. "I think that one is coming, which is good."

"I'm not looking forward to dealing with the Sansein, even if it works out in our favor," I said.

"Fall back, Path!" I shouted. "I'll cover you."

"Moving," he advised.

We took turns, his calm voice filling my helmet despite the chaos around us. The smaller, more human versions of the Neverseen swarmed through the maintenance buildings, trying to get ahead of us. When we were beyond the landing pads, they chased us into the rundown neighborhood around the compound.

"I've taken a moment to analyze the distress signal from the center of the starport," X-37 said.

"If it's not going to help me stay alive, I'm not interested," I said. "Can you tell me where Elise and the others are? Are we able to communicate with Jelly yet?

"I'm processing your request," X-37 said.

"Process faster."

Running to catch up with the others, we were unable to move in a straight line. Geography we'd already been over was surprisingly confusing and we kept running into enemies. I thought I saw ships from the normal part of the city. There was definitely a sound from that direction I couldn't identify.

"I have not located Elise or the others, but I am in communication with Jelly," X-37 said. "She advises that Coranth is rapidly advancing upon your location."

I hesitated, looking around for a place Jelly might be able to pick us up. It was an uncharacteristic waste of time. I already knew that if she could help us, she would be here. I cursed the quarantine, this planet, and my decisions. Nothing they had here could be worth losing my friends, even if it benefited the exodus fleet.

There were other systems and other planets. I was ready to scrap this entire mission if we could stay alive long enough to escape.

A sound ripped between the buildings with such force that I could see the shockwave. Even inside my helmet, with all of its protective properties, my ears hurt. I fought to even keep my eyes open and stay moving.

A quick glance at Path revealed he was having the same problems.

The enemy swarm melted away from the Sansein warrior's sonic attack. Coranth came around the corner, looking more bizarre than I remembered. He looked half starved. Short white fur that had been white was now yellow in places like the color of dried bone or the decayed ruins of an ancient civilization. Nearly as tall as Briggs, he was a bone rack with barely enough muscle to move—but move he did. Anger shone in his gaze despite a milky white sheath covering his eyes.

He charged liked a Union assault ship, fury blazing ahead of him. Snapping out my Reaper blade, I blocked him from attacking Briggs. "Stop! We were trying to help your brother."

He slammed forward, pushing me backward with both hands. Tentacles slashed toward me but stopped just short of my face. Falling back to dodge the attack, I immediately kicked up to my feet and prepared to fight. Briggs and Path moved to better flanking positions but waited. We didn't need this now.

"What did you do to my brother?" Coranth demanded.

"I didn't do a damn thing," I said. "He's the only Sansein that doesn't seem to want to kill me. Why would I harm him?"

"He is trapped. I can hear his wailing cries. Probably every one of my kind can hear him all the way across the galaxy," Coranth said.

"Help me help you." I motioned for Path and Briggs to start edging backward. If I could keep them talking, and the Neverseen were still scared of him, we might be able to get out of this alive. All we had to do was keep retreating and keep him talking.

"Why would you help me, human?" Coranth asked. "You fraternize with an abomination. It must be destroyed. Its mere existence sounds like a discarded rib in the fabric of the galaxy to me and those like me."

"Keep him talking, Reaper Cain," X-37 said. "This is important information for my analysis."

"You're the evilest of your kind," Coranth said.

"I've been called a lot of things, but that's crossing the line," I said, not sure I disagreed with the alien. I certainly wasn't good.

"Get out of my way, Reaper. Let me kill the abomination and then we can talk about my brother." Coranth moved forward.

"The Neverseen have overcome their fear of Coranth," X-37 warned.

The biggest of the behemoth Neverseen shoved aside the others and began to jog down the street, something I hadn't seen. Until now, the big ones had ambled along with heavy, plodding strides. Now it was picking up speed and shaking the entire street.

Coranth looked over his shoulder, but only briefly. When he faced me, I was afraid I had miscalculated and waited too long. "Give me the abomination now, Reaper."

"It's not the time for that, Coranth," I shouted, wishing the Sansein warrior understood the middle finger, because I really wanted to give him one. "Do something useful and kill this Neverseen freak."

"Why would I fight your enemies?" Coranth asked, face wrinkled in confusion. "These things are also abominations; another product of what humans do in pursuit of their God science."

"You can't lump us all in together," I said. "Briggs is just one man. Forget about him. Right now, you and I need to be working together to save your brother. It's a one-time offer and I'm losing my patience."

"How dare you talk to me in this way," he said.

"Listen, I thought these Neverseen freaks would be just the type of thing you crusade against. You might've scared them off with your sonic blast, but that's not going to kill them. You've got about thirty seconds to make a decision. This thing is coming, and it'll kill you just as quickly as it will kill us," I said.

"He is an abomination of your species as well. How can you look at him and not want him to die?" Coranth said.

"Well, first of all, it's not his fault. Second of all, don't you understand compassion?" I asked.

The tortured looking Sansein warrior hesitated. "What is compassion?"

"It's about the best thing ever," I said, getting nervous at the approach of the Neverseen monster. "Vital to peace. I'll teach you all about it when this is over."

"Do I have your pledge that you will do this?" Coranth asked.

"Double pinky swear," I said. "According to Elise, that's the most sacred vow a human being can make."

"Then perhaps it is enough. I will not kill the Slayer today, we will drive back these Neverseen monsters, and you will teach me about compassion when we rescue my brother from his foolishness," Coranth said.

"Good." I faced the charging Neverseen behemoth. The ground was shaking so badly now that I almost lost my balance. I aimed my HDK, wishing I had my chain gun, wishing I had close air support from jelly, wishing for a lot of things.

Coranth walked confidently toward the charging beast.

"I find it interesting that a Reaper is going to teach an alien warrior about compassion," X-37 said.

"Not now, X."

"I suggest you and Path direct all of your fire toward the

monster's feet, as you did the smaller ones. This will perhaps unbalance it so that the Sansein and the Slayer can engage it in close quarters combat," X-37 said.

"On it," I said.

Path acknowledged with a radio click. We fired at its feet, striking him in the ankles and lower legs mostly. It barely faltered. Coranth retracted all its tentacles and raised its fists, and I thought he was about to launch a flurry of death toward the thing. Briggs climbed up the fire escape of one of the nearby buildings and prepared to jump onto its back.

"Elise for Cain, I've dropped off my package. Headed your way," Elise said.

I didn't answer but kept shooting.

"Reloading," Path advised.

Elise joined the fight with a frenzy of violence—shooting at their feet, but also frequently aiming for eyes, throats, or groins.

Coranth jumped into the air, seeming to hover for a second before he landed square on the beast's snout. Every time we touched the monster, I could see it a little bit better. The stealth properties worked best when it was moving, and we were finally affecting its forward momentum.

Briggs jumped from his high perch and landed on the back of his neck, stabbing downward with his claws. When they were embedded deep in the Neverseen's flesh, he unleashed the tentacles, which had a disturbing burrowing effect.

"Reloading!" I shouted.

"Jelly says she can offer close air support," X-37 said. "But only for a short time."

"Fan fucking tastic," I said, aiming for a new target.

"It seems that the Kalon Regulars are focusing on their invasion of the compound and similar rebel areas. Their air traffic control has slipped. Would you like an update on the battle Melina and the others are facing?" X-37 asked.

"Yeah, X. I'd love that. Unfortunately, I'm a little bit busy." This entire place was coming apart. So, the mission to Yansden was going pretty much the same as every planet I set foot on.

"I don't think your girlfriend and her brothers are going to stay away for long," Elise said. "Reloading."

"Covering!" Path and I said at the same time, shooting with deadly effect while Elise switched magazines.

The Neverseen behemoth staggered then fell to one of its knees, snapping its teeth at Coranth and Briggs but never quite biting onto them. Its jaws were huge, easily large enough for my entire squad to be gobbled up in one bite.

Coranth reached into its throat and did something with his Sansein tentacles I really didn't want to see...or hear. The wet tearing sounds were immediately lost in the creature's screams.

Three or four blocks behind it, the other Neverseen creatures were gathering, and among them, there were at least two more of the behemoths.

"We can't sustain this," I said. "We need to look for another way to the center of the spaceport."

The Neverseen behemoth bellowed its death cry, a sound so miserable that I felt it in my bones.

"All right," I shouted. "It's time to haul ass."

15

Elise led the way through the neighborhood like she was born to do it. Her map of the area synchronized to my Archangel HUD where X-37 made notations for both of us. Path's observations also overlaid into our common database. Coranth and Briggs ran almost side-by-side, which was strange. I would've thought they'd be killing each other by now but maybe that was just something that would come later.

"I have my own ship," Coranth said.

"We'd ask for a ride, but my last visit to one of your ships left a bad taste in my mouth," I said.

The Sansein warrior didn't reply. X-37 suggested that I had confused him, and maybe I had. I probably confused my LAI as well.

"Elise, how much farther to the safe zone?" I asked.

"Two blocks." She disappeared around the corner before I

could catch up with the others. "It's the only place we could find where Jelly could touch down without interference from the Kalon Regulars. She's reporting a spike in drone traffic, and I don't think they're the kind we saw directing traffic and checking subway passes."

"Do not forget your promise," Coranth said. "I wish to know the value of compassion."

He peeled away from us and headed for his own ship, completely undaunted by the danger of the growing numbers of Neverseen.

"I'm just gonna say it, Reaper," Elise said. "That was the strangest conversation I've ever heard."

"He'll probably kill all of us when it's done," I said. "He doesn't think like we do. I'll bet a case of cigars compassion isn't what he thinks it is."

"That's no lie," Elise said. "Oh, look, your annoying kid friend is here."

I slowed to a walk as we reached the edge of the small landing area. Parked along one edge was the white van. Manager didn't have his friends with him this time, but his older brother and sister were there.

"Great," I said.

Tatiana stepped forward. "You still need a guide, and we still want to know what is in the center of the spaceport that kept us prisoner for generations. Maybe there is something we can salvage, or a new route we can open that cuts across the landing zones. Either way, we're coming with you."

"We might be better able to protect them once they are on the *Jellybird*," X-37 said privately.

My LAI was right. At least I would know where they were. Manager had a habit of going wherever he wanted. Kind of like Bug. "We need to pick up Bug and Hannah," I said.

"Agreed," Elise said. "I left them with this kid and his van. Maybe he can tell you where they are."

The profanity that streamed out of my mouth threatened to lock up X. I stomped toward Manager in the van. Tatiana and Brecken instinctively stood taller and seemed ready to defend their little brother, who looked suitably guilty. I stopped short, so as not to force a confrontation.

"Manager, where the hell are my sister and Bug?" I demanded.

"They went looking for you," Manager said. "I tried to stop them."

"Why can't anything be easy?" I asked the sky, fists clenched and no cigar in sight.

"This is a question you ask frequently," X-37 said. "And yet, when I attempt to refute your false conclusion, you respond unpleasantly."

"Where's the last place you saw them, Manager?" I asked. "X, use my Archangel armor to project a map on the ground."

"Done."

Manager stepped forward, eyes wide with amazement. His older brother and sister seemed equally interested in the map. "I last saw them here, and they were headed that way. At the time, it seemed like a pretty good route, but after you guys had your big fight, I think they started heading right into the middle of a very bad situation."

"That's putting it mildly," I said. "X, where the hell is Jelly?"

"She is inbound. Thirty seconds," X-37 said.

I looked to the sky and saw the *Jellybird* slanting down on an aggressive dissent vector. It made me wince to think about what Tom was going through inside the ship. Drones or micro-fighters were made for that sort of thing. The little smuggling frigate wasn't made for such hard-atmospheric flying. When she got close enough to land, I could see her wings shaking from the force it took to brake and set down this fast.

"As soon as the ramp drops, anybody who's going needs to get on. We won't be waiting around," I said.

I boarded last, watching the forbidden part of the city come alive with Neverseen marauders. A quick glance toward the compound revealed there were fewer in that direction, but I thought I could detect the Kalon Regulars beginning their assault on Melina's people.

The moment we were inside, I pulled Tatiana aside. "Are you sure about this? Your home is being attacked."

"Not for the first time," she said. "And I think our people have a common future together whether we like it or not."

"I get it, Tatiana. But saying it is one thing and living with the consequences is another," I said, knowing we weren't done with this conversation.

Her gaze left mine and I could tell she was deep in thought but not about to reverse her decision so easily.

"Welcome aboard, Captain," Jelly said. "It's good to have you with us once again."

"Glad you made it, Hal," Tom said. "It's been frustrating watching you guys fight and not being able to help."

"It's good to be back. I'd come up there for a cigar, but it would be too crowded in the cockpit with all this Archangel armor. We need to scoop up Bug and my sister."

"Already working on the coordinates," Tom said. "Jelly thinks we can reach them but is worried about flying between the buildings. We may need to wait until they are clear of this neighborhood. Every structure gets shorter and more blast resistant the closer they get to the landing pads, and beyond that, there is only the blast off zone and the launch needle of the spaceport."

"Sooner would be better than later," I said.

Tatiana, Brecken, and Manager stared at the interior of the ship, especially at the micro-fighters bolted down on the other side of the bay. I wanted to give them a tour. Maybe, if things worked out, they would live long enough for me to show it off.

"Jelly, put up a view of the city below us on the loading bay screen."

"Right away, Captain."

Tatiana held on to the emergency harness, looking vaguely ill from the motion of the ship. She kept her balance but was clearly not used to the pitching deck as the ship twisted and turned to avoid interference by the drones. A good pilot would order them to strap-in properly, but that would slow us down. Hopefully, this was going to be a short trip.

"I've never been on a ship like this," she said, then swallowed her words before she lost her lunch.

"Best ship in the galaxy," I said.

Near the door that was also the loading ramp, a screen came to life. We didn't use it much because it was made for a bigger crew—half for entertainment, but also for giving instructions or training videos. It was a simple thing, not even a holograph.

The view of the city was discouraging. Groups of Neverseen roamed the area between the compound and the center of the spaceport that was our destination. The larger ones looked like angry building-sized children breaking things. The sun was still up, cutting harshly across the terrain. Their stealth fields partially hid them, which made my stomach feel about like Tatiana's was probably feeling from the ship ride.

Jelly swooped low over building tops. I was getting used to the layout of this city. Everything made more sense from the air. A lot of planning had gone into the construction of this place, even if they would have been better off building more of their ships in space. Every few kilometers, there was a cluster of support structures like those we had used to hide from the Neverseen. X-37 filled my HUD with notations on all the places that would need to be cleared of enemies if we had to cover this distance on foot.

"Wow, X, look who is a soul breaking pessimist," I muttered, minimizing the icons to reduce distractions.

"I merely give you facts," X-37 said. "Foot traffic is a poor option from this point forward."

"I am one hundred percent with you on this one. Walking is for chumps. Who exactly is enforcing the no-fly zone?" I asked.

"I suspect there will be an obnoxiously strong drone response, but rule nothing out. We've learned less than one percent of what there is to know about Yansden," my LAI said. "This area was once a thriving support zone for the spaceport and the launch needle."

I tried to calculate how many small ships could take off from this place but understood it didn't matter. The central structure had been designed to launch large pieces of capital ships into orbit.

I couldn't even imagine the blast from such a launch.

"Right there," Elise said, pointing toward the display we had put up for Tatiana and the others. It showed a view from the front of the *Jellybird*. A half kilometer ahead of us, Bug and Hannah fled from a trio of Neverseen humanoids.

"Why don't they turn and fight?" Brecken asked. "They clearly have the armor and weapons to do it."

"They haven't been trained," I said.

Brecken, a soldier at heart even if he lacked formal training, seemed to accept that.

"Jelly, come in as low as you can. Tom, take the shots if we have them. I don't want to get into an air to ground gun battle using the *Jellybird*, but they should be something you can handle quickly," I said.

"Sure thing, Hal," Tom replied.

The ship flared its atmosphere ready wings, a sight I didn't see often, and pulsed its engines. But the simple maneuver gave Jelly problems. We slipped sideways and dropped roughly. Precision was not a word I would have used to describe the maneuver.

"I'm ready to be done with this planet," Jelly said.

"Are you getting frustrated?" I asked, surprised that such a thing was possible with my ship AI.

"Of course not, Captain."

"I am taking a shot," Tom said, then fired. Several energy bolts darted toward the Neverseen trio but veered off at random angles.

"What the hell was that?" I asked.

"Something is interfering with my targeting computers," Jelly said.

"Fine, just land on them. The harder the better," I said. "Everyone brace yourselves."

"Landing on enemy pedestrians," Jelly advised. "In three, two, one. Touching down now. Be advised, there are still Yansden drones in pursuit."

The cameras didn't show the effect of our attack, which was probably a good thing. Jelly dropped the ramp, and moments later Hannah and Bug raced on board.

"Are you okay?" I asked my sister.

"Perfect." She sounded out of breath.

I returned my attention to the mission and other people I needed to keep alive. "Tom, can you get us to the center of the spaceport?"

"Jelly and I are working on it. Half the problem is due to the aggressive jamming protocols of the local government, and half to whatever caused the problem at the spaceport. We've been banging our heads on the exact nature of the quarantine all day."

"All right, do your best," I said. "Everyone find a place to strap in. The ride is only going to get rougher. We'll stay here in the loading bay for a quick deployment."

Jelly stayed low, barely clearing the buildings in this sector. Almost immediately, a dozen Yansden drones came after us. They abandoned their patrol of the compound the moment Jelly lifted off.

I watched on my HUD, not bothering to take off my Archangel helmet. That would lead to smoking cigars, which would lead to not being ready when the time came. The resolution wasn't as good, but I could see the basics. The drones were fast, quickly surrounding the *Jellybird*. For short distances, they were too fast to avoid.

"I can outdistance them, but then we would overshoot our objective," Jelly said.

"Just do what you can," I said. "I don't see them firing weapons. Are they doing something else to interfere with your flight?"

"They are, Captain," Jelly said. "I've learned to defend my systems from the drone attacks, but it takes time and processing power. I will be glad when we're done with them. The bigger problem lies in the planet itself. Still searching for the source of the interference. Most likely it is coming from the launch spire itself."

"Can you shoot them down?" Elise asked. "Maybe that would save some of your processing power to deal with other problems."

"Let's hold off on that option," I said. "Until we can get our targeting systems worked out. "

"Understood, Captain," Jelly said.

"X, make sure Jelly understands how to interpret their data. I don't want her getting confused by the Neverseen stealth fields," I said.

"Of course, Reaper Cain," X-37 said. "I have to say, this is much better than walking."

"Don't jinx us," I said.

"We have discussed the irrational nature of your superstitions," X-37 said.

Below us, right when Jelly dipped low to avoid another group of Yansden drones, one of the behemoths scooped up a handful of the smaller, human-sized Neverseen. The monster cocked back its massive arm like a catapult.

"Oh shit," I said.

"Please tell me it's not going to do that!" Elise shouted.

The Neverseen behemoth hurled its smaller companions into the air. One bounced off the ship. Others went pinwheeling into the air, destined for a very hard landing.

"I'm not sure what that's supposed to do," Tom said via comms. "The impact didn't cause any damage."

"I'm not sure whether I should laugh or cry," I said as dozens of the behemoths began to pick up their brethren, and bits of debris, and chunks out of buildings to throw at us.

"Coranth is flying higher than we are. I'm going to take us up a bit," Tom said, sounding disgusted with the development.

"Are you sure?" Jelly asked. "That will draw the attention of the Yansden security forces. They could have worse surprises for us than the drones."

"Yeah, that's probably the bigger threat," Tom admitted. "But I just can't stand watching them throw their own kind to their deaths."

"Maybe they could throw a few more of them," Briggs growled in the corner. "Or all of them. Less for us to fight. You're soft, mechanic."

To my surprise, Tatiana and her family looked at the Slayer. "Some of them were human not that long ago. They just got weak. Couldn't stand life in the mines, or the factory, or whatever. Thought they would see what is on the other side."

"We're almost to the spaceport," X-37 said. "Coranth has veered away. My analysis of his possible motives is inconclusive. It may be that he detected a danger we have yet to realize."

"Great," I said.

"The Yansden security forces are sending us strongly worded messages to steer away from the spaceport hub," Jelly advised. "They were scrambling ships, but I now believe they're going for a different option. On the bright side, they've recalled their drones."

"Put it up on my HUD, tactical icons only," I said. Clouds of Yansden drones streamed away from us, and while I should have been relieved, the sight caused a sinking feeling in my gut. "Elise, you may have to move Tatiana and the others to a more secure location, someplace with real crash chairs."

"There won't be time for that, Reaper," Elise said.

Rockets streaked across the city, gaining more speed the farther they went from their launchpad. Two other rocket batteries activated and fired. The Neverseen monsters continued to throw bigger and bigger chunks of buildings into the air, creating a distracting chaff for Jelly to navigate.

We had two choices, go high and face rockets, or swoop low and get stoned to death.

"Jelly, raise shields," I said.

"Raising shields," Jelly said. "My calibration makes this dangerous while operating within atmosphere. Do you remember what happened when we attempted to fire energy weapons?"

"I know, Jelly. Tell me when it's time to shut the shields down." I flipped through options on my HUD and tried to keep track of my guests as well. They were being battered by the evasive maneuvers of the ship but were hanging in there. "And don't shoot anything until we get the targeting problem solved."

"Doesn't anything on this ship work?" Tatiana asked.

"Best ship in the galaxy," I repeated. "Come on, Jelly. You're embarrassing me in front of our guests."

"We are doing our best, Reaper Cain," X-37 said. "And we are almost to our objective. It seems this planet was quarantined for a reason. The spaceport is putting off a field that interferes with all types of electronic communication, including that internal to a ship. More alarming, however, is that the energy signature keeps disappearing, much like the Neverseen are wont to do."

"Keep it together, X. I see it just fine." A hollow feeling grew in the pit of my stomach as one of the behemoths vanished from existence.

What the actual fuck?

"An energy field just pulsed from the center of this facility,"

Tom said. "Godsdammit. Whoever built this place was trying to make their own slip tunnels. Or something worse, if that is possible."

As though on cue, the *Jellybird* dropped ten feet for no reason as though she had lost power or hit unexplained turbulence. Warning klaxons blared throughout the ship and in my helmet. One thing after another went wrong, and I suddenly understood why the people of Yansden relied on such primitive ground cars, railways, or walking.

"You're talking about dimensional tampering. That science was outlawed a thousand years ago," Hannah said. "No wonder our instruments are so unreliable."

"We need to get out of this thing," Manager shouted.

"Calm down," Tatiana said. "We're almost there."

"Elise, Path, Briggs—you're going with me the moment the door opens," I said. "Let's secure the landing zone and get our passengers off into some sort of safety."

I wanted to clarify what the hell Tom was talking about. Science wasn't my strong point, but I knew there had been attempts at faster than light space travel that failed. The Union never released the details of the worst disasters. Had we come all this way just to get killed by a back-system scientific fuck up? Maybe Coranth had the right idea, or maybe he was just watching what happened to us before he made his move.

"And what exactly would you consider safe?" Elise asked. "Part of the spaceport? More of the support structures that are crawling with Neverseen? Or maybe you want to go underground again like on Dreadmax, because what could possibly be bad below the surface of this place?"

The *Jellybird* swooped low and flared her engines as we landed. Another alarm rang near the loading ramp and I wondered if we were locked inside. The ship also lost control for a second, sliding sideways and landing roughly.

"Let's go!" I shouted when the ramp did finally drop. Elise and Briggs were the first out, clearing to the left and right. I moved straight forward. Path held the middle of our security zone.

"All clear," Elise said. "But I don't think that will last. The Neverseen are out hunting and it's only a matter of time before they return."

"Jelly, can you take off and run a support pattern?" I asked.

"That would be ideal, Captain, but I fear we might not be able to land again. My systems are being overloaded," Jelly said. "Tom's observations about the rogue science they experimented with might be correct. This place is dangerous. We shouldn't have come here."

"To the planet?" I asked.

"To the system," Jelly answered.

"Fantastic." I did a quick review of where everyone was and what we needed to do if we were going to survive. At this point, I wasn't sure if there was anything in this system the exodus fleet could use. The good news was that the fleet wasn't here. Losing everything due to one small mistake would have earned me a special place in hell. Why the fuck had I listened to my enemy during a duel to the death?

Dumbass. Secret to defeating the Sansein my ass.

"All right, let's do this quickly," I said. "We've got to get inside the spaceport, secure it, and see if we can't put a stop to whatever is causing all these problems."

"Sounds easy," Elise said. "Barely an inconvenience."

"Tatiana, Brecken," I said. "You're up. Stay inside our perimeter. We'll be moving fast."

"We're on the way," Tatiana said. Her brother, despite his reputation as a hard charging soldier of the compound, let her take the lead. Their relationship seemed natural and fluid. I was curious about how they would act in a non-crisis situation. Which was dumb, because my life was never going to be normal.

"I'm keeping Bug and this other kid here," Tom said. "Say the word, and I'll come running if I can."

"I know you would, Tom, but I need you on the ship." When I checked to see that I had everyone, I realized there was one more person in my assault team than I had originally accounted for.

"Hannah," I said, not sure if I could effectively order her back onto the ship.

"I know what I'm doing," she said. "Don't expect me to fight your battles, but there may be other things I can do to help. This armor will protect me."

"Are we moving or not?" Elise asked.

"We're moving," I said. "Everyone knows their places. Stay in formation. Once we enter the spaceport, we need to clear some rooms and make a safe space. As soon as we can, I want to stop and re-evaluate what we have. With luck we might hack their tech—shut down their electronic jammers."

"You're assuming the interference they are causing with our electronics is intentional," X-37 said. "But it is much more likely to be accidental and thus uncorrectable."

"X, can you just wait to give me bad news until there actually is bad news?"

"Of course, Reaper Cain," X-37 said. "I'm sure it won't be long."

"You're killing me, X," I said. "I'm dead."

"Please stop, Reaper Cain."

"You can't talk to me, X. Because you murdered my soul. I'm an ex-Reaper."

"Seriously, Reaper Cain. You're being ridiculous," X-37 said. "If you don't stop with the jokes, I'm going to manipulate your hormonal profile in an attempt to make you grow up."

"Settle down. I told you to stop doing that a long time ago, and I meant it."

We reached the main doors, which were three meters by three meters and designed to withstand a nuclear blast. The control panels were dark, and I was certain our mission had failed before it even got started.

"Path and Elise, you have to protect us while we work on these doors," I said. "Briggs, if you can, run a short patrol of the area and don't be seen. But most of all, don't get in a fight. We might not be able to come help you. Hannah, Tatiana, Brecken —put your thinking caps on because we've got to figure out these doors."

Everyone went to their assignments with minimal conversation.

"All right, I'm open to suggestions," I said as I examined the hinges and seams.

Tatiana and her brother moved closer and began looking over the blast doors. I felt pulses of energy radiating from the spaceport needle. Looking up at it, I realized that it was designed to be much taller. The simple AI in my Archangel armor took measurements and told me it was approximately one hundred and twenty-five meters high. I knew it had to be taller if it was the type of facility I thought it was.

"Talk to me, X," I said.

"I believe that the tower can extend to a greater height and possibly connect with other machinery in order to support launch craft," X-37 said.

I wracked my brain for something more. "Or part of it's missing."

"That is a possibility," X-37 said.

"I think we can open it at ground level." Tatiana briefly checked her gear.

"Really? That's fucking outstanding news," I said. "How?"

"For one thing, we're familiar with the technology. This isn't the first time we've faced a difficult salvage," she said. "Not that we're on a salvage mission exactly, but you know what I mean. The strength of your team's armor will go a long way toward mechanical manipulation of this beast. But the big thing is, it seems to be locked to keep something inside rather than keep us out."

"Whoa," I said. "Pump the brakes. That could change what we're doing here. Could that be someone holding Envoy prisoner?"

Elise, leaning close to the door, held up one hand. "I'm listening and not liking what I'm hearing. This place is big and probably goes deep underground. I'm not great at math, but I'm betting there could be a lot more of the Neverseen in there than we can deal with."

"I agree with her," Brecken said. "We have to be careful. But we also must hurry. The Neverseen are always on the move and they will be coming this way soon, especially if they realize we are trying to raid this place."

"Just give me a second," I said, running half a dozen scenarios in my head. "Question—how hard will it be to shut if we open it and we don't like what we see?"

Tatiana looked me up and down. "If your suits are as strong as they seem, I think we can shut it relatively quickly. But that assumes ideal conditions. If we get attacked while we are trying to close it, there are no guarantees."

"There never are," I muttered.

"Hal, I hate to add to your problems, but Jelly is telling me a large mass of the Neverseen are converging on your position from all directions. Estimated arrival time, ten minutes—probably less," Tom said. "It's actually kind of fascinating to watch— like the tide coming in."

"You're going to have to take off," I said.

"Agreed, Captain," Jelly said. "I must warn you that I have no clear idea when I will be able to return. I'm having cascading systems failures due to the proximity to the spaceport needle."

"Everyone stand clear," I said as the *Jellybird* lifted into the air and gained altitude. Before long, she was high above and I felt abandoned.

"That doesn't give me a happy feeling inside," Elise commented.

"It is what it is," I said. "Jelly and Tom will be back when we need them. Now let's get in this place. I'll go first. Elise and Path clear right and left. Tatiana and Brecken bring up the rear. And keep an eye on Hannah."

"I can keep an eye on myself," my sister said.

Tatiana and her brother went to work with the pry bars, moving them millimeters at a time.

"Let me help," Hannah said. "I have the armor."

"Good idea," Tatiana said.

"Elise, give Briggs a whistle. He's pretty freaking strong," I said. "But let's not wait for him."

"Way ahead of you, brother." Hannah gripped the bar and pulled. Tatiana and Brecken scrunched close to her and heaved against her armor for added leverage. Elise's shrill whistling, amplified by her helmet, was an eerie soundtrack to the scene.

Working as a team, Hannah, Tatiana, and Brecken opened the doors and stepped aside. I rushed into a large room with a high ceiling and encountered Envoy waiting for me.

"Are there Neverseen in here?" I demanded, sweeping my weapon across the darkness of the large room as my friends started to clear it section by section.

Envoy took a moment to interpret my question. "You call them the Neverseen?"

"Local name. Long story," I said.

"They haven't come inside." Envoy looked decidedly healthier than his brother. "Where is Coranth?"

"On his way, I think." I waved for someone to close the door before we got swarmed.

For a moment, I had Envoy all to myself. "Why are you locked in here?"

The Sansein's strange eyes pulsed with reflected light. X-37 shot me several warnings not to assume Envoy was the good alien. I didn't bother to admit I had already made that mistake more than once and would probably do it again.

"When I deactivated the external door defenses and crossed the threshold, I encountered a man. He had a device that I think you would call a tablet. Perhaps it was something else—a housing for an AI or a star map would be my guess," Envoy said. "If I had been able to use it, I could've taken it and left the system."

"But you didn't, and he escaped after locking you inside? That seems pretty fucking unbelievable," I said.

"He was very clever, and I made the mistake of treating them the same way they treat you and your friends," Envoy said. "Like ignorant, poorly behaved children."

"Ouch. That hurts," I said. "Are you sure he wasn't carrying a weapon?"

"I am sure of nothing."

16

"YOU NEED TO *GET SURE*, ENVOY," I said.

The Sansein considered me with a new kind of intensity, something that made me want to turn on all the lights and huddle close to my friends. I had to remember he wasn't human and didn't think, behave, or believe like we did. For all I knew, his moral code allowed him to murder all of us for no reason.

"You have additional questions," he said.

"Let's go back to what the hell's going on here and how you got yourself trapped. If this place is quarantined and even your people don't go here, why are you here now? How did one man ditch you like some kind of naive chump?"

"I'm here because you are here, on this planet. And I already explained that the stranger was clever and devious. Violating the quarantine was worth the risk. "

"I'm going to stop you right there and warn you not to assume I'm going to save you every time you get in a bind."

Envoy made no response for several seconds. "Do you need to consult with your limited artificial intelligence? I don't mind. There is no need to worry about social niceties with me. Go ahead and talk to yourself."

"Uh, sure. Thanks, I guess," I said, stalling for X-37 to comment.

"If Victon was telling the truth about a secret weapon, it makes sense that Envoy and his kind would want to control or destroy it," X-37 said. "You could go full Reaper and stab him in the face now but securing at least one ally among the Sansein might be worth more than any secret weapon."

I hand signaled X that he was absolutely no fun and was making my life really freaking difficult.

Envoy continued, unaware of my LAI's suggestions. "I've consulted with many humans like you, some without their knowing. There is only one reasonable conclusion: your purpose is to save your people. I've had a contentious debate with my brother as to whether or not this applies to nonhuman species."

"Let me simplify things," I said. "If you're not my enemy, we could be friends. So long as you don't hurt anybody I care about, I'm willing to help you if I can, and if there's something in it for me."

"Or something in it for your people is what you really mean," Envoy said.

"Whatever." The more I talked to this alien, the more I felt like I was getting the shaft. Didn't I already have enough problems?

"I will not harm you or your people at this time," Envoy said.

"As reassurances go, that's lame," I said. "I need your promise. I need an oath that you will never kill, capture, or otherwise mistreat my friends or my family."

"Done."

"That seemed rather abrupt," X-37 said. "My advice is not to trust such an easy declaration of fidelity."

I studied Envoy, aware that the clock was ticking and we needed a solution to the spaceport problem. This mission would be done already if he hadn't allowed this phantom, tablet carrying man to get the jump on him.

"I repeat, Reaper Cain, Envoy's declaration—"

"I think we can work together. Give me something in good faith," I said.

"Very well," he said. "We have known about Yansden for a long time. It is one of many human colonies we have observed. Some ended even more poorly than this one did."

"Yansden is still here," I said. "It hasn't really ended."

"It is suffering a slow decline, but it will deteriorate without intervention," Envoy said. "Like many of your kind, their mistake was trying to manipulate science beyond their understanding."

"We're clever." I pointed at my cybernetic eye. "Always looking for a hack."

"Self-improvement is a worthy objective," Envoy said. "In the case of Yansden, they attempted two very ambitious experiments that brought them to this state of decay. First, as is a common problem with your kind, they sought to develop a novel way of traveling faster than the speed of light. When they began this project, they had not discovered slip tunnels and were trying to find a way back to their home."

I wanted to ask about that but didn't. It seemed like questions about a mythological Earth would only confuse the Sansein who had finally decided to talk.

"During their experimentation, one of their scientists was ordered to adapt the new discoveries for military purposes," Envoy said.

"I can't believe it."

X-37 beeped me with a warning tone. "Do not confuse the Sansein with your lame sarcasm."

Envoy never missed a beat. "This is a common problem for your kind. Before long, they were attempting to create something like a slip tunnel, but they were also trying to create a shielding device using multidimensional theory." Envoy studied my cool response for a long time, never looking away. I had a feeling that he saw everything in the room, but his nonverbal behavior didn't offer the same clues a human would.

"I'm listening." I motioned toward my friends. "We all are, and so is my limited artificial intelligence."

"Yes, of course. Perhaps, in another conversation, I can assist you with upgrades," Envoy said, and I thought he was speaking directly to X. "The Yansden project was all-consuming, requiring total compliance from all citizens of the planet and most of its resources. The power running the spaceport needle will never run out."

"Never?" I asked.

"It is a geothermal source, rooted deep in the planet," Envoy said.

"Can we get to the source from here and shut it down? Will that remove the need for quarantine, maybe allow my ship to fly without seeming like it's drunk?" I asked.

"Perhaps," Envoy said.

"This is a significant development," X-37 said. "I suggest you consult with your team. Handling this problem is necessary before tracking down the man who imprisoned Envoy here."

"Way ahead of you, X." I motioned for everyone to come closer. "You heard Envoy. Thoughts?"

"We've been arguing for generations about why the quarantine is still in place," Tatiana said. "All of our cities suffer from power shortages. It's always seemed strange that the spaceport continued to exert its effect on our signals and other technology."

Brecken looked thoughtful but didn't say anything.

"We can worry about the mechanics later," Elise said. "For now, we just need to get to the source and turn it off. Not that complicated. We've done other missions like this."

She stared at me a second longer than needed, suggesting that X-37 had forwarded my conversation with Envoy.

"Agreed," I said, slowly realizing that the spaceport needle was trying to send the entire planet through—what, a slip tunnel or whatever equivalent technology the drunk assholes had dreamed up? "Envoy, can you help us with the schematics? There has to be a map of the power grid."

"There is, Reaper." Envoy waved one of his tentacled hands,

causing a screen on one wall to come to life. The simple flat screen representation of the area was overwhelming.

"Can you simplify it?" Elise asked. "Only show places we can go. The rest isn't much use to us."

One of Envoy's tentacles twitched, and I thought he did something with his gaze but couldn't be sure. The wire diagram vanished almost completely, leaving only a pair of hallways and a ladder way that descended less than twenty meters below the surface.

"That doesn't look like access to the geothermal power grid," I said.

"It isn't," Tatiana said. "But it makes sense. If they put that here, a single attack could disable the entire system. Or if a ship launch overloaded the heat vents, everything would be ruined. Whatever failsafes they have in place, they must be far below the surface. Well beyond our ability to access them."

"So that's it? We're going to give up?" Elise asked.

"Yep." I clapped my hands together like I was ready to leave and call it quits.

Neither Elise nor anyone else in my group thought it was funny.

"You people really need to relax," I said. "Let's talk about options. X, what do you think?"

"No facility like this would exist without some way to turn it off," X-37 said. "We merely need to find where the shut off terminals are located."

"Terminals as in plural? You think there are more than one?"

I said. "That might actually be good news. Surely one of them is still working."

"I will begin searching the records now," Envoy said. "Their operating system is a poor imitation of my people's language."

"Why can't you do that, X?" I asked, joking but also a little curious.

"My ability to hack into local computer networks relies on my partnership with Jelly. Since she is unable to function properly, I am limited in what I can do," X-37 said.

"I can't get into these computers at all," Tatiana said.

"Then we wait," Brecken said. "If the alien can give us a location, I say we go there immediately. This could change everything for our people."

17

WE WERE WAITING IMPATIENTLY when Coranth arrived. I heard the noise first, which made me want to harass my limited artificial intelligence. He was supposed to be on high alert.

Metal twisted and peeled away from the door, separating in seconds what had taken us several minutes to manipulate. The difference was that Coranth didn't seem to care about the door working after he was done with it. Which would leave us in a bit of a bind when the Neverseen attacked.

"What the hell!" Elise shouted, moving to the door to face not only Coranth, but the swarm of blurry, half formed images gathering near the opening.

"That thing just ripped apart those blast doors like they were nothing," Brecken said in amazement.

His sister and the rest of my friends argued and commented but I ignored them. Facing the Sansein, I wondered how long it would be before the asshole tried to kill Briggs again. "Why did you try to ditch us?"

"My ship warned me the spaceport was going to have a critical incident," Coranth said. He looked past me to his brother. "You're alive, brother."

"I am," Envoy said.

Slowly, with deliberation that sent a chill up my spine, Coranth faced me. "Now you will teach me about compassion."

"I suggest you think quickly," X-37 said. "I have no clear curriculum for this instruction. In fact, I'm slightly confused about the value of it myself."

"You would be, X." I motioned for my friends to stay back and stepped closer to Coranth. "All right, a promise is a promise. But I'm warning you, it's a multi part lesson and can often take a lifetime to learn."

"I do not feel like that is what you promised me," Coranth said.

I spread my hands as though none of this was my fault. "Nevertheless, it is what it is. The first lesson is, don't kill everyone you disagree with or who is a little bit slow on fulfilling their obligations."

"This seems very self-serving on your part," Coranth said.

"Talk quickly, Reaper Cain," X-37 advised.

"The second lesson requires class participation," I said. "You can't understand compassion unless you spend some time working together toward a common goal."

"And what goal would be worthy of this sacrifice?" Coranth asked.

"You're all about putting the kibosh on scientific abominations, so let's work together. Help us turn off the power to the spaceport before it warps reality to the point everyone dies." I didn't mention Envoy's stranger or the tablet that might not be a tablet.

"It seems much simpler just to kill the abomination you call Briggs. Wouldn't that teach the same lesson?" Coranth asked.

I smiled winningly. "Not at all, my friend. Don't forget who's the master and who is the student."

Coranth stared at me with zero evident emotion. X-37 warned me I had probably miscalculated and that we would all die a horrible Sansein induced death.

"This planet has been under quarantine for centuries. Everyone wins if we can stop the spaceport from generating these energy fluctuations," I said.

"Then what do you need me and my brother Envoy to do?"

"Well, we could do something about that door before the Neverseen come in here and kill us, or we could leave," I said. "X, can you get in touch with the *Jellybird* and see if she can pick us up?"

"She cannot, Reaper Cain."

"He has a ship," Tatiana pointed at Coranth. "Why can't he take us to the remote terminal?"

Elise answered for me. "Going on one of their ships is a big deal."

Tatiana pointed toward the encroaching swarm of Neverseen. "*That's* a big deal. We're going to die if we don't get out of here. I'm not seeing another way back to the compound."

"I don't think the compound is going to be such a safe place anyway," Brecken said, without explaining.

I assumed he was talking about the Kalon raid. Coranth and Envoy seemed to be talking without words, not something I was super excited about. But maybe that meant they were considering options.

Tatiana grew frustrated and snatched up her prybar from where she had leaned it against the wall. "Well we have to do something. Help me get this door closed."

"Can't be closed." Briggs started pacing like he was ready for a fight to the death, which I supposed he always was.

"Coranth," I said.

He looked away from his brother, then at me in a way that made me feel like he really missed the whole compassion lesson. Whether I lived or died probably meant nothing to the alien. "We are discussing the human woman's request."

"Would it help if I said not letting us all get ripped limb from limb by the Neverseen was a good lesson in compassion?" I asked.

"I am beginning to doubt the value of this thing you call compassion," Coranth said.

"Just hang in there a little bit longer, Coranth buddy," I said. "You and all of your friends will thank me in the long run."

"I am doubting this very much," he said. "But I believe my brother has convinced me there is precedent for transporting you and your people away from this spaceport and its field generator. He has pointed out that you have already defiled my ship and I might as well soil it further."

"Well that's not exactly complementary, but we'll take it," I said. "Elise, get everyone ready. We're going to have to move quickly."

Outside the ruined door there was twenty meters to Coranth's ship. Elise gathered everyone around me. "We're going to have to run for it."

"You first, Reaper," Elise said with an inappropriate chuckle.

Neverseen that had been wandering aimlessly saw us and gathered for an attack.

We were halfway to the ship when Tatiana and Brecken froze in their tracks.

"What the hell are you doing?" I demanded, aiming my HDK Dominator toward the nearest Neverseen and shooting it in the face. This time, it dropped. I did learn from our previous encounters that accuracy mattered. A bullet in the eye was always a winner. Any strike on its other surfaces would be ineffective.

"It's a signal from the compound." Tatiana pointed toward a pattern of flashing lights I suspected was a mirror of some sort.

"It's one of the few ways to communicate with the electronics that are being interfered with," Brecken said.

"The Kalon Regulars are massing to approach the compound," Tatiana said. "Melina's calling everyone in to man the defenses."

"Get to the ship," I said. "That's all that matters right now."

With a brief nod, Tatiana and her brother sprinted toward Coranth's ship. The alien waved one of its tentacled hands and a portal opened like an aperture rather than a normal boarding ramp. We rushed inside. The disorientation of being in a Sansein ship hit me hard. The others had it even worse.

Perception was doubled inside of a Sansein ship because that was how they saw the world.

"Envoy, can you get your brother to do something about this?" I waved my hand vaguely toward what I hoped he interpreted as what we were seeing.

To my surprise, the Sansein understood immediately. "My brother is directing the ship to leave the surface."

"You mean take off?"

"Yes." Envoy went through an aperture door without explanation. Slowly, I began to feel normal. My vision cleared and I regained my balance even though the ship was gaining altitude and banking aggressively.

"Are we being attacked, X?" I asked.

"I know less than you do, Reaper Cain," X-37 said.

The hallways inside Coranth's ship were more like tubes than what I was used to. They went up or down by some design that made no sense to me or any of my friends. We huddled in a space just big enough for all of us. I was able to maintain my balance in my Archangel armor, as were Elise, Path, and Hannah.

Briggs didn't seem to be affected at all. It was almost like he was at home in this place. But he didn't look happy with that realization.

Tatiana and Brecken clung to the floor like they might get flung out of the ship each time it turned. I grabbed them and held them firmly. What was more reassuring than the death grip of a Reaper?

"X, can you make contact with Envoy or Coranth?" I asked.

"Coranth has sent me a very concise message that he is flying the ship. He's using a binary code that is very much like machine language, a welcome change from your bizarre and tortured colloquialisms," X-37 said. "Envoy is on his way back to this compartment to wait with us."

"Great, X. You have a way with words," I said.

"I do try, Reaper Cain."

I looked to Tatiana's pale face. "Coranth could leave you and your brother at the compound so you can help your people defend themselves."

I had no idea if this was true, and X-37 chastised me for making such a promise, but I needed to give my new friends the choice. If they wanted off the ship, I would do whatever was necessary to make it happen.

18

"What would you do if someone gave you that kind of choice, Cain?" Tatiana asked me. She was beautiful despite the sickly pallor this ride was causing her. Her hair was damp with sweat and her hands were shaking but I thought she was a long way from giving up, which I respected.

"It's a tough choice," I said. "But if I had to pick between helping my people and going on some stranger's quest, I'd choose my people."

"What if you knew the stranger's quest would help your people more in the long run?" she asked.

"Well, I guess that's more complicated." I didn't really know how to answer her question, even though it was a concise summary of what my entire life had been since death row on the BSMP.

She looked at her brother then made an internal decision.

"We're going to regret meeting you, Cain. But Brecken and I have wanted something more for the compound for a long time. If your people are like you and your team, it gives us hope."

"Don't get all sentimental," I said. My LAI made a sound that really seemed like laughter, despite the complete impossibility of the algorithm being that cool.

"Yeah, we forgot to tell you the part where my mentor is the most feared assassin in the Union, or *was* before we fled the place," Elise said.

"Boundaries," I said to my protégé.

"What? I thought we are all about transparency," Elise said, then went back to working on her armor. Her teenage attitude flared up and leveled off like a force of nature.

"Assassin?" Tatiana asked. "Do I have the right word? This isn't another bastardization of our dialect?"

"It was another life, and I thought I was on the right side."

"You don't make this decision easy," she said. "I want to go back and fight beside my people, but my instincts tell me their future lies in the outcome of this mission."

"That's good," X-37 said to me privately. "Because her window of opportunity has passed. We would have to turn the ship around to take her to the compound now. If you were trying to stall her, you did an excellent job."

"That wasn't what I was doing, X," I muttered without thinking about it. This didn't seem to put Tatiana or her brother at ease, but there wasn't anything to be done.

Coranth's ship picked up speed, gaining altitude as it raced out of the city. Tatiana and her brother sat on the uncomfortably sloping floor and stared at each other without a word.

"Are they communicating with each other?" X-37 asked.

"Not really, X. It's something siblings do." I looked to see Hannah watching me, then I went over to her and sat down.

Elise and path joined us.

"X, estimate our location and project a map of the planet on the wall," I said.

My limited artificial intelligence provided a low-resolution representation of where we were going.

"Those are the Soft Mounts, barely mountains compared to what else Yansden has to offer," Tatiana said.

Brecken shifted awkwardly, sharing more than he intended. "I've always wanted to go there."

"There will not be a lot of time for sightseeing," I said. "Let's review. Yansden's power grid stretches across the entire planet. Who knew? Given what we saw at the spaceport, and the power it would take to run their experimental insult to physics, I guess it makes sense."

"Do you really think that once we find the secondary location, we can fix everything?" Tatiana was clearly having second thoughts.

"I don't know if we can fix anything, but we can shut off the power to the spaceport and that's a start." Keeping secrets sucked. For all I knew, Tatiana was related to the man with the mystery tablet. Bringing her into the mystery might be the way to go, or it might not. Instinct told me the time wasn't right.

And I was all about following my instincts.

She thought about that for a while, looking at her hands and not meeting my eyes. Now that I knew she probably despised me for what I was, I regretted not having kept the information secret. Suddenly, I was lonely and wanted a companion—her.

"Are you going to punch something?" X-37 asked me.

I gave him an impatient hand signal that suggested he should mind his own business and possibly fornicate with himself. Reaper LAI's were not equipped for managing love-life issues and I wasn't ready for a lecture.

"Are you okay?" Tatiana asked me.

Caught off guard, I looked up from my brooding. "It's been a long day."

"Yeah," she said. "Full of surprises."

The way she said it, I thought she meant full of disappointment. Which I understood, and not just because of how she made me feel. Her people were fighting against the Kalon Regulars and we were taking a trip across the planet's surface. Maybe this meant there was some mutual attraction between us, maybe not. I seriously sucked at this kind of thing despite all my training to read the way people expressed emotions.

It drove me crazy to abandon them, and they weren't even my people. I didn't even really like Melina.

"My suggestion, Reaper Cain, is to get some sleep if you can," X-37 said.

I ignored my LAI. Everyone looked as tired as I felt. Conversation dwindled to nothing, and we finally began to take our rest with the Sansein ship pulsing around us.

19

I AWOKE before the others and took a tour of the ship. Some passages ended without explanation or apparent reason. Others turned and went straight up or straight down. X-37 attempted to keep a map but kept asking me for additional input. So I kept moving, scanning the ship's interior and wondering why none of it looked as I remembered.

"The lighting is different here. I believe you are entering a private area. Proceed with caution. Violation of our host's security protocols could result in your death. And, since we're talking about aliens who might want to take you apart to see how you tick..." X-37 began.

"Dial it down a notch, X." I was not in the mood.

"The warning remains. Spying on your hosts, regardless of who they are, always has serious repercussions," X-37 said.

"We can't be that far from our destination," I said. "They're probably arguing about who should drive."

The sound of Sansein raising their voices caused my bones to ache and my guts to clench. The last thing I wanted was to be between them when their angry tentacles started flying with their insults and accusations. But then again, for all I knew, they were telling jokes I couldn't even understand.

"Hey, I'm coming in," I said before entering the room.

Both Sansein stopped making angry noises and separated.

"Sorry about that. I couldn't sleep," I said. "Are we almost there?"

"Yes, the destination is near," Envoy said. "Go back to your room."

"It's not really a room," I said. "More like a wide space in the hallway that's reasonably level compared to the rest of this ship."

"Then go there. This argument is none of your business," Envoy said. "My brother believes I was trapped because I am weak, like you. He believes that I went to the spaceport to try and save everyone, rather than choose who should die."

"Your brother may have a point," I said. "Don't get me wrong, I appreciate your help. I'm also a big fan of your willingness to accept Briggs as a sentient creature with the right to live just like the rest of us."

"I have accepted no such thing," Envoy said.

"We must be done with this association," Coranth said. "I see how the humans have affected you and worry they are doing the same to me. It is not natural, and they are not good."

"We might be a little good," I said.

"I do not understand their sense of humor," Coranth said, cutting me out of the conversation.

"I usually just ignore it," Envoy said. "If you listen closely there is wisdom in it."

"You've become soft and deluded by your excessive contact with the human race. I was wrong to attempt to understand even one of their beliefs," Coranth said.

"I'm standing right here," I said. "We don't have to understand each other. It's probably impossible, but we need to work together. Do no harm. Go our separate ways if we can't have peace. The galaxy is a big place. Should be a piece of cake."

"Cake? Is that a system in your part of the galaxy?" Envoy asked.

"No. It's something we eat. A dessert. Almost as good as pie." I quickly moved on when I saw zero understanding on their faces. "I promise we will stay away from you and your home after this is over."

"That is a good promise," Coranth said. "Go back and be among your team. I will fly the ship. My brother will help me."

"Sure, Coranth. But I'm watching you. No face eating on my watch," I said, making my retreat. "And you, Envoy, better not cut me out of the deal when we find the dude who locked you up. I want what is on that tablet, or whatever he used to dupe you."

"I will not attempt to apprehend him alone this time," Envoy said.

"Good."

"Leave us," Coranth said.

Wanting to fire off a snappy comeback, I opted for caution

and restraint. Probably because I was tired and getting old. Which was unusual for a Reaper—getting old, that is—so I'd earned my cockiness.

"That went well," X-37 said.

When I made it to the room we were calling our quarters, Elise and the others were looking at the floor. Our Sansein hosts had turned it into a screen that revealed the terrain we flew over with perfect clarity—far better than we could project from our Archangel helmets.

I stumbled at the sight of mountains rushing below us. "Shit!"

Elise laughed first, but they all laughed eventually.

"Where have you been, Reaper?" Elise asked.

"Went for a walk. Talked to Coranth and Envoy. They're not going to kill us for a while," I said. "At least I think that is what they said."

"Very reassuring." Elise squatted low, still in her armor but with the helmet off. Hannah was almost completely out of hers, while Path stood to one side like a statue.

"Is your friend sleeping?" Brecken asked.

"Probably meditating."

"What's that?"

I rubbed the back of my neck. "It's like sleeping. Time for a smoke, I think."

Elise shook her head.

"This is a small room, brother," Hannah said.

I almost rolled my eyes. "Sorry."

"Really?" she asked.

"No."

"We have a problem," Elise said.

"Give it to me." I leaned back, exhaling a tiny portion of what I had breathed in toward the ceiling.

"I've been using the combined LAIs of the Archangel gear to analyze the terrain and compare it to what Tatiana and Brecken know about the planet. X-37 might be able to help put the pieces together but..."

I waited for her to gather her thoughts and finish, but no one said a word. Apparently, they'd been discussing this while I was chatting with our Sansein hosts and had run out of things to say.

"But what?"

X-37 answered. "They haven't been able to locate the power shut off locations. One moment."

I waited.

"Interesting," X-37 said through my armor's external speaker. Tatiana and Brecken took the new voice well. They'd been through a lot. Not much was going to surprise them from here on out.

"What?" I asked.

"There is more than one location," X-37 said. "I've sent the best option to Coranth and will continue to work on this puzzle. Whoever created this power grid was paranoid and thorough."

20

CORANTH LANDED like he was trying to kill us with bad flying.

"Hey, X, tell that alien freak to go easy!" I stowed my unlit cigar and donned my helmet. Seconds later, the start-up procedure confirmed everything was working and my LAI had integrated with the armor's LAI.

"I'm doing my best," X-37 said. "It may be that our hosts have grown weary of our presence. As you recall from our first encounter with the Sansein, occupying their ship is a deeply personal affront they rarely tolerate."

"Desperate times and desperate measures," I said.

"I love the way you abuse quotes from literature," my sister said. Surprisingly, she had equipped herself despite being unfamiliar with the armor and led the way out of the ship.

I pointed right, then left. Elise and Path quickly secured the perimeter. I moved forward and studied the most beautiful foothills I had seen in a long time. There was something about the place that reminded me of the planet where we had encountered the world killing butterflies that tried to nuke us. But that was then. This was a new day with new problems.

Looking down from the mountain foothills, I could see the coastline and the cities in the distance. More than one of them had spaceport spires reaching hundreds of meters into the air. They still looked too short for what they were intended to do, but I hadn't seen them in action so I assumed they could extend higher, or the original design had anticipated orbital platforms dropping down some sort of connecting cable.

"I really wish I knew what they were thinking when they designed this whole set up," I said.

"It's fascinating," Hannah replied. "I'd like to know more about this place."

"You always were the curious one in the family."

Briggs, surprisingly, was the last person off the ship other than Coranth and Envoy. For about two heartbeats, I worried our hosts had finally decided to take him out despite their promises to postpone judgment.

The Slayer squinted against the brightness of the day, raising one hand to shield his eyes. Hair-like fibers bristled along his arms and I realized he was growing another crop of tentacles.

"How long is he going to experience these changes?"

X-37 barely paused. "Unknown. I've run several calculations but cannot offer a better analysis."

I thought about the spec ops commander as I gathered my team.

Hannah and Elise worked well together, taking stock of available gear and distributing several useful items to Tatiana and Brecken. Most of the nutrients we consumed in the Archangel armor were liquid, but each unit had a pack of bars and water purifying tablets.

Before long, the Yansden siblings were ready to hike.

We headed up a trail toward the facility. Vines and algae covered parts of the structure, but it looked in good repair. Arboreal creatures paused to watch us pass below the tree branches as we approached.

"They're cute," Elise said.

"Chita-chee-cita-cute," one babbled before swinging away from us.

"Hard to catch," Tatiana said. "But once you make friends with one, they're hard to get rid of. That's the real reason you see kids in the city with so many pets. Sure, they're useful for sniffing out Neverseen, but mostly they're a nuisance."

I held up a hand for everyone to stay back as I made the final approach. "It doesn't look like anyone's been here for a while, X," I said.

"I'm running a scan of your visuals now," X-37 said. "I detect no human trespass to this area. The small creatures that have been watching us from the trees have been here, but not recently."

"You need some help, Reaper?" Elise asked.

"Take Path and check the perimeter."

"On it," she answered. "I've got Path on the path."

Tatiana and Brecken both laughed. Hannah joined me by the

front door. Briggs loitered near the edge of the trees, still moody from our ride on the Sansein ship.

"Do you know how to scan the door?" I asked my sister.

"I could use some practice with the Archangel sensors," she said.

"There's no time like the present. I'll start with visual scans then follow the LAI prompts. This should be simple, but who knows," I said, then waited.

Elise and Path returned. Briggs joined us, his presence clearly making Tatiana and Brecken more nervous than Envoy and Coranth made them. The Sansein were brilliantly white in this environment, feathers covering their hide where my former commander had scales and disturbing splotches of camouflage. Coranth was still in poor health, or so it appeared. But the longer he was around his brother, the more he improved.

A strong breeze pushed clouds far overhead and shifted trees branches. Everything was clean and fresh, as far away from the city as we could be. Not for the first time, I thought this planet might be a decent place to live for a while if not for the quarantine and the threat of imminent destruction to the entire system.

"I've run every scan the Archangel LAI suggested and found no dangerous countermeasures," Hannah said. "I'm worried because it seems like there should be something to prevent any tampering."

"My thoughts exactly," I said. Nothing looked more like a trap than a top-secret control center without a lock. "I'll go in with Elise. Something goes wrong, Path will get everyone back to the Sansein ship."

"We will also accompany you," Envoy said.

"Not this time." I braced for another argument.

"You don't have a choice."

"I do, and you might be surprised what I can do in this armor while under planetary gravity and atmosphere," I said. "Don't push your luck."

"You assume many things," Envoy said. "But we'll wait outside."

Elise and I entered the station, turning on lights that had been off for a long time. There was dust on the floor, but it seemed caused by internal sources rather than something that had blown in through an open door. The power station felt like a tomb.

"I've got a really bad feeling we are going to be disappointed," Elise said.

"Same." The hallway was short, the layout of the facility simple, and there wasn't a single defensive measure or security protocol in place. Anyone with a basic understanding of how to open doors could walk in and do whatever they wanted.

We found a console in the center of the main room with a bank of view screens and microphones. There was one switch.

"Not it." Elise raised both hands and backed away.

Flipping the switch with one gauntleted finger, I braced myself for whatever diabolical countermeasure the facility architects had left for intergalactic trespassers. A screen came on, revealing four additional facilities of a similar design.

"Shit," Elise said. "That explains the complete lack of security."

"Do you want to go outside and tell everyone, or do I have to do it?" I asked.

"Let's just bring them in and figure out how we are going to access all four of these power stations," Elise said.

"X, can you get into this computer?" I asked.

"I can, but if you're looking for good news, I must disappoint you," X-37 said.

The information didn't improve no matter how many times I went over it. Elise drew her own conclusions, silently considering my reactions. One power station was in the mountains not far from here, another was near the coast, a third was on a small island, and a fourth was on the other side of the planet.

"Talk to me, Reaper," Elise said.

"I wish I could say it's just a matter of checking the boxes, handling one station at a time. But I think they need to be shut down simultaneously," I said. "Let's call everyone inside and work this out. It's going to be teamwork or nothing."

"Good idea, Reaper." Elise took off her helmet and sat it next to the terminal, not something I expected of her on a mission.

"Are you comfortable?"

She wrinkled her nose at me, then added a slight eye roll. "Yeah. But that isn't why I took my helmet off. Don't you worry about what Tatiana and her brother think of us always talking through helmets like we're machines? If we are asking them to risk their lives—really risk their lives—it might as well be face to face."

Rather than admit she was right, I took off my helmet and

went outside to break the bad news to the team, strange as that team was.

TATIANA, Brecken, Hannah, and Path formed a protective barrier around Briggs. The Slayer was breathing heavily and staring at Coranth, who had three parallel slashes across one arm.

"What's going on, Briggs?" I asked.

"He tried to grab me."

I stood between Coranth and Briggs, feeling my team backing me up. "Explain yourself, Sansein."

"If it is not compassionate to kill him, then he must at least be confined, and since you already ruined my ship, it is the best prison for him," Coranth said.

"The agreement was that you wouldn't touch my friends," I said, one hand on my HDK Dominator. There wasn't time for this, and I knew the mission was doomed if I was forced to use the weapon.

"I promised not to kill him until this was over," Coranth said. "Ask your artificial consciousness."

"Checking for the agreement now," X-37 said.

"Don't bother, X. This is my fault. I should have never put you two so near each other. Fortunately, the mission is going to fix that problem."

"What are you talking about, Reaper?" Coranth asked.

"Come inside. We need to look at some maps and a live video feed," I said.

No one moved.

"Briggs," I said. "I need you to be cool."

"I'm cool as ice, Reaper. Talk to your friend. Tell him to keep his hands off me, or he's gonna find out what kind of abomination I really am."

"Listen, Briggs. I'm with you on this. If Coranth wants a piece of you, he is going to have to fight me first."

Elise stepped up beside me. "And me, even though I still think you're a freak."

The standoff continued. Neither of the Sansein warriors argued. Hannah finally escorted Tatiana and Brecken inside, and I followed with the others a short time later. Envoy and Coranth came last. The room felt small inside once we were all crammed around the terminal to review the planetwide schematics of the power grid.

21

"We're going to divide into four groups," I said. "Group one: me, Hannah, Briggs, and Tatiana. Group two: Elise, Path, and Bracken. Group three: Tom, Bug, and Manager on the *Jellybird*. Group four will be Envoy and Coranth.

"This would've been a lot easier if we'd picked up the shuttle," Elise said. "Imagine just flying to our destination."

"We don't have time for that now," I said. "Tom, did you get all of that?"

"I read your message loud and clear." The mechanic sounded serious. I had no doubt he would do his part. I just hoped they didn't run into a fight.

"You're on your own this time, Tom," I said.

"I'll be careful," he said. "But I have Jelly. She'll look after us."

Bug and Manager protested in the background. The essence

of their message was that they could do this by themselves without the help of some stuffy book reading dude.

"We are nearly at your drop off point," Envoy said.

"Thanks." I gave Hannah, Briggs, and Tatiana a look. "Ready?"

Hannah and Tatiana nodded. Briggs made one of his disgusting Slayer sounds.

"Okay, Envoy. Tell your brother to take us down," I said.

The descent was more rapid than I anticipated, and I cursed myself for being surprised. Sooner or later, I was going to need to remember that the Sansein had different physiology than we did.

The aperture door opened to reveal a field of flowers. Red, yellow, and green, they were waist high and thick. Tatiana jumped down without a second thought and sunk almost to her chin. My estimation had been for someone wearing Archangel armor.

"What are you laughing at?" Hannah asked, then slipped down into the field.

"Nothing," I said. "The look on her face was priceless."

Tatiana touched her radio earpiece, reassuring me that she had heard the entire conversation. "Just be thankful I don't have allergies. These things are covered with pollen."

At about that time, Briggs went into a sneezing fit.

"Great." I took the murderous human-alien hybrid by the arm and led him to the other side of the clearing. He had a wild look in his eyes and was gushing fluid from his nose by the time we found a stream to wash him off.

The Sansein ship was gone, already on its way to drop off the next team. We started hiking. I took the lead, and once I was sure Briggs was okay, I asked him to bring up the rear. Hopefully, his training and his senses would keep us from being followed.

"Are you expecting an ambush or pursuit?" Hannah asked.

"Just standard procedure," I said. "No point in getting surprised.

Tatiana approved, I could tell. Her situational awareness was as good as any commando I'd ever worked with. She also seemed to have put aside the revelation I was an assassin. Maybe if I didn't bring it up again, it wouldn't be a big deal.

Traveling on foot took time, giving me an excuse to let my mind work through things that had been bothering me. I wondered what type of assassinations happened on Yansden. Thoughts of political intrigue and the kinds of things a benevolent tyrant like Melina would do to hold power made me consider Tatiana and Brecken in a different light.

She didn't seem bitter or like she was plotting an overthrow, but what did I know. They were related. Probably everyone in the compound was related. This wasn't Wallach or Xad. Neither of those places had been easy places to survive, but neither had their entire systems been in danger of blinking out.

"It's lucky we came here, X." I was far enough away from my companions to have a private conversation with X-37.

"How so, Reaper Cain?"

"They were just going to let the spaceport pulse until one of the energy fluctuations destroyed everything."

"In their defense, I doubt they had any idea how to stop it," X-37 said. "In fact, there is no guarantee we're doing the right thing. For all you know, shutting down the spaceport needle will be the final act."

"Don't tell me that, X." I looked up the trail at Tatiana. She wasn't talking much. The incline was unforgiving. "She never complains."

"Your powers of observation are adequate, Reaper Cain," X-37 said. "As for the likelihood we are going to doom this planet, it is low. The most likely result of shutting down the power source will be the cessation of the disruptive field generation."

"Good," I said. "Maybe next time you don't just freak me out with theoretical possibilities for failure."

"There are a lot of other ways we can fail," X-37 said.

"Save it." I caught up with Tatiana, then we waited for Hannah and Briggs. We found a small clearing with good visibility of the way we'd come as well as the final stretch we needed to climb.

"I could get used to being out here," Tatiana said. "It's a lot different than in pictures and stories."

"This should be a good place to connect with the other teams," I said. "X, can you try to raise Jelly?"

"Right away, Reaper Cain. Communications are much more manageable in this part of the planet."

We didn't have to wait long but I enjoyed the break. For a few minutes at least. Tatiana was always fighting for survival and was restricted in her movements.

"How does this compare to your world?" Tatiana asked.

I breathed in the cool mountain air and looked at the clear

blue sky. Yansden was a deceptively peaceful planet. Centuries ago, people had decided to risk everything to leave. After fighting the monsters on Wallach and witnessing the salvage fields in the Xad system, I wondered why the Yansdeninians were so hot to vacate. I mean, people lived on Gronic, and that place was a shit hole.

"It's different but the same," I said. "Why did your ancestors start an exodus?"

She looked surprised. "They didn't. Not until things started to go wrong. In the beginning, it was all in the spirit of exploration, or that's what they tell us."

"Makes sense," I said.

"I have a connection with the *Jellybird*," X-37 said.

"Are you there, Captain?" Jelly asked.

"Yes," I replied. "Can you hear me?"

"Loud and clear, Hal. What is your status? We're getting close —well within the timetable we established," Tom said.

"It has to be exact," I said. "There is no room for error."

"Understood."

"Captain, I can boost your signal for Elise," Jelly said.

"Perfect. Put me through." We hadn't conducted planetary operations on this scale. The separation from Elise and the team put me on edge.

"There is one update I must give you immediately, Captain," Jelly said.

"Go ahead, Jelly."

"The Wallach and Xad fleets have combined and entered the Yansden system. I'm uncertain of why they would deviate from the plan, and I'm confused as to why they would come here when we have not sent them the all clear," Jelly said.

"Human nature," I said. "Their initial scans will show the same thing ours did—lots of resources and no obvious enemies. Not even President Coronas can resist an easy prize like Yansden."

"She won't see the dangers until it's too late," X-37 warned.

"Then we better get moving. All we had to lose before this was Yansden, but now we have the rest of humanity at risk," I said.

"They are not all of humanity." X-37's tone sounded reproving, unhappy with my undisciplined language. "There are still Union, Sarkonians, and people living in the Deadlands."

"You know what I mean, X."

"What are you talking about?" Tatiana asked. "Are the rest of your people here? Is that good news?"

"They've arrived in the system," I said. "What could possibly go wrong?"

We picked up the pace after the news about the exodus fleet. Tatiana gasped for breath and put her hands on her knees each time we stopped. Briggs raced ahead, clearing the way of local wildlife. Hannah ran beside me, tripping and falling more than once. The armor protected her and gave her strength, but it wasn't easy to use in these conditions.

"X, try to coordinate an earlier shutdown time with the other teams." I jumped over a stream. Hannah followed me, landing hard but staying on her feet.

"I am working on it, Reaper Cain," X-37 said.

"This would be fun under other circumstances," Hannah said when we'd caught up with Tatiana and Briggs.

"Speak for yourself," the Yansden woman said.

"I'll lead for a while," I said. "Briggs, go back to rear guard. Don't race ahead. We all know how fast you are."

"Rear guard is boring." He took his place in our new order of march.

I headed into the mountain pass. The cool breeze had become frigid gusts of wind. Sleet pelted my visor. When I checked Tatiana, her face looked red, her jacket damp with sweat, but she said nothing.

"I could not contact the Sansein ship," X-37 said. "So the timetable remains the same. In the past you were comforted by things like crossing your fingers or knocking on wood. Perhaps you should try that and hope the system doesn't collapse and take the people of Yansden, Wallach, and Xad with them."

"Sometimes I wonder if you are joking, X." I assessed a steep climb, looking for places to attach ropes.

"I'm never joking, Reaper Cain," X-37 said. "I approximate humor to make you feel better."

The expression on Tatiana's face told me she'd never seen mountain climbing gear before. What we had was the basic stuff included in the Archangel armor, some safety lines that could be spooled out from the storage area and some belay rings. The Union had done a good job with putting together this kit, because it could be taken out of the armor and used if the main unit was too damaged to continue.

I began explaining the process to Tatiana, going over each

detail as I would with any beginner. For a second, she seemed a bit resentful but quickly got on board with the training and started paying attention. It was my sister who was distracted.

"Hannah, you can still die if you fall in that armor," I said.

"I know." She started to wander back down the trail we had just climbed with such difficulty. "I'm listening, I really am. I learned a long time ago to tune out most of what you say but still get the information."

"Well said," I replied.

She laughed. "You're probably right, but this is important. I wouldn't start hooking up those ropes yet."

Sensing something was seriously off, I immediately took her advice. "Briggs, can you hear me?"

The Slayer stared at an alternate route, a way none of us could ever hope to traverse. His attention to the challenge was almost spiritual and it took a moment for him to face me. From about twenty meters to my right, he turned, sensed the new danger, and immediately moved into the woods.

"There's someone out here isn't there?" Tatiana said as she moved to a better position and readied her weapon.

"Talk to me, Hannah." I moved to her side. "X, what did we miss?"

"I'm not sure," my LAI said. "It would be useful to know exactly what your sister is searching for."

I put a hand on Hannah's shoulder, urging her to stop. Following her gaze, I thought I knew what was wrong. "There hasn't been any tracks coming this way. None at all, not even from animals."

"It could be nothing," Hannah said.

"Briggs," I said loud enough that I thought the Slayer could hear me through the still forest. "Find another trail and compare it to the one we climbed."

"Already doing that," he said. "Awk. Awwwwwwk. Fucking awk, awk."

"Please tell me you're not going to forget how to talk right now," I said. "Not that I'd be surprised. That seems to be how every second of this mission has gone so far."

"There is no need to be a pessimist," X-37 said. "That's actually part of my programming and nothing you should worry about."

"Thanks, X."

"It would be extremely inconvenient if commander Briggs lost the ability to communicate right after he made a critical discovery," X-37 said.

"You know what, X? You really should broadcast some of these little inspirational nuggets to the rest of the team," I said.

"Do you want to approve each time I give bad news, or should I use my best judgment?" X-37 said.

"Do whatever." I examined the trail without really attending to my conversation with my digital friend. It was something I would regret later, no doubt.

Hannah and Tatiana knelt near me, studying the perfectly clean trail. Our tracks stood out in stark relief. I wanted to punch myself in the face.

"Good catch, Hannah," I said. "Really good."

It was hard to tell if she was blushing inside the armor, but she probably was. I had surprised her with the compliment at the very least.

"Bring it in when you can, Briggs," I called, modulating my voice to be just loud enough for the Slayer to pick up with his keen hearing. I wasn't sure he heard me because he didn't answer. Seconds later, however, he appeared beside us. The human alien hybrid really could move with frightening stealth when he wanted to.

"Someone, awk, covered their tracks this way. Other trails are more natural," Briggs said.

Standing, I looked around. "This is like a park it's so neat and tidy."

"At least now we know something is out here." Tatiana moved off to my flank with her weapon at low ready, prepared to fight but not so tense that she would wear herself out. She really did have good instincts.

"We still have a timetable," I said. "Look sharp and let's keep moving."

When we returned to the ropes, there was a man waiting for us.

22

"Don't shoot," the man said, dropping his hood to reveal an older man with salt and pepper hair. A patch covered one eye, and tattoos ringed his neck.

"Loren Jacem!" Tatiana shouted, aiming her gun and moving forward like she'd just been promoted to a kill team.

"Stop," I shouted.

"He's a Kalon Regular," Tatiana growled. "He's *the* Kalon Regular—the Grand Marshal."

"Great. Good for him. He's also unarmed." I pointed at his hands. My HDK Dominator was ready. This guy was clearly dangerous and not a friend to Tatiana and her people, but I thought we had just unraveled the mystery of Envoy getting locked in the spaceport needle, which was really good news.

"You understand, Cain," Tatiana said. "If Brecken was here, this man would already be dead."

Loren raised his hands slightly to emphasize he didn't have a weapon. Then slowly, as he talked, he pulled back his long jacket to show his waist was also clear. "How is Brecken?"

"Don't talk about him. He listened to your lies and you betrayed him," Tatiana said.

"My analysis suggests Tatiana's brother was once a member of the Kalon Regulars," X-37 said.

"Thanks, X. Got it." I moved closer to the man, hoping to ensure that if there was violence it would be between him and me. It wasn't that I doubted Tatiana's ability to do the job, it was that I thought she might do it before I had answers.

"My helmet and my weapons are behind me, tucked behind this rock," Loren said.

"Just keep your hands where I can see them and don't move," I said. "Why'd you lock Envoy in the spaceport?"

"That was an accident," the man said. "I needed the tablet. It's been my life's purpose. When I saw the creature, I reacted quickly. You understand, of course."

"I'm surprised you didn't try to kill him," I said.

"That seemed risky, and shutting the door was easier. I'd already been to the spaceport a dozen times and failed. By the time I met whatever that thing was, I had learned all there was to know about the spaceport needle security and how to get past the Neverseen."

He paused. I could feel the tension between him and Tatiana. They stared at each other for several moments like I wasn't there, then he slowly returned his attention to me—almost like he was a swimmer coming out the bottom of the pool.

"Yansden is my home and I love her dearly. There are some on this planet who still believe leaving is the only option. Did Tatiana tell you that? No?"

"Never came up," she explained.

"There are always people who want to run away from problems," I said. "Tell me about the tablet. That's why we're here, isn't it?"

"Yes. I thought it would turn off the power grid and shut off the unstable field generators that exist below every spaceport needle on the planet," Loren said. "But I've recently learned there are four remote stations that must be operated in perfect unison to kill the grid."

Tatiana laughed bitterly.

"I wouldn't have approached you if I didn't need your help," he said.

"I admire your honesty," I said. "Let me introduce myself, just so we can stay on the same page. My job is to kill anyone who threatens people I care about. And I'm good at it."

Loren stiffened, probably realizing the truth of my words.

"We already know how to shut off the power," I said. "Don't really need you."

Loren said nothing, clearly hoping I'd forgotten about the tablet. The guy was devious, but not in a nasty way. I almost thought we could be on the same side if things went well.

"Don't hold back on me, Loren. It's bad for your health," I said.

"I can see that it would be. The fact that you were able to

survive the Neverseen by brute force says a lot. It won't be long before you run into them here."

"He's lying," Tatiana said. "The Neverseen can't leave the spaceport. That's why they've never overrun the compound or the rest of the city."

Loren looked grim, not arguing immediately. In my professional opinion, this gave him serious credibility and made my guts tighten.

"You're full of shit, Loren." Tatiana turned to me. "He's a fear monger. That's how he lured my brother away and tried to brainwash him against the compound."

"That's unfair, Tatiana." Loren's stiff posture suggested this was an old argument and he knew she was right. "It was also a long time ago. We don't have time for history lessons, so I will tell you how the Neverseen survive this far from the city."

I crossed my arms, holding my gaze.

He stammered, unable to put his argument into words under the power of Tatiana's hostile stare.

"Spit it out, Loren," I demanded.

"You've seen the behemoths, fought them. Out here there is a Neverseen Lord, not as large as the behemoths, but smarter and able to carry a field generator. It has enough power to last several months and maintain a squad of servants," Loren said.

"You've observed this Neverseen Lord?" I asked.

His eyes went from me, to Tatiana, and back to me. "Well, no. But there have been disturbing sounds in the forest."

"Typical," Tatiana said. "The man built his career on fear mongering. Ignore him, or better yet, throw him off a cliff."

I needed information, so I didn't take her advice. "What does the tablet do? You thought it controlled the power grid, but I can tell by looking at you it's something even more game changing."

"It's a map." He held my gaze.

"Of Yansden?" I said, shushing X-37 before my LAI could chastise me for asking a bullshit question.

"Of the galaxy. There is a place called Maglan. A planet from children's stories. Useless," he said.

"To you, maybe," Hannah said.

"I'm not lying about the Neverseen. They're here and we need to be ready for them." He pointed into the woods as he spoke. "They wouldn't have come this far without a purpose. The only rational explanation is that they guard the remote shut off switch."

Changing to a private comm link with my sister via Archangel armor, I carefully phrased my words. "Let's play this smart. If he thinks the tablet is worthless, maybe he will just give it to us."

"If that's the case, why would he show himself? Why not just watch us solve his problems and step in if we need help? The man looks smart and must be dangerous. Your girlfriend is shaking with anger."

"Not my girlfriend." I needed to think. Hannah was right. This Loren Jacem guy was trying to play us. I just didn't know his game yet. Despite Tatiana's conviction the man was inventing ghost stories to set us off balance, or whatever, I scanned the trees with my cybernetic eye and the helmet optics, searching for any sign of a Neverseen presence.

Nothing. Not one single blurry figure for as far as I could see.

"Why do you hesitate?" Loren asked. "And why not remove your helmets? I took mine off in a show of good faith."

"More likely you didn't want to get shot on sight," Tatiana said.

"And that." He narrowed his gaze on the woman who definitely wasn't my girlfriend. "Should I just talk to you then? Since you are the only person honest enough to show her face?"

Briggs emerged from the tree line, stalking slowly but intentionally toward Loren.

"By the gods!" the Kalon Regular shouted, springing to his feet and retreating instinctively toward his helmet and weapons.

"Not so fast." I aimed my HDK Dominator. "The Slayer is with us. If you'd been watching us, you'd know that."

"I never saw that thing." He stopped edging toward his weapons stash but seemed nervous. "What the hell is it? I thought the other alien was strange. At least it didn't look like it wanted to eat me."

"Don't worry about it. The Slayer is with me and won't hurt you unless you piss me off," I said. "Briggs, did you find anything we need to worry about out there?"

"Not sure." The look on the Slayer's face warned me not to ask more until he had a chance to find what was bothering him.

"Our new friend says there are Neverseen here." I let the statement hang.

Briggs considered my words but said nothing.

"I'm telling the truth," Loren insisted.

"Maybe you are, maybe you aren't. Now hand over that

tablet as a gesture of good faith and we'll help you shut off the power grid."

The only thing that happened for several seconds was X-37 pestering me about being behind schedule.

"I think I will retain the tablet for now, as insurance. Let's work together and renegotiate after the spaceport stops collapsing energy fields," he said.

"Collapsing or creating?" I asked, wishing I had consulted X-37 or one of my smart friends first.

"Both. That is the problem. My science team believes it is the fall of the energy wall that will be the end for us."

"Where is your science team?" I asked.

He smiled, then shook his head fondly. "People from the city don't come into the wilderness. It is an eccentricity of mine. I've always wanted to explore all the way to the ancient ruins beyond these mountains."

The man looked like he was holding something back, but he also seemed ready to share a secret—nothing that would put him at a disadvantage, but a guilty pleasure.

"There is a second part to the tablet map," he said. "I believe it can be found in the ruins of the Hard Mounts."

"Yeah, well that isn't our problem, is it?" Tatiana said. "The clock is ticking. We need to get to the power station and be ready."

"What do you mean?" Loren asked.

"Should I tell him, or do you want to?" Tatiana asked.

I stepped past Loren and picked up his gear, then I checked the helmet to see if it had any comm capabilities—which it did.

Of course. The asshole was live streaming our entire conversation. Without reacting, I took the helmet and motioned toward the weapons. "Take your weapons. You might need them. Don't even think about trying to fight me or my friends."

He opened his mouth to argue.

"We already have people on the way to the other power shutoff stations. And a prescheduled time. So let's stop screwing around here," I said.

"I can't let you keep my helmet. It's a mark of honor. I will be punished if I surrender it," Loren said.

"Can you tap into this thing's signal, X?" I asked.

"Already done," X-37 said.

"Are they saying anything interesting?"

"Well, since there is no way to put this politely, the scientists and soldiers listening have come to the consensus you are too dumb to realize they are listening. Something about the helmet looking old and battered, not a likely candidate for high tech listening devices," X-37 said.

The helmet was a one-piece design, painted red a long time ago and kicked around a lot since then. There were snapped off antenna and missing seals. I tossed it to Loren.

"I'm not helping you take that piece of junk off if it gets stuck on your head." I grabbed the ropes and rechecked them. "If owning one is such a big deal, you ought to think about an upgrade."

"The Yansden audience is laughing at you," X-37 advised.

Tatiana hissed to get my attention. "You can't let him keep that thing."

I pretended not to hear or understand her. "Let's climb these rocks before it's too late. You first, Slayer."

"I've lost contact with Jelly and Coranth's ship," X-37 said.

"Work on it. We'll need to coordinate with them. The preplanned action probably won't work." I watched Briggs ascend the cliff without a safety line. The Slayer dragged our ropes to the top, saving me the need to deploy the grappling hook, which looked too lightweight for comfort.

23

CLIMBING WAS a nice change from verbal duels and getting tossed around in an alien ship. Tatiana followed me, stopping on each ledge I cleared, waiting until I signaled her to keep going.

"You can't let him have that helmet. They use them to communicate. It looks like a piece of junk, but the one thing the Kalon Regulars have a strangle hold on is communications. They were one of the first organizations to develop a stable work-around for radios.

"I know. The man has a team of scientists and soldiers listening to us," I said. "But they don't know I know. So, keep up the act. Keep trying to convince me to take away the helmet."

We climbed to the next ledge, the freezing wind cutting through Tatiana's clothing. She shivered, then took one hand from the rope and opened and closed it to improve circulation.

I extended a shorter tactical cable from the belt area of my gear. "Hook onto me."

"Thanks, Cain. But there's no need for us both to die," she said with a laugh.

Thoughts of Novasdaughter's mother falling from the bridge tortured me. More than once I'd awoken from nightmares wishing I was the one who had fallen. Maybe the galaxy would have been a better place if my captain hadn't shot my arm off to make her fall, or if I had somehow hooked myself to her and shared her fate.

"Hey, Cain. I was joking. I don't want either of us to fall," Tatiana said.

"Snap out of it, Reaper Cain," X-37 said.

"Sorry, Tatiana. Was just thinking of another time. Don't worry. I'm back and neither of us are going to fall."

"Good. I'm holding you to that promise."

Tied together, we worked our way to a shallow cave where Briggs squatted on his haunches, watching us, his thoughts unreadable.

"Can't do that from here to the top. You will need, awk, to have the good shit. Need to work individually. Awk."

"Fine," I said. "Get off that ledge and let her rest. She needs to get out of the wind and warm up."

"Okay, Reaper," Briggs said.

Tatiana moved into the shallow cave—more of an eroded spot in the rock than a hole—and hugged herself to get warm. The Slayer started to ascend but stopped. "Your sister and the red helmet are coming fast. Tat won't be able to rest long."

"I know," Tatiana said. "I already feel better. Might as well get this over with."

"Be smart. Don't rush." Moving off to one side of the climbing route, I drove my Reaper blade into a crevasse and rested against it.

Tatiana nodded, rubbed her gloved hands vigorously, then started pulling herself up the rope toward Briggs. I watched, waited, then took my turn on the next section of the climb.

"Cain!" Tatiana shouted, then she fell away from the rope right when I looked up.

Briggs lunged, grabbed her, and held on. His own grip on the rope put his arm at a bad angle. No normal person would have attempted such a grab. I scurried upward as X-37 warned me they were slipping and I should shelter in the small cave to avoid getting hit as they fell.

Instead, I pushed up on Tatiana until both she and the Slayer could recover.

We were all breathing hard by the time it was done. "Get moving, Briggs. The top can't be that much farther."

Without another word, the Slayer started again. Tatiana followed him. I looked down and saw Loren followed by my sister. They stared in amazement, or at least that was how I interpreted the tilt of their helmets, and their rigid death grips on their ropes.

"That was too close for comfort, Reaper Cain," X-37 said.

"You're telling me," I said. "Almost dropped my cigars."

"Did your armor come open?" X-37 asked.

"Joking, X."

"Of course. I shall make a note about how funny that is."

Briggs, then Tatiana disappeared over a ledge I couldn't see beyond and I assumed they'd made it to easier terrain. "Check on Elise and her team."

"I'm unable to establish communication with them," X-37 said.

"Not what I was hoping to hear, X."

24

WE CAME to a mountain clearing more beautiful than anyplace I'd seen. Loren pointed out the manmade structure, otherwise we would have had to search for it. The blast proof door was overgrown with flowers and surrounded by crystal clear streams than flowed from the black rock wall on the north edge. In places, the dark stone was polished by erosion but there were also beams of sunlight that revealed blue and orange mineral residue. Insects like I'd never seen drifted across the fields, buzzing from flower to flower and bush to bush.

"Something's wrong," Briggs said.

"Talk to me, Slayer." I swept my HDK Dominator sights over the scene, finger near the trigger and ready to do work.

"I don't see the tree creatures. They've been dogging us the entire trip. Now, poof. Gone."

"Kids use them in the city to spot Neverseen raiders," Tatiana said, moving toward a two-foot-high bolder near the edge of the clearing. It would be good cover if someone shot at her but would be less useful against a swarm of the ghostlike killers we'd faced near the spaceport.

I moved the other direction and motioned for Hannah to follow me.

"There are Neverseen guarding this place. They didn't attack the first time I was here, but I could sense them watching me," Loren said.

"He might be telling the truth." Tatiana's admission sounded like it hurt her. "I still think you're a fear mongering liar, Loren. Don't piss me off."

"Let's sweep the area just to be sure," I said. "Tatiana, Hannah, and Loren—wait near the station entrance. Briggs and I will clear. If we need help, Tatiana, you're our backup."

"Got it," she acknowledged.

I picked her because she knew what she was doing and had been in battles before we met. Hannah had high tech gear but no combat experience. The Yansden woman was better suited for what I would need if things went bad.

The clearing was just big enough that Briggs and I relied on hand signals to communicate. I tried more than once to get him to use a radio, but he refused and wouldn't explain why. Maybe it was difficult for him to operate, just like a rifle or other tools. His hands were large, and his talons made simple tasks difficult.

Moving across the field, I relaxed and thought about nothing but what I saw around me. There were enemies here, I knew it. Whether or not it was Loren's Neverseen ghosts I couldn't say, but that seemed like the most likely scenario. If the power grid to the spaceport field generators went down, the Neverseen would wither and die. Or that was the theory. And that meant they would defend against any attempt to shut the grid down.

I wondered what would happen to the more human versions of the creatures, the ones who had only recently fallen under the spaceport's influence.

Briggs gave me a sharp hand signal, indicating he had eyes on an enemy. Seconds later, I spotted the first of the Neverseen as they advanced toward us. It looked like at least a full squad and they moved with more purpose than others I had encountered.

These were difficult to see, even with my enhanced optics. Heat signatures were distorted, blending with the background more often than not. But I knew what to look for and picked them out one by one.

The Neverseen in the city had been gray blurs. These were dark green and brown with flecks of color from the wildflowers and streaks of blue from the streams cutting across the scene. I didn't have long to evaluate them because they charged soon after I aimed my HDK Dominator.

Briggs screamed the war cry and charged ahead, lacking a weapon to strike from a greater range. Aiming carefully, I picked my shots for maximum effect. We'd already learned that the standard practice of going for a body shot—normally the easiest and most effective target—didn't work with them. Something about their physiology and the clothing they wore repelled bullets almost as effectively as armor.

The speed of their movement also helped them stay alive when bullets started flying.

I hit the first right between his eyes, and he dropped. The second and third staggered after taking bullets in their throats. I moved, running up the side of a flat rock and shooting another Neverseen attacker in the pelvis. This didn't kill him, but others ran past him when he fell.

"Reloading!" I shouted out of habit, forgetting that I had no one to cover me during the maneuver.

A big Neverseen the color of trees and gold leapt at me. Side-stepping, I extended my Reaper blade and stabbed him in the stomach. He fell on me as I twisted away.

"I'm coming, Cain," Tatiana said, darting across the field with her weapon held high enough not to get struck by the wild-flowers that were nearly as tall as she was in places.

There was no point in arguing, so I fired on two more Neverseen then looked for Briggs. All I could find was a tangle of violence, blurred images rolling over the Slayer as he tumbled between trees and over rocks. He was fighting like a cat in a dogfight.

Tatiana opened fire, and to my surprise, Hannah arrived seconds later, firing the shotgun I had chosen for her armor hoping she would never use it. It was difficult to tell if she struck her targets, but I hoped it was at least having a suppressive effect on the enemy.

Tatiana stayed close to my sister, probably to avoid taking an accidental blast.

Ignoring them, I changed positions, shooting another

Neverseen in his temple while he looked at Briggs and the other monsters.

"You are becoming much more efficient in fighting the Neverseen," X-37 stated. "I'm keeping a careful record of your target selection and accuracy for future reference."

"Thanks, X," I said, then ran toward Briggs. There weren't many around Tatiana and Hannah, and they looked like they were taking care of business on their own anyway. The Slayer, by contrast, was making a mess of things.

Small trees were smashed. Ground was torn up. And blood spattered the bushes and flowers all around the conflict. I fired on the move, hammering several of the Neverseen in the backs of their heads and realizing my concern about shot selection in this situation was well-founded. The hoods they wore were armored. My bullets had a less than lethal effect.

I was able to stun them, but not put them down for good.

This time, when the HDK Dominator ran out of ammunition, I clipped it to my armor in one fluid move and jumped on the first Neverseen I came to. Landing hard, I drove my victim face down into rocky soil.

He spun to face me, but I held on. We rolled over and over, slamming into a tree with sufficient force that I felt it through my armor. Using a jiu jitsu reversal technique, I twisted its arm backward, snapping it at the elbow joint and nearly pulling it out of the shoulder junction.

I shoved it away as it screamed in pain and agony. Briggs ripped off the head of another just as I looked his way. Blood looped through the air in crazy, semi-random patterns.

I stood, extended my Reaper blade once again, and drew my pistol. The Neverseen came at me and I fought like hell. Before it was over, Briggs, Tatiana, and Hannah were at my side fighting them off.

The battle ended abruptly. The twisted bodies of our victims lay strewn across one half of the clearing. A few had fled. I could hear them howling their anguish in the distance.

I looked at my companions. "Who wants to tell Loren he was right?"

"Where is he?" Briggs snarled.

"He was fighting several near the station door when I saw him last," Tatiana said grudgingly. "I'd like to call him a coward, but it would be a lie. And I'm not about to sink to his level and start telling false stories."

We made our way back to the facility entrance and Loren who was dragging his fallen enemies to one side.

"You okay?" I asked.

He lifted his left arm to show his self-applied bandage. I realized he was hiding a limp and possibly other injuries. The man had fought, which was good, but I still didn't trust him.

"You were right about the Neverseen," I said.

He looked at his feet for a second. "Almost."

"What do you mean, almost? That was the toughest squad of Neverseen we've faced. If they had been the first that attacked us, we'd have died. They almost seemed to fight as a unit," I said.

"There should have been a Neverseen Lord giving them energy and directing them, but there isn't," he said.

"No." I did another check of the area, finding nothing. Briggs shook his head. Tatiana shrugged. Then, surprising me, she moved to Loren's side and checked his bandages, removing one and reapplying another with more skill than he had managed.

"Don't expect me to do that again," she said.

"We need to get into that power station," I said.

"I've already hacked the door and opened it," Loren said, his no-nonsense manner a welcome relief from what I expected. His personality was brusque and unpleasant, but better than the pompous asshole I expected to run the Kalon Regulars. "The problem is the shaft."

"Let me guess, it's deep and full of face eating monsters," I said.

"There weren't any dangerous animals... or aliens in the part I explored. The descent seemed pointless once I discovered there were more than one of these places." Loren took off his helmet and held it on his hip. When he thought I wasn't looking, he turned slowly to give his audience a panoramic view of the place.

"You didn't go all the way to the bottom?" Tatiana asked accusingly.

"Have a look and you'll understand my concerns," he said.

I strode toward the doors then opened them with a push of a button. "Well, you weren't lying about that part."

X-37 asked me to hold my gaze steady for a while, which was fine. The combined enhancements of my cybernetic eye and the Archangel helmet allowed me a good view of a terrifying hole in the ground, but not all of it. "How deep is this thing, X?"

"My best estimate is at least a kilometer," X-37 said.

Ladders had been removed, which was almost a relief. Who

the hell could climb a ladder for a kilometer in absolute darkness? Who would want to? I *wanted* stairs but couldn't be sure they had ever existed. Given the narrowness of the shaft, stairs would have to be in such a tight spiral that they would practically be ladders. "X, why can't anything be easy?"

"This particular mission won't be easy, but there is a remote chance it can be navigated successfully," X-37 said. "But look on the bright side, Reaper Cain, Loren's warning about the Neverseen came just in time. Navigating your way to the bottom of this facility while fighting would have made things much more difficult. So, in effect, it is easy."

"I want to punch you, X."

"You always do."

Loren, not privy to the cleverness of my LAI, shook his head. "What you can see isn't the worst of it. There are places where it narrows significantly." He pointed at my armor. "That won't fit. In all honesty, neither will you."

"Fantastic," I said, then pointed at Briggs. "What about him? He's our best climber but nearly as big as Archangel armor."

"I think he'll have problems. There are handholds, of a sort. Cracks in the shaft. Whoever built this place must have had an alternative way of getting to the bottom, but I don't know what that would be. They could probably reattach ladders and other support infrastructure in the event they needed to reopen the facility," Loren said.

"There's something else. Have all these tree climbing animals been down there?" I asked.

"That's what it looks like. They don't live underground, generally, but they store little treasures sometimes," Loren said.

"Where are they now?" I asked.

"Most likely they will return now that the Neverseen have been dealt with," Loren said, but he looked nervous.

I started taking my armor off. "You too, Hannah."

"You're going to allow me to do something dangerous? You've changed, brother." My sister laughed.

"I'm not fucking happy about it. Heights aren't really my thing." I felt my heart racing and sweat on my skin. X-37 allowed me to feel the sensations. He could reduce them, but we'd long since agreed he would only dampen my fear response in true emergencies, and honestly, by the time things went that sideways, there wasn't time to think about being scared anyway.

"Would you like me to recount the story of Novasdaughter's mother to your sister and Tatiana, or perhaps the cable crossing on Dreadmax? That might allow them to understand you better," X-37 said.

"No, X. Don't tell any stories about me to anyone." I finished my preparations for the climb. Stripped to the barest amount of gear necessary, I didn't even have my jacket where I kept my cigars and the square metal lighter I'd picked up on Yansden. All I needed was the leg and belt harness for repelling, which had never been used as far as I could tell. Unpacking it from the Archangel survival kit took far too long and it smelled like preservation chemicals.

"Let me check you." Tatiana didn't wait for me to agree. She tugged each buckle and strap to be certain everything stayed where in needed to stay. Stepping back, the Yansden woman gave me a visual once-over. "Good. Now you do me."

Once all three of us were ready, we approached the shaft and looked down. Loren hung back. Briggs stalked back and forth making angry, impatient sounds.

"Don't eat the Kalon guy," I said.

"Awk! Awwwwwwk! Fuck you, Cain," Briggs grunted.

Loren Jacem drew farther away from the Slayer and said nothing. I thought I knew what he was thinking. The man was probably calculating his poor chances of outrunning Briggs. Witnessing the way the Slayer had fought the Neverseen with his bare hands was probably a life changing moment for the leader of the Kalon Regulars.

Mountaineering, which was similar to what we were doing here, had been part of both spec ops and Reaper training. I'd been good at it, but no master. Of course, that had been before I developed my aversion to heights.

What I knew from my time bouldering and rappelling was that grip strength mattered. My left hand wouldn't have an issue but eventually my right would become fatigued. We needed to move quickly. I thought most of the handholds would be either ladders, or the mounts the ladders had been affixed to, and would thus be predictable and easy to find—much different from negotiating a natural rock formation.

"We don't have enough safety line to get all the way to the bottom. Every fifty meters, we will need to bring down the rope and reattach it," I said.

"Okay." Tatiana motioned for me to start.

There was something about the way she and my sister were looking at me, and it seemed like the women thought I was being difficult, stubborn, intent on doing too much myself. Translation, they didn't think they needed me for this mission and probably thought I was even a liability.

That didn't hurt my ego at all. It really didn't. I just didn't want them to be down there by themselves to face who only knew what.

I crossed into the darkness, activating my cybernetic eye to improve my vision in low light conditions. Then I moved quickly, always maintaining three points of contact with the wall. Sometimes I held with both hands, one foot, and reached for the next toehold with the other. Down and down I repeated the process, moving quickly and confidently, and trying not to think of what a fall would mean.

Trusting the belay line was important. And I did. Mostly. Sometimes. It wasn't like I was almost too big to fit in the shaft in the first place and weighed more than most serious climbers.

"How are you doing?" Tatiana asked.

"Good," I said, then immediately encountered a problem I knew was a dealbreaker. I made sure my microphone was off and then cursed under my breath. This kind of mistake was intolerable. It was going to cost us time, and that might cost us the entire mission. Which would endanger or doom the entire exodus fleet. Because I was an egotistical dumbass who just had to do this himself.

"What's wrong?" Tatiana asked.

"I'm coming up." I was thankful they didn't ask me for a full explanation until I was at the top.

Hannah immediately took my place and started her own climb, and I loved her for her sense of urgency and dedication to the mission. Tatiana was right behind her but paused briefly.

"I came to a narrow section. I can get through it, but I have to scrape off several layers of skin to fit. I'm not sure why it narrows and widens like that, but it's going to be a recurring problem. I'm only going to be in your way." Admitting my failure hurt a lot more than I thought it would.

"It's okay, Cain. Your sister and I can handle this," Tatiana said, and then she was gone.

I watched them for as long as I could, nervously fishing out a cigar from my discarded jacket and smoking it as I stared down into the darkness. It should've been me down there, I knew. Once I lost sight of them, even with my enhanced vision, I felt like they were never coming back.

"They're very brave women," Loren said.

"No shit, they're brave," I said. "Now shut the fuck up."

25

A cool mountain breeze touched the back of my neck and gave me shivers. I breathed in, held it, and let it out. Path hadn't taught me how to meditate. He had, instead, sold me on the true value of it and encouraged me to practice. I smiled as I thought of the times we had sat on the observation deck staring at the wall of a slip tunnel, saying nothing, doing nothing, and just breathing intensively.

"Were making good progress," Tatiana said. "We are on a ladder section now, tied off to take a short rest."

The radio comms were scratchy but understandable.

"Okay," I said. "Keep us updated. You still have time, but it's going to be close."

"Understood," Tatiana said.

I waited, and waited, and waited. Every second seemed like twenty minutes.

"Can it talk?" Loren asked, pointing at Briggs who had finally stopped pacing and squatted on a rock like some sort of primordial killer taking a sun nap.

"Why don't you ask him?" I said, not looking at either of them.

"Ask, ask, ask, awk," Briggs said, sounding like he'd just spit out something he'd eaten on the last word.

"Apologies," Loren said. "I've never seen anything or anyone like you. I just realized that there are many similarities with the other aliens, the Sansein."

"Yes. There are," Briggs said, clipping his words short.

"What do you know about them, the Sansein?"

No one said anything. Loren began again.

"I've been focused on a singular goal for most of my adult life. If you people shut down the spaceport field, ending the distortion to all our technology, my life will be complete. If not, well then who knows. We'll probably all die. But that's not my point. Meeting you and your friends has made me realize there might be a new purpose for me. I need to understand you, and the Sansein aliens, and the galaxy beyond our sun," Loren said.

Briggs hopped down from his rock and moved closer to us. This caused me to face the conversation and listen. I didn't like the leader of the Kalon Regulars much, but he seemed useful and I didn't want Briggs to hurt him.

"I have parts of their genetic code woven into my genes." Briggs sounded more like himself than he had for a while. I always valued these moments, even if they kind of sucked. I saw the man instead of the monster.

Loren listened, a thoughtful expression on his face. As hard and duplicitous as the man was, he wasn't that much different from President Coronas or Brion Rejon. Or me. He had his people and would do whatever it took to protect them.

"I hear them sometimes." Briggs's voice was so soft I barely made out the words.

"Like radio waves?"

Briggs shrugged. "More like dreams. They are not a unified race. Awk. Not sure we can really understand them."

Scratchy radio traffic caught my attention. "Hannah, Tatiana, are you trying to reach us?"

Someone was keying their mic—once, twice, then three times. I never heard any words.

"X, did you catch any of that?"

"I did not, Reaper Cain. We have lost radio contact with your sister and Tatiana."

I grabbed my climbing gear and checked it. The harness, I had left on and so I was ready in seconds.

"Wait." Briggs still had the commanding tone from his spec ops days even if it sounded strange now. "Just wait a minute."

"Cain, can you hear me?" Tatiana sounded like she was on another planet.

"I can hear you now. The connection isn't good," I said.

"Understood. You have no idea how much it hurts me to say this, but we need your help," Hannah said. "The way this is set up, it takes three people."

I pondered my options, studying Loren. There were two things working against him. First, I didn't trust him yet. Second, he'd already failed to make the descent once. I wasn't willing to risk everything on his ability to make the climb. There was no way to know if he had stopped because of lack of skill or because of fear.

"I'm on my way," I said.

The only good thing that happened during my mad rush into the vertical shaft was that we finally got an update from Tom in the *Jellybird*.

"We've arrived at our shut off terminal. I'm not sure if you figured this out yet, but it takes three people to operate the controls. We're standing by," Tom said. "Also, I used the ship guns on one of the big Neverseen creatures you described. It had little henchmen or something. Without Jelly, we'd have been dead before we knew what happened."

"We had a bit of a fight here," I said. "Hopefully Elise and Path can make quick work of the guards at their facility."

I didn't even mention how I thought Envoy and Coranth would handle a bunch of the nearly invisible jerks. All I wanted from them was confirmation they had reached their objective and figured out a way to shut down a terminal that took three people.

"What's your situation, Hal? Are you going to make it on time?" Tom asked.

"We hit a bit of a problem, but I'm on my way to Hannah and Tatiana now." I was already climbing down at a reckless pace.

Envoy and Coranth's dilemma nagged at me. "How are the Sansein going to flip three shut off switches?"

"I am confident they will manage," X-37 promised.

"You've got to give me more than that." My breath sounded loud in the confined space. Lactic acid built up in my hands and forearms right about the time I scraped my nose bad enough to draw blood.

"The Sansein can do things with their tentacles," X-37 said. "I ran simulations and concluded you wouldn't enjoy the visuals this presents."

"Probably not, X." I reached for a toehold and found myself in the place I'd gotten stuck before.

"Perhaps if you reach up and attempt to suck in your gut, you might get through this section," my LAI suggested.

"Are you calling me fat?" I asked in mock outrage.

"Of course not, I only meant—"

"Kidding, X. I'll give it a try." I stretched uncomfortably, then stuck my arm blade into a crack and pushed, careful to keep my toes on the wall. "Do you think I can make it?"

"With eighty-nine point three certainty."

"Fuck, X, that's like you saying we should just quit right now. I know the way you do numbers," I gasped, then growled as I pushed too hard and slid down. The drop forced me to grab a crack in the wall with my fingertips, but I didn't plummet to my death, so that was something.

"Don't quit your day job, Reaper Cain." X-37 made soothing, musical noises right at the edge of hearing. "I'll handle the numbers."

26

EACH TIME I came to a narrow spot in the shaft, I took a break. It was a natural place to rest because I could literally let go of the walls and not fall. That didn't mean it was comfortable. Everything about this place sucked big time.

"I should be getting close," I said. "Are there any landmarks I should be looking for? Can you shine a light or something to let me know if I'm almost there?"

No one answered.

"X, did Tom say how they dealt with their climb?" I had a hard time imagining Tom, Bob, and Manager doing this.

"I'm reviewing their mission data now. It seems that the station they located was on a raised platform, a perfect match for the fact that they are in a ship. Had we been selected to go to that location, this would've all been for nothing, given that you can't fly, Reaper Cain," X-37 said. "Tom's statement about using Jelly's guns makes much more sense now."

"Great. That makes everything better," I said, then swore as I scraped more skin off my right hand. Between blisters and abrasions, I was going to feel this later.

"You need to move faster," X-37 said. "The clock is ticking. We've not had contact with Elise and her team, so sticking to the schedule is very important."

"I'm doing my best, X."

"My analysis suggests you could in fact push yourself a little bit harder."

"Really? That's your motivational speech for the day?"

"Would you like me to play some inspirational music? I can also send you an occasional jolt of electronic stimulus if you think that might help," X-37 said.

"I told you to turn that feature off a long time ago." Talking to my LAI took a very small part of my attention. He was right about what I could do. Pain and fear were tools my mind used to keep me from destroying myself. During spec ops training, I learned the human body could do far more than most people thought.

"You did, Reaper Cain. I was hoping you had forgotten. With your permission, I will reactivate the electronic jolt function in my motivational menu and put it to use."

"Negative." I let myself slide down to the next handhold and caught it with my cybernetic hand, then I quickly reached for the next with my normal hand. "Just keep that music-ish sound in the background. Makes it less lonely in this black as sin pipeline to hell you've gotten me stuck in."

The place I needed to grab was like a living thing, or maybe I was hallucinating. The longer I descended, the more difficult it became to judge what was a dent in the laser-cut stone and what was a crack caused by hundreds of years of erosion. Exhausted, pissed off, and nearing the end of my patience, I seized the hand-hold like it owed me money. "Fuck you, stupid crack."

It took me a second to realize I'd gone too far. My right hand gripped an opening that had once been a ladder mount but shifting in the rock had distorted it. My hand went in further than I expected, almost to the wrist. When I pulled it back, I realized I was stuck.

"You don't have time for this, Reaper Cain," X-37 said.

"Less than helpful, X. I mean you've reached a new low with that fucking bullshit pain in my ass observation."

"Apologies, Reaper Cain."

"No, you're fine. I'm just a little tuned up. This blows worse than the cable crossing on Dreadmax. Really ready to be done with this crap."

Gritting my teeth, I pulled as hard as I could, knowing I would lose a lot of skin and maybe some muscle from my right hand. All I managed to do was hurt my elbow and shoulder. "Fuck me."

"Something is coming down," X-37 warned. "I believe it is some of the arboreal creatures from the forest. I do not think they are carnivorous, but if they were, it would be a good time for them to prey upon you."

"X, shut it for a second."

"Understood. I will now give you several minutes of silence," X-37 said. The silence that followed was so absolute that I almost asked him to play me some music.

The soft-furred creatures came down in a group of about nine or ten. Some were fairly large, maybe twenty pounds. Some of them weren't much bigger than my hand. I realized that I was trespassing in one of their hiding holes. They tittered at me but didn't seem angry.

"Can you help me out of this?" I asked, breathing a sigh of relief because if the fur-faced little dudes and dudettes were here, that meant we really had killed all the Neverseen in the clearing.

They chipped their little arboreal teeth at me, but I couldn't understand them. I was pretty sure they didn't understand me because their tone didn't change at all when I talked to them.

"We've received an update from Envoy. There is no audio because he sent it via binary code," X-37 said. "The Sansein are in place at their power station."

I leaned against my stuck hand, resting. "How are they going to turn it off? It takes three people."

"From the description Envoy provided, each power shut off requires three levers to be operated simultaneously—just as Tom and Tatiana have described. The distances between these devices is the reason it requires three people," X-37 said.

"That doesn't answer my question. How are they going to do that? Tentacles? Because that's not nearly as reassuring as it was about six hundred meters of climbing ago." I asked.

"Unknown, Reaper Cain," X-37 said. "I already gave you my best estimation of their methods."

"Fucking great." I braced myself for what I had to do. "I'm going to dig my hand out with my Reaper blade. It's probably gonna hurt like a son of a bitch."

"Try not to cut yourself," X-37 said.

27

THE HARDEST PART was getting the angle. With my hand locked in the hole, I had to twist my elbow and shoulder severely. Then I had to leverage my feet against the walls and push back hard. I just hoped I wouldn't plummet down and snap my safety rope.

With time running out, I aggressively chipped away at the rock, occasionally sliding the blade in the long side of my wrist and using the flat of the blade like a prybar, trying to create space. Unfortunately, that mostly meant compressing my flesh and bone, which was not enjoyable. There was already some swelling from when I initially got stuck.

My hand came out, and I slipped but didn't fall. X-37 displayed how much time I had left, and I cursed. Without over-thinking my options, I used my still extended blade to cut my safety rope. "I don't have time to keep attaching the line. If I fall, I fall."

"I understand your choice," X-37 said. "There really is no good solution. Good luck, Reaper Cain."

Just then, the moment I was free and started downward, my furry friends lost their collective minds. Cute chattering became whistling screeches.

"Cheeeeee! Cheeeee! Cheeee!" Small hands tugged at me, pulling me upward.

"Are you kidding me? Now I'm playing tug-o-war with these things." Holding my position with my feet and my left hand, I used my right to untangle them from my shirt and hair. "Give me a break, you little animals."

"Bwee! Bwee! Chee! Deee!"

I drew my pistol, aimed it into their ranks, and activated the light—blinding everyone in the shaft including myself. "I don't want to blow the shit out of you bastards, but I've got to do this."

The arboreals hesitated only a second, then doubled down on their protestations. "Chee! Chee! Cheeeeeeeeeeeeee!"

Holstering my gun, I focused my attention downward. "That is seriously going to get on my nerves."

"Would you like me to filter the frequencies they're using?"

"No, I need to be able to hear everything, including that bull-shit. We're getting close to the bottom, I hope." The furry things tugged on me several more times, but the lower I went, the less of them stayed to harass me.

One little guy who didn't say much rode on my shoulder without squawking.

"I think it is giving you a hug," X-37 said.

The creature squeezed my neck twice more, squeaked, then climbed upward as fast as he could go.

I paused, not sure how I felt about the bizarre moment. "Be careful little dude."

Scanning for new handholds, I wished I had been able to wear the Reaper mask. My initial decision to leave it topside had been correct. Every time I turned my head, I would've been bumping it. Moving quickly, I allowed myself to slide from time to time, using the levers of my feet pressed against each wall to slow my descent. The reckless maneuver dramatically increased my speed but always felt like I would lose control and go tumbling down the black tube. The dread this inspired was a close cousin to my fear of heights, the meaner, nastier cousin that would probably kill me the first time I made a mistake.

"For the record, X, this sucks," I said, breathing hard. "I'm not doing any more missions without the Archangel armor."

"That's crazy talk, Reaper Cain. Don't get soft. You know better than to rely too heavily on your equipment. You're almost to the bottom. Keep up the good work," X-37 said.

The vertical passage began to fill with light, and I knew I was close to the bottom. Not long after that, I heard Tatiana and my sister talking. They didn't seem upset by my discomfort. By the time I put my feet on the ground, I was inventing new swearwords and making sounds that were a language all their own. My right hand was so miserable I fantasized about having two reaper arms instead of one. I had abrasions all over my face and under my clothing and I didn't want to think of where else.

"You made it." Hannah helped me stand after I nearly

collapsed. "We don't have much time so let me get you to your station. We can talk about your poor hand later."

Tatiana looked at the flesh ripped from my knuckles and fingers, and she winced. At least someone understood how much I'd gone through to get here. Apparently, they were better climbers because they looked better composed and lacked similar injuries.

They showed me around the chamber, which was roughly segmented into three sections. In the center of each section was a computer terminal and a crude lever.

"Did you hear that, Reaper Cain?"

"No, X. I didn't." There was something off about the setup and my LAI's paranoia—what I called paranoia despite his frequent attempts to explain he didn't have emotions—wasn't helping me much.

"Is the shaft the only way to get down here?" I asked.

Tatiana shifted from foot to foot and glanced over her shoulder before answering. "Yes and no. There's a door between your station and mine but it's closed. I can't imagine it goes to the surface, but maybe it leads out the side of the mountain. A ventilation shaft or something."

"But it's closed. You tried to open it, and made sure it was locked tight?" I asked.

She nodded.

"The computer is off. Nothing we did activated it," Hannah said. "There is power, however. If you look, you can see a soft green light at the base of each lever. We did as much testing as we could, and it seems these will take a lot of force to move."

"How much time do we have left?" I asked.

"About one minute and fifty-eight seconds," Tatiana said. "We better get in place."

The only good thing about our situation was that I could see both of them from my station. X-37 began the countdown timer via radio gear links, but also audibly just to be sure.

"X, make one last attempt to contact the other teams. If possible, I want you to coordinate all our efforts. If this has to be simultaneous, I want it to be as perfect as possible," I said.

My LAI continued to count down the time, pausing briefly to speak. "I am unable to contact the other teams. We will have to wait until the predetermined time, which is only moments away."

"Did you hear that, Reaper Cain?"

Moving toward the supposedly secure mystery door, I drew my pistol. "Sure as hell did, X."

Tatiana and Hannah also moved toward the sound of metal twisting.

"Stay behind me," I snapped. "Back as far as you can."

They didn't argue.

"Something's coming through," I said, aiming my pistol with one hand and snapping out my Reaper blade with the other. "As soon as I engage, try to flank it or something."

"Could it be the Neverseen Lord?" Hannah asked, drawing her own pistol and looking so nervous I wished she didn't have the weapon. An untrained gun handler in this environment wasn't really a good thing.

"Do you know how to use that?"

Her response sounded indignant. "I've been to the range. Can't avoid it on a ship full of Union spec ops teams."

"I've got you covered, Cain," Tatiana promised, holding her pistol with both hands and moving to one side as far as the shape of the underground cavern allowed.

The wide door bulged in the middle and stretched along the frames. Pieces of rock broke loose around it, small bits at first but more and more as the pressure increased. A really annoying mental image of spec ops jerks hitting on my sister—inviting her to the range where they could show off—intruded at the worst possible moment, so I jammed it back where it belonged.

"The door can't hold," X-37 said, right before the metal exploded toward me.

A piece of shrapnel sliced the side of my face, narrowly missing my cybernetic eye. Other pieces peppered my chest and shoulders. I fired three rounds, moved, and fired again at a Neverseen asshole worse than any I'd met before.

"Recommendation, go full Reaper on that thing," X-37 said, a bit more calmly than fit the moment.

Firing until my pistol ran dry, I heard Tatiana and Hannah doing the same. Bullets ripped through the dust and debris and ricocheted everywhere, but they also hit the Neverseen Lord in its face and throat—which was exactly where I was going next with my blade.

"Chee chee, motherfucker!" Screaming a war cry, I leaped across the distance and drove the blade home with all my strength.

The Neverseen Lord batted me aside. After hitting the wall

upside down, I slid onto my face then rolled gracelessly to my feet.

"Reloading!" Hannah shouted.

"Me too!" Tatiana said.

"They are supposed to cover each other during reloads," X-37 said. "But since the Neverseen Lord doesn't use guns or other ranged weapons, their tactical deficiency should go unnoticed."

"Everyone's a critic, X," I muttered, staggering forward with stars clouding my vision and the entire planet shifting under my feet like I was six whiskeys past drunk.

The monster charged Hannah, who sprinted away during a fumbled reload. Tatiana charged at the thing, putting her barrel inches from its earhole and dumping several rounds.

The beast lashed out, roaring in pain as it sent her through the air, right over my head. When in doubt, attack. That was what the Union taught me in basic training.

It roared, spreading jaws big enough to bite my head off. Not wanting to become headless, I dropped low and stabbed for its waistline.

Teeth snapped near my head, the sound hurting my ears it was so close and forceful. I stood, driving for the bottom of its jaw, and found the first good target of the fight.

The blade sank into its flesh, spearing its jaws closed from the bottom. Drawing the only other weapon I could find—a small knife I used to trim cigars and always had in my pocket—I slashed across its jugular.

Or where I hoped its jugular was. That was the problem with fighting monsters. None of them were built the same.

The Neverseen Lord grabbed me with both hands, pushed me back until my arm blade came free of its jaw, then raised me overhead. I braced myself for the return trip to the ground but realized too late it was smashing me into the ceiling—and that I had lost my cigar knife. Which was fine. I'd left my fucking cigars in my jacket anyway.

Thoughts like that happened in the flicker of a second and couldn't be kept away. My brain was going all kinds of places when I needed to focus on winning.

The monster threw me. I landed hard, then rolled into a sitting position.

"Where am I, X?"

"Reaper Cain!" X-37 shouted as he jolted my nerves with a microsecond of electricity drawn from elsewhere in my nervous system.

I sprang to my feet, alert as fuck. A big, blurry…thing I'd never seen before rushed me like we had a history or something.

"You can go straight to hell, asshole," I said as I dropped to one knee, aimed my blade for its groin, and lunged for a killing strike. Driving with my arm, shoulder, and core strength, I also stood and ran forward with my legs—which were trembling like I'd climbed four thousand stairs. The blade cut deep, all the way to my knuckles, as it clawed at me. I ripped my weapon free as I continued forward, moving between its legs, dragging the sharp edge down through its hamstrings with a violent flourish.

"Very good, Reaper Cain," said a voice in my head.

"Fuck that. I'm a monster." The thing that had attacked me fell forward, which was away from where I now stood. Two women ran at me, holstering pistols and hugging me hard enough it hurt.

I thought I knew who they were.

"You're our monster." Hannah laughed.

That was her name. Hannah. She was my sister. "Didn't we come here to do something?"

Both women laughed.

"Yes we did," exclaimed the other one. She was bleeding from her nose, bruised all over, and seemed about as happy as anyone I'd ever seen. "We have to shut down the power grid to the spaceport, remember."

"Yeah, I do, actually." Everything came back thanks to the voice in my head I realized was X-37, my digital conscience or something. He gave me directions and I followed them carefully.

Hannah and the other one, Tatiana, took their places by unpowered computers and large levers with tiny lights showing they had residual power at least. I took my place, gathered my fragmented memory, and mostly understood what the fuck was happening.

"All right, X," I said. "We are ready."

A cluster of the arboreal creatures gathered to watch us. The little green one climbed onto my shoulder and gave me a neck hug. The chittering of the others didn't change much, and I wondered absently what they thought of us.

"Ten seconds," X-37 said. "Nine, eight, seven, six, five, four, three, two, now."

I slammed the lever hard, not willing to take a chance that it would get stuck halfway. The green light at the bottom of the lever changed to red. "Talk to me."

"My indicator turned red," Hannah said.

"Same," Tatiana said. A few seconds passed. "I doubt we will know if it worked until we climb out of here and contact the other teams."

I looked at my tattered right hand. "I can't wait."

We gathered below the shaft opening. Tatiana examined my hand, then she cleaned it up and wrapped it with some first-aid bandages. "You're going to have to deal with it. There's no way you can make this climb wearing gloves. And I doubt they would do you much good anyway."

"Thanks," I said, studying the vent the Neverseen had used to attack us. "I'll go last. I don't want to fall and knock you and my sister off the wall."

"You're not considering going that way, are you?" she asked.

I hesitated, wishing there was an easier way than what we faced but there never was. "It's an unknown. I just don't have the energy."

She patted my arm, nodding with a smile. "Okay. I'm pretty sure you'll make it.."

I waited until they had a good lead and began my assent.

28

DISTRACTION WAS MY BEST FRIEND. The only thing I didn't allow myself to think about was what would happen if the exodus fleet arrived just in time for the entire system to collapse in a failed slip tunnel experiment. The local scientists had been messing with things they didn't understand.

The arboreal creatures liked me more than my sister or Tatiana. They climbed over me, which was distracting, but they also followed and talked amongst themselves. Or that was what I thought they were doing. Their vocalizations were almost musical and didn't bother me as much as I thought they would when I first heard them.

"So, what brings a bunch of furry face guys and gals like you to a place like this?" I asked.

"I don't think they understand you, Reaper Cain," X-37 said.

"I know, X. I'm just having some fun."

"Chee, chee, chee," one of the creatures, not my little green buddy, said as it stopped right on my shoulder. I was stretched out to reach the next handhold. Its long ringed tail tickled my nose. "Chee, chee."

The creatures kept trading places, taking turns riding on me. I didn't mind but worried about the little one. Each time it came back, I felt better.

"Maybe next time you guys can do this for me," I said. "What do you say?"

My friend scurried down my back and disappeared amongst his fellows.

"At least they don't bite." I climbed farther, reached one of the narrow spaces, and wedged myself between the walls to take a break. My arms and legs were trembling. The pain in my hand was now joined by blisters on my feet and road rash every-place else. The only good part about my condition was that it was all running together. Nothing was acutely painful. Back in my early training, we called this the grind. Just had to get it done.

One of the orange and brown fur-faced little creatures made the chee noise again. It was bigger and probably older than the one who had stayed with me the longest on the way down to face the Neverseen Lord. Thinking back, they had tried to warn me of the danger.

I looked up and one of the green furred creatures with brown stripes looked directly at me like we were actually having a conversation.

"Perhaps you should strike up a conversation," X-37 said. "If they truly understand your language, they could be a wealth of information."

"Chee, chee," it chittered, then vanished upward. The rest of the forest creatures followed. The small green one went with them, and it looked like it was smiling.

"Finally," I said. "I thought we'd never get rid of them."

"Are you glad they're gone?"

"Yes, X. Why wouldn't I be?"

"It's very quiet and dark without them constantly moving about," X-37 said.

"Good thing we're getting close to the top. We are getting close to the top, aren't we, X?"

"Keep moving and see for yourself," my LAI said.

The last stretch of my journey sucked without the tree creatures bothering me. X-37 wasn't fooled by my indifference. I liked having them around. They made the long climb much more bearable.

For some reason, I expected them to be all over the place when I emerged from the shaft. But they were gone. Disappeared into the trees or wherever they went when they weren't pestering my team.

Hannah gave me a huge hug, then to my surprise, so did Tatiana. I held up one hand toward Briggs. "Don't even think about it, Slayer."

"Awk."

"Congratulations," Loren said. "Did it work?"

"We'll see." I didn't have the answer he wanted.

"I wasn't talking to you," Loren said.

"That's right, you have your secret council listening in," I said. "Tell them the Reaper said hello and they better not screw with my friends or they'll meet me in person."

Loren had the decency to look embarrassed.

I crossed my arms. "Well? Did it work?"

"It seems the spaceport has gone completely dark," Loren said. "We have teams of scientists running tests. So far, the prognosis is good."

He said other things, but I was focused more on lighting my cigar and ignoring my rather impressive collection of injuries. The weird part was that the little things bothered me more than the concussion and bruised bones. I had carbon fiber sheeting that kept me alive during that last fight. The memory of slamming into the wall was hazy. Studying Tatiana, I wondered how she'd lived through it.

"I'm going to help your sister back into her armor," Tatiana said. "Do you want me to help you next?"

"That'd be great, Tatiana." I said, then had a seat on a rock near a stream. "Are you okay?"

She nodded. "That thing didn't throw me like it did you. I thought you were dead."

Exhaling smoke away from her, I shook my head. "Reapers are hard to kill."

"The smoke doesn't bother me, Cain," she said. "Blow it in my face if you have to, just don't try to blow it up my ass."

Laughing hurt. The next time I exhaled, I didn't twist my neck—which did hurt a lot—but let the cigar smoke out slowly enough that neither of us were overwhelmed by it.

Loren continued his conference call. Briggs ran into the woods, and a herd of the arboreal creatures swung after him, chattering, "Chee, chee, chee."

"Awk!" Briggs roared.

"Don't go too far, Slayer. If the *Jellybird* gets here and you're still screwing off, I'm leaving you."

EPILOGUE

I LOUNGED in the captain's chair, glad to be free of my Archangel armor, Reaper mask, weapons, and the responsibility for saving multiple civilizations from total annihilation. Tom handed me a glass of whiskey.

"We really shouldn't have this on the bridge." He took a sip of his own drink.

"Agreed." I let the warmth flow into me. Looking at the glass, I thought about making a toast but didn't know what to say. "Just this once."

Tatiana's reaction to the drink suggested she'd never had anything like it. I doubted she was going to be a fan. Hannah passed on Tom's offer of alcoholic refreshment. Briggs had decided to go to his room.

That left Loren Jacem, who remained in awe of the ship. They had technology on Yansden, but not like this. The man would really freak out if he was forced to ride in the Sansein vessel. I made a note to keep that as an option if he annoyed me.

"President Coronas is hailing us," Jelly said.

"Put her through if you think she won't be offended by our casual attire," I said.

"I'm not qualified to make that assessment, Captain," Jelly said.

I circled one hand in the air, indicating she should put us through.

"Halek Cain," President Amanda Coronas said, looking crisp and regal on her end of the holographic link. Her uniform was perfect, her hair startlingly red, and her expression welcoming. "It's good to see you. When we decided to rendezvous at the system, there were some arguments that it was a bad decision. I've been told that you took action to avert a very serious disaster."

"Just doing what we do," I said.

"It looks like a nice system," she said. "Are you sure this isn't a trap? We found hundreds of ships loaded with raw materials that seem to be going back and forth between mines and asteroid fields in the planet."

"They had a bit of a glitch in their resource gathering protocols," I said. "Before we get to why everything is so messed up here, let me introduce you to Loren Jacem. He's the leader of a security force they call the Kalon Regulars."

Loren stood, then bowed his head slightly. "I'm honored to make your acquaintance."

I slid back as they exchanged pleasantries, glad that I had

convinced the man to leave his red helmet in a secure locker. He hadn't liked the idea at first, but I was persuasive.

"Your people are the ancestors of the Alon?" Coronas asked.

"It's strange to hear you describe it that way, but it must be so," Loren said. "You must understand that the Alon and the Manna were only words in our history until now. You talk as though the Alon are your enemies. Where does that leave us?"

"That's what I hope to find out," Coronas said. "Now if you don't mind, I need to speak to Halek Cain in private."

"I'll take our guest to the observation deck," Tom said. Only Hannah stayed with me.

"Thanks, Tom." I straightened up and put my whiskey aside.

"There's something more, isn't there?" Coronas asked once we were free of the Yansden soldier.

I nodded, then massaged some feeling back into my right hand. "Loren located a tablet that has a star map. From what I can tell, it's extensive and probably the most valuable thing on this planet. It references a system called Maglan. They talk about it like it's a garden paradise."

Coronas considered my words. I knew her well enough to read her expression. In her eyes, we'd hit the jackpot here and venturing back into another long journey probably seemed exhausting.

"I don't think we can stay here," I said quietly.

"Why do you say that, Hal?" she asked, equally somber.

"There's more to this place then we're being told. Someone quarantined this entire system because of their scientific screw up, but they were very interested in space travel before that.

Loren wants to lead an expedition to the planet's interior to explore ancient ruins."

"And you think you should go with him?" Coronas asked.

"Yep. He won't like it, and I'm betting that he'll try to take enough muscle to keep me from stealing whatever we find." I smiled, showing my teeth.

The President gave me a little nod. "I don't think he'll have enough to keep you from whatever it is you plan to do."

"No, no he won't," I replied.

CAIN, X-37, and ELISE return in HUNT OF THE REAPER, available now on Amazon.

For more updates on this series, be sure to join the Facebook Group, "J.N. Chaney's Renegade Readers."

RENEGADE STAR UNIVERSE

The Renegade Star Universe
Available on Amazon now

The Renegade Star Series

They say the Earth is just a myth. Something to tell your children when you put them to sleep, the lost homeworld of humanity. Everyone knows it isn't real, though. It can't be.

But when Captain Jace Hughes encounters a nun with a mysterious piece of cargo and a bold secret, he soon discovers that everything he thought he knew about Earth is wrong. So very, very wrong.

Climb aboard The Renegade Star and assemble a crew, follow the clues, uncover the truth, and most importantly, try to stay alive.

The Last Reaper Series

When a high value scientist is taken hostage inside the galaxy's most dangerous prison, Halek Cain is the only man for the job.

The last remaining survivor of the Reaper program, Hal is an unstoppable force of fuel and madness. A veteran amputee-turned-cyborg, he has a history of violence and a talent for killing that is unmatched by any soldier.

With the promise of freedom as his only incentive, he'll stop at nothing to earn back his life from the people who made him, imprisoned him, and were too afraid to let him die.

The Orion Colony Series

Humanity's Exodus is about to begin.

When half of mankind revolts and demands more opportunity, those at the top decide on a compromise: they will build the first colony ships and allow those who are willing to discover new worlds to leave and start over.

Twelve ships are built, the first of which is called Orion. Many are eager to go, but only one hundred thousand are chosen for each vessel. Far from Earth, a new life awaits, and it promises the prosperity they've always wanted.

But still, resistance stirs, eager to sabotage this new expansion effort, threatening the promise of a new life. As Orion moves through the void of space, towards a distant world, its passengers must fight for survival in an unprecedented conflict.

Win or lose, their future will be forever changed.

The Fifth Column Series

After a soldier is left for dead, Eva Delgado's life begins to unravel.

The truth of what happened remains a mystery, and the government will stop at nothing to keep it buried.

Together with the unit's medic, Eva finds herself branded a terrorist and enemy of the State, hunted by two opposing governments.

When the pair uncover a plot that could have ramifications for the whole galaxy, they know they have to act, but it will take all of their training, cunning and just a bit of luck to do what no one else has achieved.

But what do you do when every secret begets another? And how far will you go to find the truth?

<u>Nameless (Abigail's Story)</u>

Abigail and Clementine were just a couple of orphans looking for a home.

But when the two girls witness something terrible, they have no choice but to leave their orphanage and go into hiding. The only person willing to take them in is a man named Mulberry, but his home isn't the safest place for two innocent children.

Abigail and Clementine quickly discover that their new care-taker is the head of a guild of assassins, and the two are thrown into a whole new world of danger. To survive, they'll need to adapt, focus, and learn how to survive in a world of killers.

The Constable (Alphonse's Story)

My name is Alphonse Malloy, and I see everything.

From a simple glance, I know your hobbies, what you ate for breakfast, how well you slept, and whether or not your wife is secretly seeing the high school biology teacher when you're not around.

I can't explain how or why I get these feelings, only that I know they're true.

All the little secrets you're too afraid to tell.

Sometimes, that means helping people. Other times, it means staring down the barrel of a loaded gun.

I wish I could tell you I was using this ability for good.

I wish I could tell you a lot of things.

The Constable Returns

Alphonse Malloy may just be the smartest man alive.

A year has passed since Alphonse joined the Constables, but his work is only just beginning. In order to graduate and achieve full Constable status, Alphonse will need to complete one final mission.

When new information about an old enemy arises, Al and his mentor Dorian must head deep into the Deadlands in search of answers.

But in a galaxy of secrets, the truth is often more elusive than it seems.

As the search continues, Alphonse's talents will be pushed to their absolute limit, and he'll need everything he's learned to make it out of this one alive.

<u>Warrior Queen (Lucia's Story)</u>

On a lost world, far removed from Earth, a group of humans struggle to survive.

Two thousand years after their ancestors lost control of a hidden genetics research facility, the descendants of mankind have been reduced to a tribe of two hundred survivors. They fight, kill, and die in an endless cycle, all in the hope that things will get better.

Lucia is one of these colonists and the daughter of the tribe's leader, the Director. Together with several other candidates, she must soon undergo a trial to decide her father's replacement. The winner will shape the future of the entire colony.

But the trial is dangerous, meant to test each candidate's wits and strengths to see who is truly worthy. To claim victory, Lucia will need to venture out into the tunnels near the city to search for lost artifacts known as Cores--small but powerful devices capable of harnessing endless energy.

But there are monsters here, waiting in the dark, and they are always hungry. Beware the Boneclaw, Lucia's father use to tell her, for it lives only to kill and to feed.

Lucia must do whatever it takes, learn as much as she can, and fight with every ounce of strength if she hopes to make it through the day.

Forget winning the trial. The real challenge is staying alive.

Resonant Son Series

30 floors of nightmare fueled action. An ex-cop with nothing left to lose.

After losing his job and family, Flint Reed finds himself in the middle of a terrorist attack. With nothing but his wits and experience as a former Union police officer, he must do everything he can to stay alive.

As he soon discovers, however, there are also hostages, and no one is coming to save them.

All hope falls to Flint.

But as he fights to navigate the building, the real answers begin to unravel. What are the terrorists really after, and why are they so intent on getting into the vault?

Experience the beginning of the Resonant Son series. If you're a fan of Die Hard, Renegade Star, or the Last Reaper, you'll love this epic scifi thrill ride.

GET A FREE BOOK

Join the conversation and get updates on new and upcoming releases in the Facebook group called "JN Chaney's Renegade Readers." This is a hotspot where readers come together and share their lives and interests, discuss the series, and speak directly to J.N. Chaney and his co-authors.

https://www.facebook.com/groups/jnchaneyreaders/

He also post updates, official art, and other awesome stuff on his website and you can also follow him on Instagram, Facebook, and Twitter.

For email updates about new releases, as well as exclusive promotions, visit his website and sign up for the VIP mailing list. Head there now to receive a free copy of *The Other Side of Nowhere.*

https://www.jnchaney.com/last-reaper-subscribe

Enjoying the series? Help others discover *The Last Reaper* series by leaving a review on Amazon.

Scott Moon also offers free stories and other cool stuff when you sign up for his newsletter. Head to the link below for more details.

https://www.subscribepage.com/Fromthemoon

ABOUT THE AUTHORS

J. N. Chaney is a USA Today Bestselling author and has a Master's of Fine Arts in Creative Writing. He fancies himself quite the Super Mario Bros. fan. When he isn't writing or gaming, you can find him online at **www.jnchaney.com**.

He migrates often, but was last seen in Las Vegas, NV. Any sightings should be reported, as they are rare.

Scott Moon has been writing fantasy, science fiction, and urban fantasy since he was a kid. When not reading, writing, or spending time with his awesome family, he enjoys playing the guitar or learning Brazilian Jiu-Jitsu. He loves dogs and plans to have a ranch full of them when he makes it big. One will be a Rottweiler named Frodo. He is also a co-host of the popular Keystroke Medium show. You can find him online at **http://www.scottmoonwriter.com**

Made in the USA
Columbia, SC
08 February 2020